DOUBTING THOMAS

C. Daniel Pugh Sr.

Doubting Thomas

Copyright © 2026 by Jade Chapters Publishing

The following is a work of fiction. The names, characters, and incidents described within this story are the product of the author's imagination. Any resemblance to persons living or dead is entirely coincidental.

ISBN: 979-8-9943287-0-5

Contact the Author:

didipugh@gmail.com

To Chon, my wife of fifty years, thank you for encouraging, prodding, questioning, and loving me through this entire project. Words cannot express how amazing my life has been simply because you were in it.

Chapter 1

A CHARCOAL HONDA Accord rolled in beside the curb in front of the Boston three-story townhouse. The driver hesitated for a moment before getting out. The man was late thirties, average height with dark wavy hair and wore a light blue golf shirt with shorts and sandals. He stretched and scanned the front of the house before moving.

Two blocks away and facing him from the opposite curb, a white van with a red Merson Cable company logo printed on the side sat double-parked. Two men sat crammed inside the cargo space, which held six wall-mounted video monitors. Sweat was beading on both of their foreheads in the unseasonably warm June weather. At the moment, they were focusing on the top left monitor, which was zeroed in on the Honda.

"Run the plate," said the one in charge.

The other swiveled on his stool, wiped his forehead with a sleeve and began poking at a laptop with cigar-sized index fingers. After several miscues and swear words, he got the seven-digit plate number hammered into the MVD console application. After a few seconds, the plate registration popped up.

"Thomas Braden," said the second man.

"Okay," said the first. "The prodigal grandson has returned. I think things are about to get interesting. According to the boss, the kid hasn't been around to visit the old man for a couple of months at least."

"He doesn't look too excited to be here now," replied the second man.

"Where's Donaldson?" the first man asked.

"He's walking around the block. Should come alongside the Honda any minute."

"Donaldson," said the first, while holding a button on his lanyard. "We want to track the kid parked out front. After he goes inside, let's take care of that."

"Got it," came Donaldson's voice over the tinny speaker.

"All right," said the man in charge. "The boss will want a tap on this kid's phone. Call it in, then let's call Harrison and fill him in."

***

Thomas trudged up the brick steps of the aging brownstone, fighting the urge to u-turn every step of the way. Being summoned to his grandfather's house, though considered an honor by others, was just this side of torture for him, which was something that Thomas avoided.... although there was that one girl at M.I.T.

"Focus, dummy," he snapped to himself. "Whatever the old man wants, the old man gets." Then, in his best uppity English accent, "You have an audience with the world-renowned archaeologist, purveyor of rare artifacts and antiques, muckety-muck to the stars. The Great and Powerful Oz has requested your presence, no doubt to inform you that you are not only cowardly, but stupid and heartless to complete the Emerald City trifecta."

He gathered himself at the top step, but before he hit the bell, the door opened, and filling the frame was the man-mountain butler, Carson. He stood six feet seven inches tall, and the Braden family had employed him for most of the last sixty years. Thomas was positive that if he googled either the oldest or the tallest living manservant on the planet, Carson's picture would pop up. He wore, as always, a dark mortician's suit with a white shirt and black tie. His eyes were too small and too close together for his face. He stared down his Roman nose at Thomas like a vulture over roadkill.

"Master Thomas, you are fifteen minutes late," the butler said.

"Yeah, I was just finishing up my fifteen minutes of fame before I came over," Thomas dead-panned back. Conversing with Carson was akin to a jousting match. One had to be wary of the constant thrusts and parries.

"How nice for you. Do have a seat in the parlor, and I will inform your grandfather that you have arrived."

"Well, I wouldn't say that I have arrived, but I have

socked away twelve hundred and fourteen dollars in my IRA. I know what you're thinking. That's not half bad for a guy who translates books all day, every day. Well, thanks for the kind thoughts. I appreciate it."

Carson glared at him, refusing to acknowledge Thomas's feeble attempt at levity. In all his years, Thomas had never once seen the behemoth crack a smile, let alone laugh. Yet, that didn't discourage him from throwing out a few lines to see if he could reel in a reaction, any reaction. After a moment and without another word, the would-be Sasquatch turned and ambled down the hall.

"By the way, who uses the word 'parlor' anymore? I mean, other than Jed Clampett?" Thomas said behind him.

Satisfied that he had gotten in the last word, even though he figured the old geezer was deaf as Grandma's ironing board when his back was turned, Thomas slumped into the most uncomfortable chair ever fashioned after wandering into the so-called parlor. The upholstery stank from decades of sitting in the airless room, and the old mahogany frame had petrified into something harder and more unforgiving than the parent tree. Thomas knew something about engineering, and for the life of him, he could not fathom how any chair-maker from the eighteenth century or any century could have come up with a more useless design.

"Did you actually put your keester in this thing, buddy, or did you just assume it's all good?" Thomas mumbled to himself, thinking about the chair maker from another time. "Or did you intentionally design a chair that could instigate thoughts of suicide?"

Although he had always heard that talking to oneself

may be a sign of insanity, the exact opposite idea occurred to him. Talking to himself had a way of grounding him in whatever current reality he found himself in, and therefore he considered it proof positive that he was very sane. Of course, he didn't dismiss the possibility that an insane person might subscribe to the same rationale. Time spent whispering into his own ear during his roller-coaster childhood had always felt like time well spent, and he saw no reason to give it up now.

As he pondered the reason for this out-of-the-blue invitation from his grandfather, he studied, not for the first time, the various antiques that cluttered the room. He knew that this room did not differ from any other room in the house. All were brimming with relics that had qualified for antique status long before they came to rest in the Braden estate, and they had been sitting in their assigned locations throughout the dwelling long enough to become antiques all over again. He doubted his grandfather had opened the door to most of the rooms in the estate in decades, and even Thomas himself had avoided some rooms just because their ominous countenance proved stronger than even his adolescent boy's curiosity.

Carson's hulking presence materialized in the hallway and wrestled Thomas from his thoughts. "Mr. Braden will see you now."

"Not if I see him first," Thomas murmured.

"What's that, Master Thomas?"

"Nothing. Hey, I love what you've done with the place," he said, with a sweeping gesture toward the mausoleum known as the parlor.

"It is as your grandfather likes it. That is all that matters to me, Master Thomas. I should think that what he likes would be important to you as well. At any rate, your indifference is not my concern. I will show you to him."

"I can find my way to the study, Carson. Feel free to go do whatever it is you do."

"I'm afraid he is not in his study. He is in his bedroom in his bed, and he requested I show you in," Carson responded as he turned and left Thomas standing there with his mouth hanging open. "Please come with me," he added, as he began the long march down the hallway.

As far as Thomas knew, Stewart Braden had not been sick a day in his life, and he'd rather slam his hand in the car door than spend the day lounging in his bedroom. The Marines had nothing on his grandfather when it came to knocking out a to-do list before breakfast. As Thomas followed Goliath down the hallway to the primary suite, a sudden and distinctly foreign dread folded over him. His Catholic upbringing had taught him to use the same C and E approach to visiting his grandfather as he did to going to church. Every Christmas and Easter he would come by for a cup of tea with two lumps of, well, lumps. He had endured plenty of disappointing grandfatherly sighs and many long, lonely nights in this house.

While most kids he knew adored their grandfathers and went fishing or played cards with them, his grandfather had subjected him to daily teaching and testing of his knowledge. After his parents died in a horrific car accident, leaving him and his brother, Caleb, orphans, their grandfather took them in and provided nominal care and zero compassion. The man invented the "spare the rod, spoil the child" motto, and soon the two boys were studying calculus or French while everyone else was splashing girls at the pool or buying popcorn at the Fairlane Cinema.

But now, guilt about his cavalier ways regarding the old man was visiting Thomas' soul, and it was both unexpected and unwelcome.

"Maybe I should have come on the Fourth of July too," he rasped from a dry throat, but the humor rang hollow as he approached the "inner sanctum," also known as his grandparents' room.

"I'm afraid I must ask you to leave your cell phone," Carson said, blocking the door.

"Don't be afraid, Carson. It doesn't suit you. Why do you need my phone?" he asked as he held it up.

"It might interfere with the machines," Carson answered as he pinched it from Thomas' fingers and threw it on an ancient hallway table.

"What machines?" Thomas asked.

Carson pushed open the heavy door and stood aside. Thomas stepped over the threshold into an assault on his senses. A blast of near-arctic air rushed past him into the hallway, seeking warmer climes. The smell of disinfectant was on a seek and destroy mission of all other scents. Someone had transformed the ostentatious bedroom into a hospital room equipped with the latest and, Thomas was sure, the most expensive digital displays and whooshing technology that money could buy. A kind of boudoir civil war between old and new was in full view. A sixteenth-century writing desk that his grandfather had received as a gift from the Prime Minister of England labored under the weight of two medical monitors. The giant four-poster oak bed he had discovered in the Canadian Rockies and brought back to Thomas' grandmother was now relegated to the far side of the room like a vanquished warship. In its place stood a metal bed on wheels that looked as if it could assume more positions than a yoga instructor. Twin IV poles stood at attention on either side of it, guarding the prisoner, his grandfather. More monitors hung above his head, beeping, whining, gurgling and screaming their war cries while sucking the very life from the walls. Clips, buckets, smaller monitors and IV bags hung from various poles and stands like ornaments on a macabre Christmas tree. A floor-to-ceiling curtain hung open on a track that circled the bed from above. On a small table next to the bed, a machine spewed a continuous paper stream with markings that looked like the results of a lie detector test. As Thomas tried to take it all in, one monitor began urgently beeping, prompting a nurse to appear from behind him. She wore dark blue scrubs and matching clogs and whisked past him to quiet the offending machine and check the leads attached to the old man's chest.

"You need to take some deep breaths," she said to her patient.

"I know. I know. I'm still breathing, dear. You worry too much."

She lifted his head and pushed another pillow under it. He noticed Thomas standing just inside the door for the first time.

"Emma," he said. "This is my grandson, Thomas."

The nurse turned and smiled at him. She had dark brown, caring eyes and light brown hair cut short that framed her face just right.

"Nice to meet you. I'll leave you two alone for a bit,

but don't make me come back in here," she said, wagging her finger at the elder Braden.

She slipped past Thomas again, who stood still, bolted to the floor, and gently closed the door behind her as she left.

"Papa," he said. "What the hell is going on?"

His grandfather's eyes locked with his, and Thomas could sense that this was a moment that he would never forget.

"I'm dying, son."

Chapter 2

"WHAT ARE YOU talking about, Papa? Last time I saw you, you were planning another trip to Europe. Remember? You wanted to know if I could take some time off and go with you."

"Pancreatic cancer doesn't need a lot of time to ramp up," the old man said before breaking into a coughing jag.

He crooked a finger at Thomas, imploring him to come and sit.

"Close the curtain, will you, son?" he said when Thomas had gotten close enough.

Thomas did as he was told and plopped into the lone chair near the bed.

"Are you in pain?" he asked.

"No, Emma does a marvelous job keeping me afloat on

morphine."

The elder Braden seemed to slip out of consciousness, so Thomas sat and waited. He had stepped into something that he couldn't get his head around and did not know what to do about it. Beneath the sheets, his grandfather's body had withered away to straw, and his shallow breaths empowered one machine to bark at him again. They sat there like that for several awkward minutes. Then his grandfather lifted a frail hand as if he wanted to hold Thomas'. Thomas grabbed it but felt a foreign object trapped between their palms. He arched an eyebrow at his grandfather, but Stewart held his hand with surprising strength and stared into his eyes as if trying to convey a message. They sat that way for a few moments before the old man reached over with his other hand and forced Thomas to close his fist around the object. He put a finger to his lips in a shush motion and then looked down at Thomas' hand, encouraging him to look at what he had given him.

Thomas, though stunned by the urgency of his grandfather's movements, placed the object in his lap and unwrapped it. Inside, he found a key. It was smallish with a rounded end and had the number 47 engraved on the head. On the paper, there was frenetic handwriting that Thomas at once recognized as his grandfather's.

It read: 'We are being watched. You could be in danger. Trust no one! I love you.'

Then, there were four series of numbers.

29 16 24 16 24 13 16 29
26 32 29
33 12 14 12 31 20 26 25

24 13 31 31 19 16 34 127 154

Thomas looked up only to see that his grandfather's eyes were closed, and he appeared to be sleeping. He re-wrapped the key, still holding it in his lap, and then slipped it in the buttoned pocket of his cargo shorts. He was numb from the shock of the last few minutes, including the part where this man, who had never uttered such words, said he loved him. His grandfather did not reopen his eyes. Thomas had no idea what to make of these bizarre circumstances, so he just sat and stared off into the distance, thinking about nothing. Instead of his mind whirring along trying to decipher the coded message on the paper, if there was a code to be found, it idled blankly like a freshly rebooted computer. The only sounds bouncing around the room were the rhythmic symphony of the medical equipment. His grandfather was very ill and possibly delusional. There was no way of knowing that just yet, and he was loath to ask Carson anything. Besides, the note said trust no one, and there was little doubt that Carson should be at the top of that list. As the seconds ticked on, Thomas's brain ignited. If he was being watched, who was doing the watching, and why? What kind of danger were we talking about? Grave danger? "Is there another kind?" he heard Colonel Jessup from 'A Few Good Men' ask in his head. At the moment, Thomas wasn't sure he could handle the truth.

Then, with monumental effort, Stewart Braden turned his head and gazed into his grandson's eyes. They stared like that for a long moment before either of them spoke.

"I have been a terrible stand-in father to you and Caleb, Thomas," the elder Braden began. "Your father, rest his soul, would have expected more from me. I was ill-equipped to parent him properly, and I didn't do any better for the two of you."

"Let's not go there, Papa. It won't do either of us any good."

"No, hear me out, please, son. I have done countless things in my life for which I am ashamed, but disregarding and discounting my own flesh and blood tops the list. It's just that losing him, plus your grandmother in the space of a year, damaged me much more than I would have guessed. Their deaths ripped out my soul, and it took many, many years to grow back."

The old man broke into another coughing spasm that took several uncomfortable minutes to run its course. At last, he took a determined breath and set his jaw as if the very words he needed to say would fight him every inch of the way as they emerged from his throat. He was either in agonizing pain or in line for the best actor in a supporting role Oscar. Either way, it entrenched Thomas in the moment. The next time Stewart spoke, he did so in French.

"You know, when your grandmother first told me she was pregnant with your dad, I was so elated that I grabbed her and we danced around the kitchen table. I had concluded that I would never become a father. And now, all these years later, it is still one of the happiest moments of my life. I bought us a motor home a week later and took her on an extended road trip. We visited so many grand and exciting places, like New Orleans for Mardi Gras and the roller coasters at Six Flags Over Texas. We traveled to Graceland and visited the Bahai House of Worship. Your grandmother was never more beautiful, and I was never more in love than that year."

"That sounds wonderful, Papa," Thomas responded in French as well, even though he didn't know why.

"Thomas, if you take nothing else from what I am telling you, remember this: your father was an answer to a prayer, and your grandmother and I celebrated his birth with great joy."

"So, you became a family man. It was all good, at least for a while."

"It was perfect," his grandfather said with his eyes closed. "And the only reason it didn't last is all on me. I mistreated him because I thought he was a dope, but I was wrong. He knew how to love, and you and your brother could have had wonderful lives with him and your mother. Instead, a tragedy ripped you from the lives you could have had and left you both stuck with me. So here we are. I'm not long for this earth, and I have called you here, not to mourn the loss of a grandfather you never had, but to ask you a favor."

"Favor?" Thomas asked.

"Yes, it is imperative that I impress upon you the importance of what I am about to tell you, but first I have to ask you a question."

Thomas squirmed in his seat and nodded as if he were being interviewed while Stewart switched back to English.

"What do you believe?" the old man asked with piercing eyes.

"I believe in music," Thomas quipped.

"Your penchant for diving into humor whenever you get nervous has always annoyed me."

"And your penchant for getting annoyed at me has always made me nervous. So, I guess we are even. Now, what are you really asking me?"

"I am asking you if you believe in God," his grandfather sputtered, as the coughing demon took over again.

"Come on, Papa. We've been through this a million times. And why aren't you asking Caleb this if you want a better answer? And for that matter, why isn't Caleb here? Why aren't you telling him all of this? Do we really have to plow this same ground now?"

Stewart Braden struggled to rise in his bed and pointed a bony finger at his grandson. "Yes, we have to do this, and we have to do it now," he managed before falling back onto his pillow, exhausted.

"Okay, okay. Can I get you some water or something?"

"No, I need you to answer the question, please," the old man pleaded.

"I don't know, Papa. I'm not sure what I believe. The things I saw in Iraq will never go away. People dying in the streets. Kids killing soldiers. The horrors that news reporters rush to get in front of millions of viewers make me question the existence of a God. I think the first monkey that picked up a stick and whacked another monkey with it evolved into man. And we've been clubbing each other over the head ever since."

"Are you that jaded?"

"Well, I had little guidance in peace and understanding. Isn't that right?" Thomas shot back.

"I guess I deserved that," Stewart sighed. "But to answer your previous question, your brother is not here because he is too much like your father. His belief is strong and unshakable. He doesn't have the wherewithal to question authority. You do."

"Look, what's this all about? What does my belief or lack thereof in God have to do with anything as we sit here today?"

"It means everything to me. If you don't or can't ever believe in God, then I have failed as a grandfather and a Christian." He paused and got his breath. "I'd like to tell you a story."

"Should I get the popcorn?"

"Don't be flippant, son."

Thomas looked around the room contemplating making a run for it, but his legs did not move, and he stayed seated in yet another uncomfortable chair, but this discomfort was more emotional than physical. He waited while the old man gathered his thoughts and began speaking in German.

"I have only been truly frightened once in my life. When I was twenty-three and fresh out of Harvard, I was fortunate enough to get hooked up with an expedition that was traveling to the Middle East for a dig. I was the youngest of the four archaeologists and was so proud to be included. After the first discovery of the ancient texts that became known as the Dead Sea Scrolls in 1947, archaeologists from all over the world launched many such expeditions. Even ten years later, there was still a flurry of activity as more parchments were being discovered in various caves in and around the ancient site of Qumran. This was January 1956."

Thomas listened, both because he was still struggling to understand the secret note from his grandfather, and because he already knew that this story would be new to him. As a matter of course, the man never shared tales from any of his archaeological digs. All Thomas ever knew about them was what his father told him. His grandfather would disappear for weeks or even months at a time to exotic locales around the world, and no one knew when or if he would return. For all Thomas knew, the guy could have been James Bond's stunt double while he was in Beirut or Istanbul or on the moon.

"We were digging," his grandfather continued, "in a newly found cave that was just north of Cave 3 in the Qumran area. The north side of the cave wall had collapsed many decades earlier, so from the outside it didn't look like a cave at all. We had been at it for several weeks when the news came to us that a large cache of scrolls had been unearthed in what the archaeologists were calling Cave 11."

Stewart stopped speaking for a moment as his mind went back to that frantic night, replaying every sight and sound. He sighed loudly before continuing the story, but now back in French.

"The news of the find at Cave 11 ignited a spark in all the amateur diggers that had come there looking for hidden riches. Hordes of Bedouins began roving the desert like landlocked pirates, and within a flash, all semblance of order vaporized as they began looting every encampment, no longer just looking for lost and found treasures, but robbing and beating anyone they found. Across the desert floor, we could hear gunshots and screams. We were terrified, and there was no way we could outrun or stand and fight against the pillaging gangs. So, we kicked out our fire and hid in the very cave we had dug out to explore. Even after our excavation work, the entrance was invisible to the casual eye, so we sat and prayed together. We were strangers, having only met each other a few weeks before, and didn't know each other's religious beliefs. But on that night, it didn't matter. We all expected to meet our God before sunrise, and we prepared to do just that. It was the longest night of my life."

He paused to catch his breath again as one machine beeped faster for a moment, then slowed again is if to say, false alarm. He continued, this time in Arabic. Thomas was getting whiplash playing language Whack-a-mole, but he didn't interrupt.

"When the looters arrived at our site, we heard them laughing and yelling as they scavenged what they wanted and destroyed the rest. They assumed that we had run away, and they toasted themselves on having conquered another camp. I have met many men of science in my life who profess that there is no God, but I tell you on that night while we huddled like frightened schoolchildren, there were no atheists among us. Sure, we could have questioned the existence of God as we listened to the decaying souls that were masquerading as human beings just a few feet away. Evil certainly exists in the hearts of humankind, but that does not prevent God from coexisting as well."

The old man paused for effect and held Thomas with his eyes. Thomas knew in an instant there was more. He heard Paul Harvey in his head: "And now for the rest of the story." But his grandfather concluded the story right there and converted back to English.

"So, this is the favor that I ask of you. I ask that you try to believe. I ask that you open your heart to the possibility that a greater power reigns supreme. It is my last wish. Can you do that for me, son?"

Thomas stared into the man's fading eyes and, for the only time in his life, he watched his grandfather cry. Thomas stood and held the dying man's bony hand. The two of them had been drifting apart for many years, but this was the first time that he had ever considered that they might never come to terms again. The old man shivered violently, and Thomas clenched his hand tighter.

"I'll try, Papa," he said. "I will try."

The elder Braden relaxed at Thomas's words and turned his head as if to sleep.

"Papa, I don't know why we turned out the way we did, but for my part in it I am sorry. I love you."

With that he turned and left the room, half-expecting to see Carson snooping by the door. Carson wasn't in the hallway or anywhere near the front of the house, though. Thomas grabbed his phone off the hallway table, let himself out, double-timed down the stairs, and hustled to his car. He did not possess an intuitive bone in his body, but at that moment he was absolutely certain that he and his pseudo-father had just had their last conversation.

Watching out of the kitchen window, Carson picked up the phone and dialed a number from memory. The man answered it on the first ring.

"He just left," Carson said.

"Did the old man give him anything?" the voice on the other end inquired.

"I don't know. The boy closed the curtain, so I could only hear what they said. A lot of talk about God, but they kept changing languages."

"Did you understand any of it?"

"For God's sakes, no. I don't work at the U.N. It was

nothing but gobbledygook to me. Sounded like the ravings of a lunatic."

"Is that so? Did you download the app as requested?"

"I did," Carson replied.

"Very well then, we will take it from here. We will compensate you as agreed. Just keep an eye out for the young Braden in case he returns or if the other brother comes to see the old man."

The line went dead. Carson set the phone down and scowled at it. These imbeciles were a means to an end, but he detested dealing with them. A man of his age needed a retirement plan. It was as simple as that, and he could no longer count on the renowned Stewart Braden to take care of him. After decades of dedicated service, Carson knew two things for sure. One, when Stewart Braden passed, the smart-ass brothers would inherit everything, and two, he, Carson Prewitt, could not survive on a butler's pension.

Chapter 3

THOMAS BANGED THROUGH the front door and dropped his keys on the credenza in the hallway. He already knew that Dani was not home. She had a peculiar habit of locking the door when she was in during the day and leaving it unlocked when she was out; exactly the opposite strategy from what Thomas would do. But that was just one example in a long list of things where Thomas and his wife were different. Whoever first said opposites attract was speaking from personal experience.

After leaving his grandfather's house, Thomas went straight to the gym. He didn't consider himself an athlete by any stretch of the imagination. As a linguist and a translator, he was more likely to talk someone into submission, but Caleb was at the opposite end of the athletic spectrum and had talked him into trying boxing back in the day. While not his brother's equal, Thomas quickly discovered he had a knack for hitting things and over time learned to love the sport. He never tired of working out frustrations on the heavy bag or zoning out to the rhythm of the speed bag. Even the simple act of wrapping his hands snatched him away from the world and opened newly painted doors in his mind to explore and ponder. For this reason alone, he always carried a set of wraps in his pocket.

He took a quick shower, then headed for the den to his thinking place. He plopped into his overstuffed recliner, ratcheted it back, took a deep breath, and closed his eyes.

"Now this is what a chair is supposed to feel like," he said aloud.

He replayed the strange meeting with his grandfather, trying to get his mind around what took place there. In his past, because of his language skills, he worked as a translator for the military, and many times, translating was only part of the process. He quickly became a code-breaker as well, and his Papa knew it. So, he examined every element of their interaction and conversation from different angles, hoping that somewhere a light would come on. Deep in the recesses of his mind, he kept hearing him use the word danger. Thomas did not really believe that danger in any form was lurking around the corner, but he had seen the unmistakable imprint of concern etched on the old guy's face. What could make a man as sure of himself as his grandfather so unnerved? Thomas was meditating over the scared look in his Papa's eyes when the back door opened and slammed shut, causing him to flinch. He opened his eyes and stared at the doorway from the kitchen. He saw Dani whisk into the room wearing gym shorts, a t-shirt that was a little too tight, thank you very much, and a pair of pink sneakers she had bought at a breast cancer awareness rally. She stared at him like a one-eyed fish while she chugged down a bottle of water in one fell swoop. She finished, wiped her mouth with the back of one hand while she crushed the bottle with the other and tossed it cleanly into a recycling bin full of its brothers and cousins.

"How did it go at your grandfather's?" she asked without preamble.

"Carson was rude, the house was stale, and my visit with Papa set a record for bizarre family encounters."

"In other words, same as always," she said with a smile.

"No, actually, on the Richter scale of weirdness, this would register about an 8.8," he replied.

"No wonder you look so shaken," she said with a wink. "You want to tell me about it?"

"Yes, but I still need a little time to get things straight in my head first."

"Okay, tell you what. I've got to get cleaned up, and you try to straighten out your head if that is possible. But when I come back, I expect a full report. Got it?" she snapped.

Thomas nodded and watched her jog out of the room, blond ponytail swinging back and forth behind her. He thought back six years to when he first met Dani at a teacher's conference. From the moment he saw her, he knew she was way out of his league, but he didn't care. If they had been feds, she would have been above his pay grade and strictly on a need-to-know basis. It didn't matter because he desperately needed to know her. She was a

Scandinavian blond with a killer smile, and he was a dork who spoke seven languages and offered little more than a dry, sarcastic wit. He maneuvered to sit next to her at the conference lunch and eventually summoned up the courage to strike up a conversation with her. She was funny and bright and possessed a laugh that could tame wild boars. He was smitten immediately, and to his great surprise, she seemed to like his company too. That night when he got home, he sat in the dark in this very chair and stared at the ceiling, replaying every smile, every laugh, every morsel of the day in his head.

Within a few weeks, he was meeting her family. They were all a bunch of tall blond Swedes with last names that needed to buy a vowel, but to their credit, not one of them seemed to notice that Dani's escort was more like a Ford Escort next to her Mercedes elegance. Her dad in particular, a six foot six broad-shouldered man with hams for hands appropriately named Max, seemed to like Thomas a great deal. He was always jovial, laughed at all of Thomas' jokes, and enjoyed smacking him on the back a lot. Thomas appreciated Max, and all of Dani's family really, because he really had no one to listen to him or see him for who he was before he met her.

A few months later, he found out that he and Dani might have met once before when they were kids at somebody or other's birthday bash. Dani's grandfather had worked with Thomas' grandfather on translation projects, so the Livdahl family wound up on the guest list. Neither he nor Dani remembered meeting the other, but twelve-year-old boys don't travel in the same galaxy as six-year-old girls. One is running, throwing a ball and sweating while the other is giggling on the swing set. Thomas remembered that party fondly. It was the last time that he and his father had thrown the football together. Thomas' parents died a week later.

Before he knew it, their whirlwind romance landed him on one knee along the Freedom Trail by Paul Revere's statue. Dani taught high school history, and he thought he had a better chance of her saying yes if there was a historical landmark nearby.

His grandfather's strange words abruptly brought Thomas back to the present. "We are being watched. You could be in danger. I love you," Thomas repeated them aloud.

"I love you too," Dani responded as she entered the room, toweling her hair. She was wearing a fresh pair of shorts and a T-shirt with a picture of a horse lying on a kitchen floor on it. The caption read: 'Help! I've fallen and I can't giddy-up'.

Thomas smiled at her ever-present sense of humor.

"I wasn't talking to you," he said. "That jury is still out."

"Well, fine then. I take mine back. If one responds with what she thinks is an obligatory return 'I love you' and then later discovers that there was no starting sentiment of like kind, she is no longer liable for the response. It's all written out in black and white in our prenup."

"We don't have a prenuptial agreement," he countered.

"We don't? Crap, I knew something would fall through the cracks in all of those wedding preparations. That could be a biggie. I still don't know if I even like you," she said sweetly as she sat across his lap and wrapped her arms around his neck. "It's only been six years. You're still basically in your probationary period," she added as she kissed him lightly on the lips.

"My grandfather told me he loved me," he said, getting lost in those blue eyes for about the millionth time.

He kissed her back, feeling a familiar urge rising within him.

She backed her face away from his and stared at him. "Has he ever done that before?" she asked.

"Not as long as I can remember. He's dying, Dani," he whispered. "He's hooked up to enough machines to run a small dot-com business and is credit-card thin. In my whole life, I never imagined I'd see him that way. He was always so strong, so vibrant, so indestructible. He's Stewart Braden, for God's sake!"

"I'm so sorry," she said. "Maybe I can comfort you a little."

She climbed out of his lap and then straddled him in the chair.

Thomas pulled her close and kissed her. He let her freshly shampooed hair fall over his face. His breathing quickened.

"Whatever is going on with your grandfather, you will not figure it out right now."

"Why is that?"

"Because you're thinking with the wrong head right now."

"Yeah, you're right."

He pushed the recliner back as far as it would go as she climbed further onto him.

"Have I told you how much I love this chair?" he said.

"Shush, no talking," she said, kissing him hungrily.

A few minutes later, Dani hugged him fiercely while catching her breath. He was deep-breathing with his eyes closed. She felt tiny earthquakes inside him, rising from his core like underwater bubbles desperately seeking the surface. She clung to him and buried her face even deeper into him until he pushed her back and looked at her with damp eyes.

"I'm so glad I have you," he said. "I don't know how I would deal with losing him if I didn't have you."

"Well, I'm not going anywhere," she said. "He has always been a great man, but everyone reaches the end at some point."

"I know, but that's not the worst of it," he said. "He is losing his grip on reality. We're talking about a man who could name every U.S. president, what years they were in office, where they were born and what they had for breakfast on their inauguration day."

He paused for a moment and gazed out over her head as if he needed to recall something important. It was like a night creature nibbling at the edges of his memory but remaining just out of sight. He struggled to catch a glimpse but finally gave up.

"Now," he continued, "his head is full of conspiracies and riddles."

"What do you mean?" she asked.

"I don't know. He was talking all crazy mumbo-jumbo; said we were being watched and that there might be danger. And he was acting paranoid as well; waited until Carson left the room to give me something and made it clear that it was a secret. Then he told me this story from a dig he was on when he was still basically a rookie archaeologist.

Honestly, I don't even know if the story was real, but he seemed to relive it as he told it."

"What did he give you?" she asked.

His cell phone chimed out "Take Me Out to the Ball Game", and Thomas glanced at the screen.

"It's Papa," he mouthed before saying hello.

"Master Braden," Carson's nails-on-the-blackboard voice blared out of the phone. "I'm afraid I have some terrible news."

Thomas swallowed hard. He didn't want to hear this.

"What?"

"Your grandfather has just passed away."

Thomas hung up the phone. There were already tears in Dani's eyes, and he could not suppress his own. They flowed through his eyelids no matter how tightly he tried to keep them in. Death had come again, and with it the pain. His grandfather had asked him if he believed in God, and this is the answer he hadn't wanted to give. This was the very reason he could not believe. If there were a God, and that God had the power to do absolutely anything, then why did people have to die? Why did the people he loved and cared about have to die? Why?

Chapter 4

CALEB SAT ACROSS from them in the hearse, like in a stagecoach scene from the Old West. He was the XL version of Thomas. Same curly hair, same eyes, different demeanor. The big Cadillac's air conditioner was good, but it couldn't hold a candle to the ice storm brewing in the back seat.

"When was the last time you saw him?" Thomas asked his brother.

"Week ago, Sunday. He liked me to visit on Sundays."

"You saw him every Sunday?"

"Mostly."

"And you didn't bother to call me or, I don't know, drop me a text that the man had nine toes in the grave?"

"He told me not to bother you and said that if you

wanted to know how he was doing, you'd reach out," Caleb replied.

"He hated me, Caleb! Did you somehow forget that? Has your mind blocked out all those times I spent locked in my room conjugating verbs or some shit while you were outside taking batting practice or putting in your ten miles?"

"He knew you were the smart one. That's why he pushed you. I could study French from now until the Rapture, and I still could never order coffee in Paris."

"Bullshit, Caleb. You just pretended to be dumb so that he would leave you alone. You were his favorite because you reminded him of our father. He as much as told me so," Thomas said.

"What do you mean he told you? When?" Caleb asked.

Thomas shifted in his seat.

"The day he died," he whispered.

The pendulum of outrage swung back to Caleb.

"Are you fucking kidding me right now! Did you ever think to call me, or, I don't know, drop me a text that you visited with our grandfather just before he took his last breath?"

"Boys!" Dani stepped in. "This isn't the time or place for all of this brotherly love to erupt. When this is over, you can put the gloves on, climb into the ring and hash it out, but for now, put a cork in it."

The two brothers glared at each other as the car came to a stop on a narrow road in the Mt. Calvary Cemetery. The driver got out, opened the back door without a word, and waited.

"This isn't over, Thomas. Not by a long shot," Caleb

said.

A well-suited man with Santa Claus eyebrows approached them as they got out.

"This sucks," Thomas muttered.

"Father Caleb, Mr. and Mrs. Braden, if you will follow me, please," the cemetery greeter said.

***

Thomas stood dry-eyed behind sunglasses as well-wishers paraded past, first shaking his hand and then Dani's, and offering their condolences. He stared out over their shoulders and watched as a brisk breeze tickled the evenly cut grass and whipped the tiny American flags to attention. Above, ominous gray clouds elbowed their way into a low ceiling, bringing with them the slight scent of rain. A flock of crows cackled loudly from a towering oak in the distance as if cheering on the festivities below. A single-lane road snaked through the cemetery. Along its shoulders, an impressive line of limousines and town cars idled together, like a grazing herd on a cattle drive. He methodically said thanks every few seconds to the dozens upon dozens of Stewart Braden's friends, colleagues and admirers. There were politicians, scientists in several fields, and minor celebrities in attendance. The only things Thomas could feel were Dani's hand squeezing his arm gently while greeting the stream of people herself and his left hand fiddling with the hand wraps in his pocket. He really needed to hit something or someone right now.

Caleb was a few feet away, working his own receiving line, accepting hugs and praying with lost souls. Someone

— Thomas didn't know who — thought the line would move faster if it were split in two, but he didn't care if no one came by to see him.

He spotted Carson standing near the gravesite like an overgrown ogre in an undertaker's suit. High above, the sound of jet engines reverberated through the clouds. Thomas wished he were on that plane. He longed to take Dani and fly away. He wanted to scream to the heavens and run across the grass to a better place, any place.

"You know, I never realized before how much you favor him," an elderly woman with light purple hair and a kind smile said to him.

"Thank you," he replied.

When the last of them finally said their peace and drifted off to their rides and back to their lives, Thomas plopped into the wooden folding chair under the family's tarp and stared at the coffee-colored coffin that held his grandfather. A couple of ripe drops of rain splashed on its top and drizzled off the side. Dani sat next to him, rubbing his back while Carson consumed a chair in the second row. Not long after, Caleb took a seat on the other side of Dani in an attempt to put Switzerland between them, Thomas surmised. They sat quietly like that while the sky opened up, no longer able to hold back the force of the rampaging clouds. The gravediggers huddled at a discreet distance under the tarp with them while instant waterfalls swirled from every corner of the tent.

"The irony of all this is that almost every single person who was consoling me knew my grandfather better than I did," he finally said.

"It doesn't matter," Dani responded. "Their world

didn't change today. Yours did. Caleb's did. It will never be the same as it was before. Whether or not you were close to him does not change the fact that he was your grandfather."

Carson leaned forward from behind Thomas like the Grim Reaper. "Master Thomas and Father Caleb," he began, "your grandfather was a great and generous man. It was my honor to serve him for so many years, and I would consider it a privilege if you would allow me to help you through this trying time. I know he has many artifacts and collectibles that need to be identified, and I'm sure that the estate will need to be inventoried, etcetera. I would like to offer my services in whatever capacity is helpful to the two of you."

Dani made a gagging face before turning away. Thomas watched the rain dwindle as if someone in the clouds was turning off the faucet. He stood, stretched his neck, and turned to the butler.

"I think," he said to Carson, "that the best service you can be to me is in the capacity of being invisible. Consider yourself retired as of this moment. I'll have the attorney draw up your last check and a bonus for all those years of service, as you say. Are you in agreement, Caleb?"

His brother nodded without looking over.

"Whatever you say, Thomas," Carson replied dryly, dropping all pretense of an employee-employer relationship. He stood to his full height and for a moment hovered over Thomas before walking away.

"I am really turned on right now," Dani whispered in her husband's ear as the giant faded into the light rain. They stood arm in arm as the gravediggers lowered the coffin into the ground with large straps, and Caleb offered one last blessing. Then, they noticed a man across the way step out of a black SUV and head toward them. He was clean-shaven and wore a dark suit coat, unmatched dark slacks, dark glasses and an old-fashioned derby.

"Well, who do we have here?" Caleb wondered aloud.

"Are you expecting someone?" Dani whispered.

"I'm an introvert. I never expect anyone," Thomas answered.

"Excuse me, Mr. Braden," the man said. "I just wanted to say I am sorry for your loss," he added, tipping his hat to Dani.

He glanced over at Caleb, but didn't seem interested in him.

"Thanks. Did you know my grandfather?" Thomas asked.

"Not exactly no. But I'd like to speak with you for a moment if I may. I'm Agent Harrison from Homeland Security," he said, flipping out a leather wallet.

Thomas studied the man's identification badge for a moment. Agent Harrison appeared to be built from cement blocks, and his face could have served as the prototype for the Rock'em Sock'em Robot. Other than a gravy stain on his red tie, there was nothing out of place.

"Agent Harrison, did they give you bad timing training over at Homeland?"

The agent grinned broadly. "Good one, but I wouldn't be here if it weren't important. I just need to ask you a few questions."

"Well, we're expected at a reception and we're already late, so maybe some other time."

Agent Harrison puckered his lips in disbelief for a

second, but then jumped into what was on his mind. "You visited your grandfather the same day he died, am I right?" he asked.

"I did. Why, may I ask, is that any of your or Homeland Security's business?"

"Yes," Caleb added, joining the conversation. "What business is that of yours?"

"I'll get right to the point. We have been monitoring your grandfather's house over the last few weeks."

"Wait," Thomas felt a twinge of anger mix in with his anxiety. "What does that mean: monitoring his house?"

"It means we have had the house under surveillance and are monitoring all incoming and outgoing calls."

"What? What gives you the right?" Thomas shouted.

"Well, actually Congress gave us the right, or don't you read the papers, Mr. Braden?" the agent calmly replied.

"I stopped reading them when I realized how many lies were being printed every day. I know the bar is set pretty low for you boys over at Homeland Security, but are you saying that you had his phones tapped because my grandfather, on his deathbed, presented a credible threat? To what? A bedpan? Who's next on your watchlist, SpongeBob SquarePants?"

"Did your grandfather say anything unusual to you or act out of the ordinary in any way?" the agent continued, ignoring Thomas' sarcasm.

"Yes, he confessed he was the man on the grassy knoll, so there you go. You've just broken the biggest case of the twentieth century. Congratulations."

"Look, Agent Harrison, I'm Father Caleb Braden, and we just buried our grandfather. Perhaps this conversation could take place at a more appropriate time."

"I know who you are. I'm really trying to help here, and neither of you is making it very easy. There are a lot of dangerous people in the world, and I'm assigned to keep track of them. I hope you can understand that."

For the second time in the last week, someone used the word danger or one of its derivatives in a conversation with Thomas. He was really beginning to hate that word.

"My grandfather acted like a dying man, Agent Harrison, and since he actually died, I don't think it was an act at all. He did not have the time or energy to threaten national security, if that is what you are wondering."

"What about his butler, Carson Prewitt?"

"Carson's second cousin is dirt. He's a threat to keel over from old age at any minute," Thomas replied. "Now, we really need to get going. Is there anything else?"

"No," the agent replied as he chiseled a smile back onto his granite face. "I'll just leave you my card in case you think of anything substantive. Thanks for your, uh... cooperation." He nodded to Dani for the second time, ignored Caleb for the second time, and walked away.

"What was that all about? Caleb asked.

"How the hell should I know?" Thomas answered.

"Look, Thomas, if there is something you need to tell me, let's go somewhere and talk."

"What, like the confessional? Forget it. We're going home."

Thomas grabbed Dani's arm.

"At least let me get you a ride back to the church," Caleb said.

"No," Thomas snapped. "I'll catch up with you later."

"Thomas," Caleb said, "have a little faith. It won't hurt."

***

They ordered a Lyft back to the church and then drove home. When they got there, Thomas circled the block once before parking.

"What are you doing?" Dani asked him.

"Just being cautious."

He slammed the car into park and raced for the front door, Dani trailing. Once inside, he retrieved a scrap of paper from the bedroom, plopped into a kitchen chair and started copying from it into a notebook. Once he finished, he handed Dani the original.

"When I was with Papa, he handed me this," he said, showing her the key, "wrapped in that note and then told me we were being watched."

Dani stared at the key and opened the slip of paper. She frowned at the numbers she saw written on it.

29 16 24 16 24 13 16 29
26 32 29
33 12 14 12 31 20 26 25
24 13 31 31 19 16 34 127 154

"What is this?" she asked.

"Well, depending on your perspective, it's a numerical code, the gibberish of a loon, or both. I told you I thought he was losing it. He went all cloak and dagger on me, and the conspiracy or danger or whatever he thought was out

37

there — well, I thought it was all in his head. But after the visit from our friendly neighborhood G-man, I'm having second thoughts."

"If he was just being a nutcase, why did he go to all the trouble to create a coded message to give you?" Dani asked him. "I mean, in the movies, those guys just try to tell anyone who will listen that someone is after them. They don't think to themselves; Hmm, how can I make it as difficult as possible for someone to figure out that I need help?"

Thomas contemplated that for a moment. She had a point.

"Perhaps if he thought he was being watched, he considered that the note could be intercepted, and if it was, he wanted it to be challenging for a stranger to decipher."

"Or," she countered, "he specifically decided that you were the right person to trust with whatever this is."

"Maybe so. I even asked him why he didn't just talk to Caleb about what was bothering him, but he insisted it had to be me."

"Still, there's no harm in decoding it, is there?" she asked. "You're probably right about him just being paranoid, but Stone Face Harrison admitted they were watching the house."

He turned the key over in his hand as he studied the numbers on the paper again. He looked at the number 47 engraved on the key.

"The key is the key," he announced.

"The key is the key?" she asked. "That's your brilliant insight? Is the table also a table? What about the refrigerator? Could it also be the refrigerator?"

"I mean, the number on the key is the key. The code is relatively easy to break, which makes me think he wasn't up to his normal complex self when he wrote this. More likely, he was in a big hurry and just threw this code together."

"If he just threw it together, then he must know that almost anyone could break it. That doesn't seem especially secure," Dani replied.

"Yes, except he only gave it to me, and I am probably the only person alive that knows that his favorite number is or was eleven. If anyone else got a hold of this, they would eventually break the code, but he was hoping I could do it quickly and then get rid of the note, I think."

"Why do you think eleven is important?" she asked.

"Because of the key," he answered. "The numbers add up to eleven. If you take any two-digit number where the two digits added together equal eleven, and then reverse the digits to form a second number, you will always get one hundred and twenty-one when you add them together."

"You lost me," she said.

"Okay," he said. "If you take forty-seven and add it to seventy-four, the sum is one hundred twenty-one. The same is true for thirty-eight plus eighty-three and twenty-nine plus ninety-two. The square root of one hundred and twenty-one is eleven. That is why he liked the number eleven so much. While everyone else thought of it as an odd, relatively obscure prime number, he loved the way it sort of balanced itself out. Once you know eleven is the key to the code, the rest is easy."

He took the sheet of paper where he had copied the numbers from his grandfather's message and, below each number; he wrote a letter by subtracting 11 from the number.

29 16 24 16 24 13 16 29
r e m e m b e r

26 32 29
o u r

33 12 14 12 31 20 26 25
v a c a t i o n

24 13 30 28 132 145
m a r k

"The last two numbers don't fit the code," Dani said, chewing her lower lip.

"Right, because they are numbers, not letters," Thomas surmised. He eyed the last two numbers for a few seconds.

"I've got it," he snapped. "He used one twenty-one as the base for the numerical part of the message. So, if you subtract one twenty-one, you get eleven and twenty-four."

"Mark 11:24," they said together.

Thomas looked at her for a moment and waited. He knew it wouldn't take long.

"Therefore, I tell you, whatever you ask for in prayer, believe that you have received it and it shall be yours," Dani quoted from memory.

"You should really get on Bible Jeopardy," he said.

"But what do you think it means?" she asked.

"How should I know?" Thomas said. "It could still

mean nothing."

"You haven't believed that since Stone Face paid his respects."

"You're right, but I don't know what to make of anything yet."

"What about this other half of the message?" she nudged him. "This looks like 'remember our vacation'. Does that mean anything to you?"

Thomas leaned back in his chair and rubbed his eyes. He could still hear kids laughing, music playing, and the rush of the Atlantic. His feet could feel the weathered boardwalk's uneven planks. He turned the key over in his hand, trying to elicit some hint, however subtle, from it.

"It means we're taking a trip," he announced, dropping his chair back to the floor.

Chapter 5

THOMAS AND DANI rolled up to the shuttle parking lot at Coney Island around noon after four hours of awkward driving silence. A stooping guy wearing an orange vest and waving a flashlight guided them into an unmarked spot on the dirt. A cloud of dust trailed them in.

"This guy must be moonlighting from his Wal-Mart greeter job," Thomas quipped.

"Really? After four hours of acting like I don't exist, your first words to me are some lame joke about the parking attendant?" Dani snapped at him. "Not cool, Braden! I've spent the last hundred miles asking you questions and getting nothing but shrugs from you."

"I'm sorry. This whole mess has got me jumbled up inside. At first, I didn't believe a word of my grandfather's story about being watched, and I dismissed it as the ravings of an old man, but I was wrong. Now, I'm wondering how wrong I have been about him for a long time. When Harrison showed up at the funeral, it was like a gut punch. Papa was right. What he was sensing was real, and I just blew him off. Then, worst of all, he died before I could apologize to him. He told me he loved me for the first time, and I made out like it was no big deal. I can be a real ass sometimes."

"Then let me in and help you. Are we in this together or not? I realize you like to turn to humor as your defense mechanism, but now is not the time. It's annoying."

"Wow, that's exactly what he told me. Did he tell you to say that to me?"

"Ugh," she grunted. "You really CAN be an ass sometimes."

"I know. I know. You're right," he said. "Look, I feel like I owe him something. He trusted me and confided in me. We are in this together, and believe me, I need you right now, but there is a small part of me that is wondering if there really is a chance that we could be in danger here. I want to see this through for him, but not if it means putting you at risk."

"Even if your grandfather was not imagining being watched, that doesn't mean we are in danger because of it."

"You're probably right still; we're not spies or detectives or whatever. If we sense any danger at all, I think we need to get the hell out. Agreed? The first sign of trouble and we leave it all to old Stone Face."

"Agreed. So, tell me why we are sitting in the parking area at Coney Island."

"The note said, remember our vacation. During my entire childhood, we took only one vacation as a family, and it was here. I remember I couldn't believe it. My grandfather came home one day from one of his long digs and told us we were leaving the next day for a vacation. Just like that. He gave me a riddle to break and said that it held the clue to our vacation destination. It stunned Caleb and me, but we didn't let any grass grow under our feet. We started packing that minute. Well, packing might be an overstatement. We threw swim trunks and fins into a bag and called it good. I had the coolest bath towel with sharks on it, and Caleb's had dolphins. We grabbed those and ran for the car before Papa could change his mind. I worked out the riddle in about two minutes, and we were off to Coney Island."

Dani smiled at him as his mind surfed back to that special memory. She touched his hand.

"It may have been the happiest moment that Caleb and I ever shared."

"It sounds like it was a wonderful trip. So, where does this key come from?" she asked.

"If I remember correctly, there were a couple of places where there were lockers for rent. One was near the water for storing your clothes while swimming, and the other was underneath the roller coaster where you could put stuff that you didn't want to lose on the ride."

"Okay," she said. "Let's go check them out and see if there is a locker forty-seven."

They got out and headed for the park entrance. There were hordes of people everywhere. Many of them were wearing long blond wigs and brightly colored tops with flaps on their sleeves. Some wore tight skirts with bright aqua trains trailing behind them. As they approached the entrance, they saw a huge banner saying, 'Welcome to the Mermaid Parade.'

"Well, that explains that," Thomas commented. "Try to fit in, will you?"

Dani punched him in the arm and then held on to it as they queued up at the ticket window. As the line slowly inched forward, Thomas watched a young family just ahead of them. The kids wore bathing suits and kept churning around the legs of their parents, running this way and that in perpetual motion. Once, when the father looked back, Thomas noticed the grim look on his face as if to say, 'Why did we think this was going to be fun?' Directly in front of him was a young couple dressed for the parade. Thomas almost stepped on the girl's tail twice. He looked back to see how long the line was behind them and noticed a man staring directly at him. He had long, straggly hair and was dressed more for a motorcycle rally than a carnival and certainly not for the beach. Thomas let his eyes pass over the man as if he didn't notice him. Maybe his imagination was working overtime. He turned back and didn't look back again.

"Everything okay?" Dani asked.

"Fine," he said.

After twenty minutes in line, they finally got in. Thomas headed straight for the roller coaster to check out the bank of lockers. He held Dani's hand tightly as they cut through the throng like a canoe through water. Kids were laughing and screaming on the Tilt-a-Whirl. Parents were taking pictures and smiling while toddlers in strollers looked around wide-eyed at all the sights and sounds. Thomas excused himself after bumping into a pair of mermaids trying to take a selfie. They reached what appeared to be the end of 'The Cyclone' line as the great wooden coaster came crashing down the rails amid screams of joy. He couldn't see the beginning of the line as it weaved underneath the coaster structure, but the sounds transported him right back to his childhood.

"I can remember so vividly Caleb and me standing in this line," he said. "Papa didn't care to ride it, but we were all in. We were tweens and didn't want to miss a thing. I remember my heart racing when we climbed into the car. I had chosen the ride, but as the line got closer and closer, I was having second thoughts, but I didn't let on. Caleb, though, was fearless. He said little to me usually, but on the roller coaster he was a freak. He would throw his hands in the air and scream like a high school girl at a horror movie through every drop and corner. We bought one of those pictures that they take while you're on the coaster. The looks on our faces were polar opposites. Mine was sheer terror, and his was unfettered joy."

"Papa brought us here totally out of the blue and never laughed much with us or ever praised us, but when we got off that ride he was smiling like a proud Papa. On my last day, I will still be able to recall and feel that moment."

"Sounds nice," Dani said.

"Yeah," he said, clearing his throat. "So, if I remember right, the boxes are just before you get into the main line. We'll have to stand here for a few minutes before we can reach that point, I guess," he said.

"Forget that," Dani responded as she pushed her way

through the line. "I'm looking for my daughter. She's lost," she said to the others as she passed them in line.

Thomas pushed through behind her, apologizing to the line members as he went until they reached the place where the lockers sat stacked against a wall. It didn't take but a moment for them to realize that they were not in the right place. There were no more that a dozen lockers, and most of them did not have doors on them at all. They turned and pushed their way back out of the queue in reverse order.

"Next stop is the beach area," Thomas yelled over the sound of another train plunging down the tracks.

They maneuvered their way back out onto the midway and set their sights on the ocean. The Mermaid Parade was in full swing now, and there was no way for them to cross over to the other side, so they paralleled the marching mermaids as best they could, sliding in and around onlookers as they went. Finally, they reached a point where they couldn't go on. They settled for watching the parade go by. On the other side, through a float with dolphins playing on it, Thomas saw the same man. This time, there was no question. The man was watching them. Thomas pulled Dani back from the parade line and led her back the way they had come.

"What's going on?" she asked.

"I'm pretty sure that we are being followed," he said. "I just want to fade back into the crowd and see if we can lose the guy."

"What guy?"

"I saw him in line behind us for tickets, and I felt like he was watching us. Then, just now I saw him across the way. He didn't care a bit about the parade. He was staring directly at me."

Thomas guided Dani into a side alley where there were concessions and portable johns. Next to the hot dog stand was a large tent. They ducked inside and found themselves at a kind of flea market. There were hats and shirts and scarves, and bathing suits advertising Coney Island. And on the far wall, there were mermaid costumes for all ages. Thomas led Dani to the back of the tent.

"Remember when I said I wanted you to fit in?" he said.

"You are kidding me, Braden."

"I'm not. We need to change our appearance quickly."

"This all seems like a contrived reason to get me into one of those outfits," she said.

A few minutes and a hundred and thirty dollars later, they walked out of the tent. Thomas was wearing a bright blue t-shirt that read 'Mer-man', an aqua pair of shorts, dark glasses and a Coney Island cap pulled low over his eyes. Dani was wearing a sundress with mermaids on it, a long blond wig and dark glasses of her own.

"It's best if we don't walk together," he said. "Stay a few steps behind me. If you see me take off running, go the other way."

"No way."

"Just do it!" he snapped.

Dani stared at him for a moment and then turned away as he moved back toward the beach. The parade crowd was breaking up, and people were dispersing as if a bomb had been detonated on the midway, launching human shrapnel in a million directions. Thomas waded through the crowd, keeping his eyes roving for the mystery man, and every so often glancing back to see that Dani was still in tow by some invisible rope. At last, they reached the edge of the beach and spotted a shower building to the left. Here, the crowd thinned considerably, and the carnival sounds were muted. They walked to the low-slung building and entered a flow-through entrance that opened to the sea at the other end, allowing the warm ocean breeze carrying the scent of suntan lotion to funnel through it. A sign pointed to the ladies' showers on the left and the men's on the right with big arrows made of driftwood. Lining both sides of the open area were lockers running the full length of the building and stacked three high. They quickly deciphered the number pattern and found locker forty-seven.

"This isn't at all like I remembered it, but I guess he didn't get the key twenty-five years ago. He probably only did this in the last year or two," Thomas said as he stared at the unopened locker. "I'm a little afraid of what we will find in here."

"Whatever it is, we'll deal with it," Dani said.

Thomas took the key from his pocket and inserted it into the keyhole. The key turned easily in his hand, and he flipped the latch up and swung the door open. Inside, they found one sealed envelope with Thomas' name scribbled in cursive on the front.

"It's Papa's handwriting. It was always as awful as a doctor's."

He pulled the envelope out and instinctively shook it to no avail, then closed the locker and left the key in the keyhole. He slid the envelope carefully into his back pocket just as two men entered from the carnival-side of the building.

"Must be the welcoming committee," Thomas said

under his breath. "I've been in bigger messes, but not in a long time. Let's go."

Chapter 6

THE MEN SEPARATED to block the way out. Thomas turned around, grabbed Dani's arm and headed for the beach-side exit, but after only a couple of steps two men appeared at that end of the building as well. All four men had tattooed arms and wore blue jeans, work shirts, leather jackets, and sunglasses. Thomas turned in a circle, keeping Dani close as he surveyed the situation. He recognized one of them as the man who had been watching them.

"You guys hit a buy one get three free sale at Muggers R' Us?" he asked.

No reply. Two young girls in bikinis approached the breezeway from the beach. The man at the end stepped in front of them.

"This area is closed," he growled.

Thomas saw the girls' eyes grow wide as Frisbees before they turned and ran off without another word.

The man watched them leave and then turned back. Now, all four men focused on Thomas and Dani. One of them assumed command by stepping forward. He was thin, maybe thirty-five, and had a sharp, protruding nose. He was wearing a ball cap with "Make America Great Again" stitched on the front.

"Mr. Braden," he started with a Cheshire Cat grin, "it would be better for you and your lovely wife if you would come with us, please."

"Who are you?" Thomas asked. "And how do you know my name?"

"You'll get your answers in due time. For now, we need to go."

"I don't think so," said Thomas.

With that, Thomas took his hand wraps out of his pocket and started wrapping his right hand first.

Ballcap laughed at him. "Whatever you are thinking, Mr. Braden, I suggest you reconsider. Things could go badly for you and your wife."

Thomas ignored him and wrapped his left hand.

"Lucky," Ballcap said.

One man from the beachside quickly moved in on them. Thomas turned and hit him with a quick jab to the nose, a hammer to the ribcage, and a left hook to the temple. Lucky dropped faster than a skyscraper elevator.

"Your boy needs a new nickname," Thomas said.

He turned to see that Ballcap had a gun trained on him.

"You're a funny guy," he said to Thomas. "I hate funny guys. They make me so angry I could spit. Now you have something we want, and I beg you, say something funny."

Thomas stepped in front of Dani and swallowed hard.

"I'm sure that I do not know what you're talking about. I have nothing that would interest you," Thomas said.

"You either have it or you can lead us to it," Ballcap replied, still pointing the gun directly at them. "However lovely as Mrs. Braden is, she is of no use to us at all. So, it's your choice. You either come with us, or she suffers the consequences for your comedy act."

"What is it you want?" Thomas asked.

Ballcap didn't answer. Instead, he shot a quick look at the others, and they all began moving in unison, closing the noose around the young couple. Thomas stayed in front of Dani and pushed her back against the lockers. There was no way he could get them out of this. It was now three to one, and Mr. Ballcap was being cavalier about brandishing his weapon. When they were within just a few feet, everyone stopped as they heard someone approaching.

"Say nothing, or you will both die right here, right now," Ballcap snarled. Thomas froze.

The lyrics of 'My Girl' wafted on the breeze as a tall, dark man in a loud Hawaiian shirt sauntered around the corner singing.

"Stop where you are!" snapped Ballcap.

"Say what?" Hawaiian Shirt asked.

"Turn around now and walk away before you get hurt," Ballcap replied.

"Oh, I'll only be a moment. Got to hit the little boy's room. You understand."

The man next to Ballcap turned and confronted the would-be Temptation while pulling a gun out of his pocket.

"You must leave now. Do you read me, or are you too drunk to get it?" he asked.

A million-watt smile spread across Hawaiian Shirt's face as he held his arms out, palms up in a gesture of peace.

"Now, my brother, I do in fact love to sing out the hits, but I don't drink, cuz I promised my mama I would stay away from that sort of thing. So, I think you have me all wrong, and we somehow got off on the wrong foot. My name's Cleveland Chaney."

He offered his hand to the gunman, who just stared at him. Then, as if noticing Dani for the first time, Chaney took another step forward.

"Now ain't you the most precious thing." He then looked at Thomas. "You are one lucky young man. Yes sir, no doubt about it," he continued with another step.

"That's far enough," the gunman said, grabbing Chaney by his left arm.

Immediately Chaney latched onto the assailant's left arm as well, as if they were preparing to arm wrestle. Then Chaney came over the top with a punishing right cross to the man's throat. He went down like a sack of flour, but Chaney didn't even notice. He was already on Ballcap with a ferocious chop down on the man's gun hand, sending it clattering across the concrete floor as a massive uppercut caught Ballcap under the chin and sent him crashing into the lockers. The two men at the other entrance were too slow to react and could only stare blankly as Chaney pulled a weapon from the small of his back and yelled at both of them to hit the floor. They looked confused about the instructions, but eventually complied. At the same time, the man called Lucky got to his knees while attempting to pull a pistol from his pocket. Chaney shot him smoothly in the shoulder. The bewildered man dropped the pistol and sat down awkwardly against the wall. Chaney crossed the floor, kicked the gun away and hustled the man down onto his face.

"Get their," he started to say when Ballcap got to his feet and stumbled towards his gun.

Dani saw him at the same instant and expertly kicked him between the legs. He crumpled to the floor with a "whooshing" sound escaping his lips. He did not move again.

"Cute and feisty," Chaney commented with that huge grin. "You've got to like that. Now, you two gather up all of their guns, cell phones, and IDs and put them in this bag. He threw a canvas tie-up bag at them. We've gotta move."

"Wait a minute," Thomas said, holding Dani in place before she touched anything. "Why should we go with you? For all I know, you are as bad as these guys. Actually, a quick look around here tells me you are worse."

"Can we talk about this after we get these guys secured, please?" Chaney asked. "These chumps weren't here to ask you to a Tupperware party. Agreed?"

"Yeah, I guess that's right."

"Good. Dani, you gather up their stuff while Thomas and I haul them into the bathroom."

He then ripped up his shirt and put a tourniquet on the bullet wound and, with Thomas's help, they dragged all four men into the men's shower area and put them in the back stall together where Chaney left them with a warning.

"Now, we're going to leave, but if I hear anyone screaming for help in the next ten minutes, I'm going to come back and put a bullet in each one of your sorry heads. Do I make myself clear?"

All four men acknowledged his warning with a slight nod or by being unconscious.

"Alright," he said to Dani and Thomas. "We have to move now. Don't run, but don't dawdle either."

The three of them left the shower complex toward the beach and quickly made their way toward the surf. They were instantly swallowed up by hundreds of sun-worshipers, frisbee throwers, volleyballers, swimmers, waders, sandcastle diggers and sandcastle destroyers.

"When we reach the pier, we will head back inland to my car," Chaney commanded.

"Really?" Thomas protested. "I don't think we are getting into a car with you. We have our own transportation."

"It's been compromised," Chaney replied.

"What are you talking about?" Thomas demanded.

Chaney stopped and eyed the young man for a moment.

"You have some of the old man's stubbornness in you. I can see that pretty clearly."

With that, he started traipsing through the sand again. Thomas and Dani looked at each other for a moment, then followed him.

"Give me the bag," Chaney said. "We need to dump everything."

Thomas gave him the bag with the guns and IDs in it and then grabbed Chaney's arm.

"Look," he said. "I appreciate you helping us out back there, but who are you? And why should we trust you now? We don't even know what any of this is about."

Chaney looked directly into Thomas' eyes. The smile was gone now. He was all business.

"My name's Chaney. Your grandfather sent me because he was concerned for your safety. I know less than you do about what's going on, but that's not my department. He placed his bet, and it was on you. You're going to figure this whole thing out, and I suggest you get started right away because we just tied up four bad guys and left them in a public bathroom, and whoever sent them ain't gonna be happy about it. Got it?"

Thomas stared back at the man for a moment. His grandfather's words sprang to the front of his mind. Trust no one. There could be danger. I love you.

"Okay," he said. "Get us out of here."

***

Taylor Mackie sat in a small clearing by a glass-topped lake. His tattered lawn chair squeaked every time he moved to swat a mosquito. Trees blanketed the shoreline, mostly pines and sugar maples that marched right up to the water's edge like a conquering army. Cicadas sang from the trees first on his right, then his left, like they were doing the wave at a ballgame. A thin wildlife trail wove out of the underbrush, tiptoed up to the water and then disappeared into the foliage on the other side. The bank was rocky with a three-foot drop to the water. There was a dilapidated dock that listed to the left just below his feet.

He watched as two teenage boys trolled toward the dock in a flat-bottomed boat. The one in the stern expertly cut the motor so they could coast home while the boy in the bow jumped onto the dock like a gymnast sticking a landing and tied the boat off.

"Y'all catch anything, boys?" Mackie called out.

The boy in the stern pulled up the lead wire from beside the boat and held up the bounty for inspection.

"Mostly crappie, but one catfish was dumb enough to get caught too," the boy replied.

"That's a nice-looking string, boys. Now, why don't y'all just run those on up to the big house and get'em cleaned. You hear?"

"Yes, sir, Mr. Mackie," they replied together.

As the boys headed up the hill, Mackie called after them.

"And y'all make sure that Aunt Hazel and Aunt Sudie know that there's fresh fish available. You hear?"

"Yes, sir. We'll tell them."

Mackie turned his attention back to the lake just as the phone rang. He flipped it open and took a deep breath.

"Did you get 'em?" he asked.

"No, they had help," the voice came from the other end.

"What does that mean?"

"Another man intervened. I've never seen him before. Some black dude."

"You mean a Good Samaritan?" Mackie asked.

"No, he knew them. He was there specifically for them."

"I see. There were four of y'all, right?"

"Yes, but he surprised us, and he has had some training."

Mackie took another breath. He should have gone

himself. Instead, he sent these idiots. This would not do at all. At some point, he'd have to get involved, beginning by handling the fallout from their massive failure.

"Do you have any idea where they are going next?" he asked.

"No. They tied us up in the bathroom, and the black guy shot Lucky. The medics released me just this minute. I'm using one of their phones. Braden took our phones and guns. The police are here and are asking questions. No one is talking, but I think they are going to arrest Smitty."

"For what?"

"They didn't say."

"Typical," Mackie said. "If you don't look like you work in an air-conditioned office behind a desk, they can arrest you for having the awful sense to get shot by a stranger. A black stranger, no less."

This was getting better and better. He could actually feel his blood pressure rising, but the beast in him would have to wait for satisfaction.

"Do you know where they are taking Smitty?" he asked.

"No."

"Find him, break him out of the hospital and high-tail it home. Do you understand?"

"Yes."

"Now, you have compromised this phone. Do you realize that?"

There was silence on the other end for a beat.

"So, only now you realize it. Is that a fair assessment?" Mackie asked.

"Yes."

"Good, now do as I say. Load everyone into the van,

injured or not, and drive through the night. Stop only for gas and a piss. Do not make another mistake."

He hung up the phone before the other man could respond. Then he pushed himself out of the sagging chair and flung his phone as far as he could into the lake. This mission was going to be more challenging than he had expected, but any challenge worth overcoming must be difficult and he knew when Patterson contacted him three months ago that he had brought with him an opportunity for Mackie to set the Freedom Landers up for years to come.

Chapter 7

THREE MONTHS EARLIER

A heavy black sedan wallowed along the tree-lined, pot-holed dirt road and came to a stop at an iron gate. The foliage was so thick on both sides that there was little need for fencing on the property. Cameras sat atop the bookend iron posts like medieval sentries watching the road. The sedan came to a stop and waited. There was no obvious speaker system available with which to contact people within the compound. After a moment, the driver got out and looked for a way either to open the gate or to hail someone who could. He was heading back to the car when a voice boomed from speakers hidden in the trees.

"Are you lost?" the voice asked.

Not knowing where to look while speaking, the young man stared straight through the gate, down the dirt road, and said, "We're here to see Mr. Mackie."

"Do you have an appointment?" the voice asked. "He does not entertain guests without an appointment, and I don't see one on his calendar. I think it would be best if you were on your way."

At that moment, an older man exited the back seat of the car and answered.

"We were remiss in not obtaining an appointment, sir, but if we may be allowed just a few minutes with Mr. Mackie, we will make it worth his while. We are prepared to make a sizable donation to the Freedom Landers Church of God for his time. I ask only that you relay this information to him, please."

"Standby," the voice responded.

The two men got back into the vehicle, in their respective seats, and waited.

Inside the compound, a different set of speakers called out.

"Mr. Mackie, please report to the security bunker. You have a visitor at the gate."

Taylor Mackie looked up from his sermon text, closed his Bible, and made his way to the big house. He said hello to the half-dozen kids who were shucking peas on the porch and the two women who were cutting up chickens for frying.

He reached the solid steel door in the center of the house and used his thumbprint to gain access. Inside was a two-story oval room with television monitors running along the entire main wall. There was a long steel desk that dissected the room, with four technicians monitoring various banks of monitors. Behind them was a massive U-shaped desk housing multiple monitors, with a massive man sitting at it. On the back and side walls, a constant stream of data and voice prints drifted around the room like a miniature version of the New York Stock Exchange, but this data was not Dow Jones Industrial stock prices or the latest scores on ESPN. It was indecipherable to the uneducated eye.

Mackie walked over to the man they called Junkyard, who was in charge of all video and audio surveillance. Junkyard played left tackle for the Razorbacks for one season before being discharged from the team for being too violent. He sported a long red beard down to his chest and a completely bald head. Tattoos ran up both arms and peeked out above his t-shirt collar like they were looking to further expand their empire.

"What you got for me, Junk? And why the hell is it so cold in here?" Mackie asked the big man.

"I like it cold, Mack. You've just been outside in the heat too long. There are two men at the south gate in a town car. They asked for you by name and said they wanted to make a donation to the church if they could speak with you briefly. I ran the plates already, but it's a rental out of Little Rock."

He pulled up still-shot photos of the two men as they stood by the car and zoomed in on their faces.

"I ran facial recognition on both in the standard databases, but nothing popped."

Mackie studied the photos, which sported flawless resolution. The first man was young, maybe thirty tops, and had dark hair and a meticulously trimmed beard. He wore a tight-fitting suit designed to show off his biceps. Mackie was unimpressed. The other older man had gray hair and a thin mustache. His suit easily cost five grand, and his shoes were spit-shined. He was the definition of distinguished, and Mackie did not trust him at all.

"Show them in and tell Marcus to assemble the welcome wagon," he said to Junkyard.

The gates opened without preamble, so the driver pulled through the tight opening and continued up the road. Half a mile later, they encountered another gate that was already standing open. The driver rolled through that one, and it immediately closed behind them. They continued up a small rise and flattened out into a large clearing. Straight ahead was an outdoor wooden structure with benches under a canopy. It read "Freedom Landers Church of God" above the arched entrance to the pavilion. Directly to the left was a much larger two-story building with what appeared to be an outdoor kitchen and mess hall attached to one side. On the immediate right was a one-room building that read "Schoolhouse" over the door. Further to the right and running up a long, easy slope were several cabins, all apparently built from identical kits, including the porch swings. The big sedan rolled to a stop in the clearing. The driver put his window down but didn't get out. All he could hear was the pinging of the engine cooling and the cicadas in the trees.

After a few moments, men carrying automatic weapons approached from all four points of the compass. They stood ready, and one of them signaled for the two men to get out of the car. The men complied with hands held high. From the kitchen area of the big house, two men approached. One was as big as a mountain and looked as if he could tame lions with his bare hands. The other was shorter, but still imposing. They appeared unarmed. When they got close enough, the shorter man stepped in front. He was a little over six feet tall but stout as an oak, with a clean-shaven face and a haircut that would make any marine proud. He wore full military gear with heavy boots and walked with an air of superiority.

"Well, fellas, it seems y'all are kind of off the beaten path, aren't ya?" he said. "My name's Taylor Mackie, and while I freely admit that we have a very nice and welcoming community here, I don't believe we're on any travel brochures at the moment. So, I will give you gentlemen the opportunity to hop right back in your car and go back to Little Rock right now, or I'm gonna have to ask Marcus to search you before we can visit. Your choice."

"Mr. Mackie," the older man said. "We have traveled a great distance in order to meet with you, and as I said to the man monitoring the gate, we will gladly make a donation to your church and community if you will only allow us a few minutes of your time."

"Marcus," Mackie said.

The man called Marcus handed his rifle to another guard and approached the two men.

"Hands on the roof, please, and spread your legs," he told the visitors.

They complied while he frisked them. Then he pulled a wand from his back pocket and scanned them both. He pulled their cell phones and dropped them in a heavy bag like those that commercial enterprises used to transport large deposits to the bank. He locked the bag and returned the key to his pocket, and then handed the bag to the driver and backed away.

"We don't allow smartphones of any kind on our property," Mackie said. "They provide misinformation to our people and poison our children's minds with nonsense and video games. We will hang on to them while we talk and then return them to you when you leave. Are we in agreement?"

The two men nodded.

"Very well, if you would kindly join me at the picnic table, we can have a sit-down. But just you," Mackie continued, eyeing the older man. "Tell your man to wait by the car."

He nodded to the driver, who stayed put, exchanging glances with the armed guards.

"Junk," Mackie said. "Ask Aunt Hazel to bring us some iced tea, if you will. Thank you."

The big man lumbered off to the kitchen. Mackie gestured to the weather-beaten table. He watched as the gentleman pulled a handkerchief from his pocket, shook it out and laid it on the bench before taking a seat across from him.

"Now, my friend, I'm afraid that you have me at a disadvantage. You know my name, but I don't know yours," Mackie said.

"Quite right, Mr. Mackie. I do apologize for dropping in on you out of the blue. My name is Walter Patterson, and I represent a very large and powerful organization. I have come here today with a proposal. Now, if you will permit my driver to come over only for a moment, we have a donation to your church as a show of good faith and the seriousness of our intentions."

Mackie nodded, and Patterson waved the driver over.

"Joel, please give Mr. Mackie the envelope," he said once the driver had arrived at the table.

Joel did as he was told and then walked back to the car. Mackie rifled through the contents of the envelope and looked up at Patterson.

"You will find fifty thousand dollars in there, Mr. Mackie," Patterson said. "Consider that a donation to your church and your community, and if you will listen to and accept my proposal, your church will receive many times that amount."

Mackie considered the man across the table. He certainly carried the ways of a diplomat and was nothing like the bullshitters he normally had to deal with: drug addicts, elected officials and those who were of a criminal element.

"Okay, Mr. Patterson, for fifty thousand dollars you get ten minutes," he said.

"Splendid," the gentleman responded. "I will be succinct, but I must start at the beginning in order to give you a clear understanding."

"You have the floor, and the clock is running," Mackie said.

"Right. Many years ago, over fifty to be more specific, there was a group of men who shared a passion for archeology. These men organized a dig in the Qumran area of the Holy lands. This was at a time immediately after the discovery of the first Dead Sea Scrolls and this band of scientists wanted to be in on the action and apparently, they did indeed discover some ancient texts, recover them and sequester them away from the authorities so they could study the scrolls themselves without outside interference. Are you with me so far, Mr. Mackie?"

"Tick, tock," Mackie said.

Patterson frowned at Mackie but continued on.

"So, fast forward to today, and we have it on good authority that the documents have not only been moved to this country but that the heirs of the original scientists are going to sell the ancient texts to the highest bidder."

Here, Patterson paused and changed trajectory.

"Mr. Mackie," he said, "I believe that your core beliefs and mine align. If I may be so bold, I think you and the others here have chosen this lifestyle to protect those same core values and to make sure that your children learn their values from you and not from the outside world. Am I correct in this thinking?"

"If you're asking do we believe in one true God in whose image we're made, then you are correct. If you're asking, do we believe this nation was founded on Christian principles and those same principles are under constant and nefarious attack from the Jews and the Muslims, then you are damn straight. We don't invite people from other cultures and backgrounds to commune with us, and we don't believe in a country that supports the LGB and whatever other abomination they want to add to the list community. Our children learn the King James Version of scripture. We don't let the filth of television or the internet infect their minds. We know in our hearts that we are a chosen people, and it is imperative that we maintain a simple and faithful Christian life for our children while the rest of white America is under siege from a boiling pot of sin."

"I couldn't have said it better myself." Patterson said. "I believe you are indeed the right man for the mission I am proffering. While the scrolls are certainly precious, it is our understanding that the text contained within them could prove extremely damaging to the very foundation of Christianity not only in this country but around the world. As I have stated earlier, I work for some incredibly powerful and resourceful people, and they have assured me that this threat to Christianity, especially in this time and place, is very real and possibly fatal. Every mainline denomination in this country is already feeling the sting of aging populations. The percentage of un-churched people has risen to staggering heights in both rural and urban parts of our nation. We must fight to protect our religion, and that fight is not for the faint of heart."

Aunt Hazel delivered the tea with cut lemons and a sugar bowl to the table and then quickly departed again.

"If I may interrupt here," Mackie said. "Now is the time for you to tell me how you came to be here today and have sought me out. I'm not on Facebook or any other social media. We're a small, simple, off-the-grid community that keeps to itself, so I'm at a loss as to why you think I can help with your problem."

"Well, Mr. Mackie, you needn't be coy with me. I know a lot about your operations. I know you own 144 acres around this lake, a very Biblical number by the way, and that you possess a large solar panel installation on the western pasture of the property. You operate a farm just north of this location and, of course, provide education and housing for everyone here. It's quite impressive, really, that you do all this yet remain off the grid, as you say."

"Not off it far enough, apparently," Mackie responded.

Patterson leaned close over the table and continued in a more subdued tone.

"I also know that you operate a highly successful surveillance operation, which includes forays into extortion, bribery, robbery and loan-sharking occasionally. I also know that you choose to target sinful lowlifes for these kinds of activities, which gives you both a feeling of satisfaction and justification. Am I correct?"

Mackie sat motionless for a moment and then leaned across the table himself.

"If you know all this, then you know I would do anything to preserve our way of life here, and I ain't intimidated by a stranger in an expensive suit," Mackie said.

Patterson sat back. "You misunderstand my intention, sir. I'm complimenting you, not threatening. It's these qualities that I wish to employ, and I know that you have the wherewithal to accomplish a mission that will be beneficial for both of our interests. If our information is correct, you could help us save Christianity itself from extinction. It's already headed down that path, and if what is in those scrolls becomes public knowledge, then God help us all. Now, if you agree to partner with us, I will call my superiors and approve an additional donation of two hundred thousand dollars, which will be delivered to you by this time tomorrow. Also, you are not going into this thing with no leads. We do not know the whereabouts of the scrolls, but we have a contact who can give you insight into this mission. You will meet with that person and then use your surveillance skills on the heirs of the archaeologists, all but one of whom are deceased, and I am led to believe that even he is seriously ill. Do you agree?"

"The two hundred gets me started, but there will be expenses to mount an operation on four different families," Mackie said. "If these scrolls are so valuable, it's going to cost more."

"Quite right, Mr. Mackie. The two hundred plus the fifty today is just the down payment. I know you are a shrewd businessman, and I am authorized to offer you ten million dollars delivered to or deposited for you in whatever form you choose. All you have to do is find the scrolls and deliver them to me."

"That kind of money makes me think that there may be a need for, let's say, more persuasive actions than just following someone to the treasure," Mackie said. "Are you authorized to give us the freedom to accomplish this mission by any means necessary?"

"Mr. Mackie, we are much more concerned about the scrolls falling into the wrong hands than we are about potential collateral damage that may occur while protecting our interests. You can run this operation as you see fit. All I ask is that you keep me updated on your progress."

"I believe we have a deal, Mr. Patterson."

"Excellent," the elder statesman said, standing up. "Here is the contact information of our confidential informant and my burner number. Please meet with the contact as soon as possible, and I will look forward to hearing from you."

Patterson walked briskly to the car, got in, and they turned and left with no further discussion.

Chapter 8

CHANEY LED THEM to an old Ford sedan that was double-parked on a fire hydrant just outside the Coney Island employee entrance.

"Get in the back and get down," he told the couple as he jumped in the driver's seat.

Thomas and Dani got in from opposite sides and lay down from a sitting position so that their heads were next to each other. Dani stared at his throat from their upside-down positions and then giggled.

"You realize we were about two seconds from being kidnapped until this guy came along and probably kidnapped us anyway, right?" Thomas said.

"I know, but you have to admit we've had more excitement in the last twenty-four hours than we can get in a year of working for a living."

She started laughing again, and Thomas pulled her in and kissed her, which made her laugh even louder.

"That was very Spider-Man of you, you know," she said.

"Well, you know I try to be the hero whenever there's a need."

"Hey, whenever you two lovebirds finish smooching, I need to know where we are going," Chaney called from the front seat. "I mean, right now I'm just clearing the area and watching for tails, but eventually we need to, you know, have a plan."

Thomas started to sit up.

"Stay down," Chaney yelled into the rear-view mirror. "We ain't clear yet."

"You're asking me for a plan?" he yelled out. "I don't have a clue what to do, and I don't have a clue what the thugs with guns wanted with us. What my grandfather was into or why you showed up and saved us is an absolute mystery to me. I don't know why we are lying down in the backseat of some broken-down old sedan. But mostly, I don't have a frickin' clue who you are!"

"So, you're saying you're clueless?" Dani asked before erupting in more laughter. "Look," she continued. "Mr. Chaney popped up out of the blue and saved our necks with some very cool moves, I might add, and he has never once pointed his gun at us or threatened us. And now, he is asking us what to do next. That doesn't seem like the typical MO of a kidnapper."

"Really, MO? Now you're even sounding like a bad television drama. We know nothing about this guy. Maybe he's the world's foremost expert on kidnapping people without them knowing it," Thomas said. "Maybe he won a reality show called The Amazing Kidnapper."

"You guys know I can hear you, right? I'm not a kidnapper, and I didn't show up out of the blue. Your grandfather sent me."

"And exactly how did he do that from the grave?" Thomas asked. "How do you know my grandfather, and how did he know I would figure out to go to Coney Island?"

"He had great faith in you. He had great faith period," Chaney responded, with a serious tone. "When I was sixteen, your grandfather saved me and my fourteen-year-old kid sister by getting us off the streets when our mother died from a drug overdose. He got us set up with a foster family that he trusted and made sure we had what we needed. My sister is an attorney now, thanks to Mr. Braden. And I went to college and then served in the Marine Corps for ten years. When he contacted me earlier this year to ask for my help, there was no way on earth I was going to say no. He said that if something happened to him, that I should start shadowing you and he would pay me to keep you and Dani safe. So, that's what I've been doing. I was at the funeral and saw the big cop approach you there. I was watching when you guys lit out, and I followed you to Coney Island. So, all I know is that I need to watch your back."

Thomas tried to unpack everything he was hearing, but his mind was a logjam of questions.

"So, where did those guys come from?" he questioned.

"They were following you too. So were some G-men,

but I don't know where they are now."

"Jesus, I'm like the first guy on the escalator. Everyone is following me and I don't know it," Thomas muttered. "We need to get somewhere where we can stop talking through the seat cushions."

"I know. Just hang on a bit more," Chaney responded.

An hour later, they pulled into the gravel parking lot of a diner that had lost its identity in the sixties.

"You can sit up now," Chaney told them.

They did so, stretching their arms and necks, trying to shake off the rust.

"Where are we?" Thomas asked.

"Linden, New Jersey. Population 40,499," Chaney answered. "Let's get some grub and figure out our next move."

They climbed out of the car and made their way to the entrance of the shiny, silver greasy spoon. Once inside, they dropped into a booth from which they could see the car.

"What's your sister's name?" Dani asked their newfound friend.

"Sara," he answered with a grin. "She got all the smarts in the family, and thankfully she is putting them to good use. I'm mostly good for running errands, but she, she can think through problems and come up with answers in a heartbeat."

A middle-aged waitress in an old-fashioned white apron approached the table. They quickly ordered burgers, fries and soft drinks without looking at the menus and waited for her to leave before continuing.

"Sounds like we could use her now," Dani said,

referring to Chaney's sister.

"Nope," he said, smiling at Thomas. "We got Thomas and his granddaddy trusted him to figure out this mess we are in, and that's good enough for me."

"I wish I shared your and, apparently, my grandfather's confidence in me," Thomas replied. "Which, not for nothing, is the first time I've ever felt he had faith in me, so temper your enthusiasm."

"No, he's right," Dani countered. "He gave you that key and a coded message because he believed you were the only person who could decipher its meaning. He saw Caleb every week and never gave him the key. No, you're the man, Thomas Braden. Not because you're the smartest person on the planet, but because you are uniquely qualified for this mission."

"Mission! What mission? I almost got us kidnapped or worse. Apparently, half of Boston was following us, and I had no idea. I'm not uniquely qualified. I'm just the grandson of a formidable, intelligent, somewhat mysterious and maybe delusional man."

"Those four guys at the bathhouse were not apparitions," Chaney snapped, eyeing Thomas closely. "They were real men with real guns and nasty dispositions. I don't know what they wanted, and I don't care. But your grandfather cared enough to enlist your help, and whatever those guys are after has something to do with it all. You can figure this out. So, do it already."

Thomas nodded and pulled out the envelope with his name on it.

"He left me this in locker 47. It's my Papa's handwriting," he explained to Chaney.

He turned the envelope over in his hands, like he had done countless times in his life with his grandfather's messages. He held it up to the light and felt along its surface for indentations. There were no extra markings on the outside, but there was a hard object inside. He felt it briefly, then he put the letter down on the table and studied it further.

"If you're not sure how to open it, I've got a knife," Chaney said.

"My grandfather's clues can be both right in front of your eyes and completely hidden. You don't want to destroy something important before you get the thing open."

At last, he nodded at both of them and carefully opened the letter. A second key clattered onto the scarred tabletop. All three of them stared at it as if it were radioactive. Thomas went back to the envelope and pulled out a single sheet of paper. There were four words written on it: some random letters with two underscores and then six numbers.

YOU ARE THE KEY

A F
B E
C F
D I

– –

24 12 29 22 124 122

The three of them passed around the paper without a hint of recognition. After a few minutes of head-scratching, the server approached with their food. Thomas re-folded the paper, put it back in the envelope and then back into his pocket. Chaney scarfed his burger down in three bites and gazed out the window, waiting for the others to finish.

"I've seen hungry, hungry hippos savor a meal more than you do," Dani said.

"My sister and I spent time in foster homes as we grew up because our mom couldn't stay clean or keep a job. One home we went to had nine kids in it. They said grace this way: 'In the name of the Father, Son and Holy Ghost, who eats the fastest gets the most!' And let me tell you, they weren't kidding. So, yeah, I eat when I get the chance, and I don't waste time doing it," Chaney replied, over a toothpick in the corner of his mouth. "Besides, my job is over-watch, and that's what I'm doing. Thomas has to do the rest, and apparently he is the key."

"I know," Thomas said. "But now I'm wondering if I should keep going. Maybe it would be better to leave it as is. Maybe we shouldn't go turning over any unnecessary stones. If I did something that got Dani hurt, I wouldn't be able to live with it. Right now, we're safe. If we go on, I don't know that we will be. I'm thinking we contact Agent Harrison and give him what we have and wash our hands of the rest of it."

"Look at me," Dani said. "We are in this together. If your grandfather had thought the best plan of action was to call the authorities, he would have. No, he gave this to you to follow through."

"Plus," Chaney chimed in, "we can't explain the four

guys back there. Your Agent Harrison…"

"I like to call him Stone Face," Dani interrupted.

"Okay. Well, Agent Stone Face might decide that it is in his best interest to just lock us up for assault and be done with it because we have nothing else to give him."

Thomas closed his eyes to gather his thoughts. What they were saying made sense, but deep inside him there lived a sense of dread that he could not deny. Of course, until a couple of days ago his grandfather had never told him he loved him, and according to Chaney, Papa was proud of him as well. Somehow, Thomas felt obligated not to let him down. He retrieved the envelope from his pocket.

"Okay, this is the point of no return. If we can decipher this note, we are going to see this through to the end. Agreed?"

They both nodded.

Thomas spread the paper out and placed condiment bottles on the corners to keep it open. Then he grabbed a napkin and pen and copied down the cipher. After making the copy, he studied it and doodled around the edges of the napkin.

Dani looked at Chaney and winked as if to say. 'I know it's weird, but that's how he does things.'

"Obviously, the numbers at the bottom are the same code as our previous note, which means we need Mark 13:1," Thomas said, without looking up.

"And as he came out of the temple, one of his disciples said to him, 'Look, Teacher, what wonderful stones and what wonderful buildings!'" Dani replied.

"Isn't she exceptional?" Thomas said to Chaney. "You

just mention a chapter and verse, and she spouts it out faster than Siri on her best day."

"That is a neat trick, but what does it mean?" Chaney asked.

"No idea," Thomas said.

The waitress returned and brought refills without Thomas even noticing. Finally, he looked up at the two of them with a wry grin.

"The answer for the two underscores is F D," he stated confidently. "You see, each pair of letters when converted to numbers is a squared number. A F is 16, which is 4 squared. B E is 25, which is 5 squared and then 6 squared and 7 squared. So, the next one in the progression would be 8 squared, which is 64 and translates to F D."

"So, what does that mean, Dani asked?

"Once again, it's another thing I don't know," he replied. "It's part of the solution, but obviously there must be more. It has to tell us where to take this key, and there is something else about me that is relevant to the ultimate answer."

His words made him think of Regis Philbin asking, 'Is that your final answer?' No, Regis, that is not my final answer. I need the world's biggest lifeline right now. Can I phone a friend, please, because I'm as lost as Will Robinson and in just about as much danger.

"Think, Thomas," Dani pushed. "Maybe it relates to something you and your grandfather did together."

"Belching on the couch while watching football doesn't seem like much of a clue. Other than that, we didn't do things together," Thomas said.

"Okay, let's go back to the note," Chaney suggested.

"What do we know about it? There are four words on the page. The random numbers seem to suggest squares of numbers. The two new ones that you added are F and D. What does that all tell us?"

"Come on, Thomas," Dani added. "You are the key. Think!"

"I am trying," he snapped back. "If it's so easy, then why don't you come up with an answer?"

"Thomas Jackson Braden! I am only trying to help. I know this is stressful, but you will not yell at me like that!"

"Okay, sorry. You sound like my mother. She always used my middle name when I was in trouble."

Thomas shook his head. "I am the key," he said. "I am the key."

He stopped, and his eyes widened.

"What is it?" she asked.

Thomas looked into Dani's eyes, then grabbed her and kissed her full on the mouth.

"That's it! You are a genius!" he yelled.

A few of the restaurant patrons looked up from the meals and squinted toward the threesome.

"Sorry," he said under his breath. "But you have hit on the answer, or at least part of it. All the numbers are squares. My mother always called me Jackson."

"Jackson Square," Dani finished for him.

"Right," he said. "We have to go to New Orleans."

"Hallelujah!" Chaney exclaimed. "I was afraid we would have to eat breakfast here too."

Thomas' phone rang.

"It's Caleb," he said. "I'll take it outside. Pay the bill, and then we are out of here."

He tapped the phone to answer as he pushed through the glass door to the parking lot.

"Caleb," he said.

"What the fuck, Thomas! First you got all squirrelly at Papa's funeral and ran off. Then, you drive to fucking Coney Island and get in a goddamn brawl? What did you do, cut in line for a goddamn roller coaster?"

"Calm down," Thomas said.

"The hell I will!" Caleb yelled.

Thomas held the phone away from his ear as the anger poured out into the diner's parking lot.

"I just got through talking to that Homeland asshole, Harrison. He showed up at my door asking questions about you."

"Dani calls him Stone Face," Thomas replied, trying to diffuse the situation.

"Fine, Agent Stone Face was asking me where you were and what you were doing."

"What did you tell him?"

"I didn't tell him shit, because I don't know shit!" Caleb answered, losing steam.

"I'm sorry, Caleb," Thomas said. "I know little more than you do. Papa gave me a key and a coded message. That led us to Coney Island. The key opened a locker there, you know, the ones by the beach. We were opening the locker when these four morons showed up and told us we were going with them. I've never seen them before, and I don't know who sent them. I'm sorry."

"Lucky for you, I'm in the forgiveness business," Caleb replied. "Did you at least get in a few good licks?"

"I put one down before this other asshole pulled a gun."

"Coward," Caleb responded.

"Yeah. Dani kicked one in the nuts, though," Thomas added.

"That's my girl," Caleb said. "So, what's next?"

"The locker only held another clue. So, we're going to New Orleans. It's all I know to do right now. Papa said he was being watched, but I just thought he was paranoid. Now, I know better."

"Okay," Caleb said. "But no more keeping me in the dark. We're brothers."

"I got it. I won't."

***

Two hundred miles away, Agent Harrison's phone rang.

"Harrison," he answered.

"It's Conner, sir. Braden just got off the phone with his brother. He told him they were going to New Orleans."

"Why the hell are they going to New Orleans?" Harrison asked.

"He said something about a clue, boss, but nothing else."

"Very well. I'll meet you at the airfield. I want to be in the air in an hour."

"Copy that," Conner said before disconnecting.

Chapter 9

MACKIE LET HIMSELF into the control room and walked over to the man called Junkyard. He, not for the first time, marveled at how easily the big man could watch and decipher twenty monitors at once while eating a bowl of cornflakes. If a casino ever got wind of this guy, they would throw money at him. He could hear him slurping milk as he approached.

"Hey, Junk," he said. "What do you have for me today?"

"Two potentials," Junkyard said. He typed out a command on his keyboard and pointed to one display.

"This is from yesterday afternoon," he continued. "This punk is selling crack one block from Central High School. Street name is Rollo. He's there in front of that convenience store every day when school lets out."

"Hmm," Mackie said. "Who do we have down in Little Rock right now?"

Junkyard tapped on the keyboard again, and the main console display changed to a map of Little Rock with several red dots on it.

"Marv and Batman can be there at three o'clock," he said.

Mackie smiled. Why anyone would name their kid Bruce Wayne Richards was a mystery to him.

"Okay, have them roll up on old Rollo this afternoon and relieve him of his goods and cash. Tell them to impress upon him how important it is for his well-being that he find another occupation."

"Will do, Boss."

"And there's another one?" Mackie asked.

"Yes sir. I was saving the best for last. Check out monitor nineteen," Junkyard answered. "This was from last Wednesday night?"

He tapped out the command, and a high-resolution picture popped up on the display. It showed, in vivid detail, a man lying on his back in a king-sized bed and a woman straddling him. He had a handsome, good for television face and dark, wavy hair. Even in his prone position, Mackie could tell that the man was tall with arms that spent time in a gym. The man's eyes were closed.

"Who's the hooker?" Mackie asked.

"Name's Amber. I told her that if she let me set up her condo with a camera, she would earn ten percent of our take."

"Well done. So, who's the mark?"

"That is none other than Congressman David Kelley

from District Four. Every time he flies back from D.C., he spends a couple of hours at Amber's before he heads down to Hot Springs to be with the wife and kids," Junkyard replied.

"I love predictability," Mackie said.

"It certainly helps," Junkyard said. "I've already pulled his financials. He's squirreled away over 100k in a Little Rock bank that I'm sure the Missus knows nothing about. He's got over three million in a T. Rowe Price investment account and a few thousand here and there in various operating accounts. And best of all, he has a ticket on American that arrives in Little Rock at 7:10 pm tonight."

"Well, that is opportune for us then," Mackie said. "I reckon you and I will pay a visit to the good Congressman this evening."

A doorbell sound emanated from the primary display, and with it a picture exploded onto the screen.

"Looks like the boys are back from their road trip," Junkyard said.

"Let them in," Mackie replied. "I need to have a conversation. Where are our marks on the Scroll Project?"

Junkyard checked the GPS coordinates on another screen.

"They're heading west on I-10, just outside of Mobile."

"Any idea where they're heading?" Mackie asked.

"I-10 runs all the way to L.A., so it could be just about anywhere," Junkyard said.

"Okay, keep an eye on them. I've gotta to go talk to these knuckleheads."

Mackie met the van as it drove through the second set of gates. One man opened the sliding door, and Mackie could see that the man called Lucky was lying in the back and in obvious pain.

The man who opened the door jumped out.

"We pulled him out of the intensive care unit, Boss," he said. "They took the bullet out, but he needs pain meds and probably something to fight infection."

Mackie yelled in through the passenger window to the driver.

"Take him to the infirmary and get the doc on him. Then go get yourselves cleaned up. You're going back out."

The driver nodded, and the van ambled along the dirt road and up the slope. Mackie turned his attention to the man still standing there.

"I'm waiting to hear what happened," he said.

The man removed his MAGA ball cap and wiped the sweat from his face.

"We had them cornered, Boss. Told them they needed to come with us. They got away only because this guy came into the breezeway singing."

"Singing?" Mackie asked.

"Yes, he was singing, and we told him he needed to move on, but he wouldn't. We didn't want to cause a stir with weapons, so when we closed the net, he lunged at us."

The man looked down at the ground before he spoke again.

"It was just the element of surprise. That's all."

"Look at me," Mackie demanded.

The man put his hat back on and looked up. Mackie caught him on the chin with a hard right and sent him sprawling.

"You get your ass up to the armory and load up. Get

heavier equipment and a new burner phone. Then, grab those other two idiots and get back out on the road! Junk will send you the coordinates. Find them and bring them in, and do not fail me this time."

He stomped off, leaving the man bleeding on the ground.

***

Congressional Representative David Kelley exited the garage elevator and hurried toward his car. It took close to an hour to drive to Hot Springs, and he needed to get going. He hit the button on his remote, and the BMW backed against the far wall flashed and beeped. He jumped in and hit the ignition button. The sedan did not respond. He hit again. Still nothing. He scoured the console for an idiot light. Nothing. Finally, he looked up and saw two men standing in front of the vehicle, looking directly at him. One had his hands in his pockets, and the other, a much larger man, held a briefcase. Kelley pushed the door locks and heard the satisfying clicks. Then he saw the larger of the two men point a device at the car and the doors unlocked. He frantically tried the start button again, and thankfully it cranked. He threw the car into gear only to have it die before he could hit the gas. The smaller of the two men got into the passenger seat and sat down. Before Kelley could get out, the big man pointed the device and locked the doors again.

"Congressman Kelley," the man in the passenger seat began. "This can go really easily if you will just relax and listen. There is no reason for you to be nervous. We ain't here to hurt you. If you agree, please put your hands on the steering wheel."

Kelley complied.

"Who are you?" he asked the passenger.

"That ain't the question you need to be asking right now. What you need to be asking is, what do we want?"

"So, what do you want?"

"I will tell you, but first I am going to invite my colleague to join us. If you try to get out of the car, the you won't get hurt part goes away. Do you understand?" the man asked.

Kelley nodded.

The man waved for the other to get in the back seat. The car buckled noticeably when the man climbed in.

"I hate these foreign car backseats," he said. "Didn't your daddy ever tell you to buy American?"

Kelley didn't answer and refused even to look in the backseat.

"Now, Congressman, we believe you have been a naughty boy."

"I don't know what you're talking about," Kelley replied.

"Junk," the man said.

From the backseat, the man reached over like a tree limb sprouting forward and held an iPad in his hand. The man in the passenger seat took the tablet, held it up for the congressman, and pressed play. The events earlier in the evening up in Amber's bedroom unfolded in high definition. After a moment, Kelley looked away, and the big man retrieved the tablet.

"What do you expect from me? I'm not one of those

millionaires who live in Washington. I'm a working-class man of the people," Kelley said.

"Save it for the campaign rallys," the passenger said. "Junk, if you please."

Once again the man in the back passed the tablet forward, and on it this time was a balance sheet of Kelley's financial holdings.

"Now, sir, my man Junkyard here is a genius at tracking down everything about a person's life. If it's on a website somewhere, he can find it. Like your wife's email address, for example."

"That would be monica_lloyd2002@yahoo.com," Junkyard said.

"So, out of the 100k that you have stashed at the Mooney Bank and Trust for your gambling trips to Atlantic City, you're going to give us fifty. You're going to call your wife and tell her that your flight was delayed, and you will spend the night at the Little Rock Hilton."

He stopped and looked a question back at Junkyard.

"Is it the Hilton?"

"Yes, the one on Rock Street currently has twenty-three rooms available, so that's where I would go," Junkyard answered.

"Perfect," the passenger said before continuing. "Then, in the morning, you're going to withdraw the money from that account, uh, what's that number?"

"Checking account number 105568790," Junkyard said.

"Right. So, you're going to withdraw the money and store it in our briefcase that Junkyard will leave in the back seat. After you retrieve our money, you will go to the Morning Brew across the street from the bank, order a coffee, sit down and enjoy. When you leave the cafe, simply leave the briefcase on the floor. Easy peasy. Since the wife doesn't even know about this account, she'll never miss the money. Do you understand the rules of engagement?"

"I do," Kelley said.

"Very good. Now, let me tell you, Congressman, what you're thinking right now. You're thinking that maybe you should just tell your wife about your dalliances with Miss Amber and she will forgive you and you can keep your money. What's that other email address, Junk?"

"Walter_Higby@ArkansasDemocrat-Gazette.org."

"Now, I need you to look at me, David Kelley," the passenger said, lowering his voice.

Kelley swallowed and looked into the man's eyes.

"We might not end your marriage, and maybe even your career will survive a scandal. Lord knows others have. But I can promise you that you will not survive a visit from Junkyard if you do not do exactly as I am telling you. Do I make myself clear?"

Kelley nodded.

"I need you to say it," the passenger said.

"Yes, we are clear, but how do I know that you won't come back for more even if I pay?"

"Well now, that's an easy one. That is totally up to you. Clean up your act and stay away from hookers, and you will never see us again. But if you can't keep it in your pants, well, I reckon we'll have to come around for another visit. Understand?"

"Yes."

"Very good," the man said. "Enjoy your stay at the Hilton, and we will be watching you closely tomorrow. Any sign of the authorities, even by accident, and Junkyard will take a brief trip to your house there in Hot Springs real soon. Your lovely wife and those two pixie girls will have nightmares for a long time after that. Thank you for your time."

The two men got out and walked into the darkness of the garage. Once they were out of earshot, Junkyard spoke.

"Boss, you know I'm all in for the cause, and I got no problem putting hands on the likes of that guy, but I ain't down with hurting innocents like women and kids. I told you that when I joined up."

Mackie clapped the big man on the back.

"I know, Junk, and I respect it, but the Congressman doesn't know that, and if it gives him extra incentive to do the right thing, I ain't gonna let him in on your secret. Understand?"

"Yeah, boss. I got you."

Chapter 10

THE SONG EDGED its way into Thomas' dream. Something about cruising together. He stirred against the passenger window before waking.

Thomas looked over with one scrunched eye at Chaney singing at the top of his lungs.

"Do you have to do that?" he asked.

"Well, top of the morning to you too!" Chaney said.

Thomas rubbed both eyes and tried to shake the kinks out of his neck and shoulders. They had spent a few hours at a dump somewhere in rural Alabama. Chaney said that it was safer to drive at night. The three of them took turns driving after Dani squelched any chivalrous intentions by the two men.

After a moment, Thomas realized that even though

there was light, he could see nothing outside the car. A menacing, impenetrable fog bank engulfed them on all sides like a Stephen King novel. The only breach in the white wall was the arrow-straight highway directly in front of them. The otherworldly picture served as the perfect complement to their surreal predicament, he thought.

"What the hell?" Thomas said as his phone rang out the Rocky Theme. "Shit, it's Caleb," he said.

"Hello, my brother."

"Is this what you call keeping me posted, Thomas? I haven't heard from you in hours." Caleb's voice blasted from the phone.

"I told you we were going to New Orleans. We're almost there, but there is nothing new to report. Look, Caleb, I don't want to get you involved."

"I am involved, you selfish prick! I'm your brother, and whatever is going on with you and Dani affects me. The minute Agent Stone Face darkened my door, I became a person of interest. That means I'm in the shit with you."

Dani heard Caleb shouting and popped her head over from the back seat to listen in.

"Okay, you're right," Thomas conceded. "Papa was crazy paranoid when I saw him on that last day. He was speaking in different languages, which I just attributed to some sort of dementia, but now I think it was purposeful in case someone was listening."

"Who?" Caleb asked.

"I didn't know then, and I don't know now. Maybe no one. Listen, Caleb, I don't want to say anymore over this phone, okay? I will get in touch with you later."

Thomas disconnected before his brother could argue.

"I hated to do that, but I don't know what to do about Caleb just yet," Thomas said.

"I'm not saying I believe this," Dani started, "but I wonder if your grandfather meant Caleb too when he said don't trust anyone?"

The question hung in the air like smoke over a Fourth of July cookout while they pondered it. No one spoke for a long time. Finally, Dani broke the silence.

"Man, when you go for a drive, you take it seriously," she said to Chaney. "What planet are we on?"

"Crossing Lake Pontchartrain," Chaney replied. "You'd best get that phone cranked up. We're close to Nawlins," he said with a grin.

Using the GPS, Dani navigated them off the freeway onto Esplanade and into the French Quarter. Spanish and French architecture fought for space on every corner and sometimes within the same structure. The streets were barren at this time of day except for a few delivery trucks dropping off the day's consumables. Birds lined the tops of buildings as if called in for an early morning meeting. They found parking at the New Orleans Historic Voodoo Museum and paid even though it didn't open for a couple of hours.

"No use callin' attention to ourselves," Chaney said.

With that, he reached across to the glove compartment and retrieved a spare magazine for his 9-millimeter.

"Is that really necessary?" Thomas asked.

"I sure hope not, but I'm not taking any chances," Chaney said.

"Right," Thomas replied.

They got out and headed south on Dumaine until they

got to Chartres and hung a right. Once they arrived at Jackson Square, they realized they didn't know what to look for next. They wandered into the gardens and past the fountain in front of the massive St. Louis Cathedral. On the other side of the square sat Andrew Jackson atop his rearing horse, hat in hand. The smell of freshly cut grass rose around them.

"You know, prior to 1815 this area was known as Place d'Armes and was used for public executions." Dani said.

"The less said about executions the better," Thomas said.

"Then in 1815 they renamed it Jackson Square because Andrew Jackson was their hero after he defeated the British."

"That's all well and good, Missy," Chaney said. "But right now we need to know what lock Thomas' key will open."

"And what, if anything, F D means in this equation," Thomas added.

They strolled along the perimeter of the square. Along St. Peter Street, small shops sat quietly waiting for their owners to arrive. Pigeons walked and pecked among the flagstones before flying away in a rush as the threesome approached. They made a left on Decatur, which formed the southeast border of the square, and across it people were already coming and going from the Cafe du Monde, where the smell of fresh beignets wafted above the street. The mist off of the Mississippi was retreating to the water just on the other side of the cafe. Two early-bird horse and buggies stood nose to tail just outside the gate to the square. The horses snorted and pawed as their owners brushed their coats to a shiny gleam while the brightly painted buggies gathered the morning dew.

"I have to admit I'm a bit stuck right now," Thomas told the others. "I'm sure we are in the right area. We just need to figure out more specifically what we are looking for."

"Maybe there is something in the note that we missed," Dani suggested.

He pulled his copy of the note and key back out and, while holding the key, he scanned the sights in front of him. "What was the reading from Mark 13:1 again?" he asked Dani.

"And as he came out of the temple, one of his disciples said to him, 'Look, Teacher, what wonderful stones and what wonderful buildings!'," she answered.

Thomas looked at the St. Louis Cathedral. "What wonderful buildings," he said. "Let's go."

As they approached the gigantic double doors of the church, they noticed a bronze plaque attached to the stone wall.

"Father Dimitri Boudreaux," Dani said. She looked at Thomas. "F D," she added.

He nodded, and they stepped inside the huge cathedral. The sanctuary emitted a dark, musky odor, as if all of its forgiven sins over the years had been stacked on the altar. There were hundreds of candles flickering in the cavernous space. Enormous chandeliers hung above the long rows of wooden pews, their lights emitting a dim glow. Ornate paintings of the Virgin Mary and child, along with depictions of Jesus preaching to crowds, floated on the ceiling. Tall white columns lifted twin balconies that ran the full length of the church. The wide center aisle paved the way to the marble altar adorned with even more candles.

"The acolyte for this place must get a stipend," Thomas said.

"Shush. Let's go over to the confessionals and see if we can find a priest," Dani whispered.

They made their way around the stately wooden pews to the far-right side. There they found two deep red velvet curtains, both of which were standing open. The posted schedule showed that they were in time for early-morning confessions.

"What do we do now?" Thomas asked.

"You go in and kneel to confess your sins," Chaney said. "Ain't you ever been to confession?"

"Uh, yes, when I was a kid. I don't remember caring for it though," Thomas answered.

"Well, try it, dude. It ain't gonna hurt ya."

Thomas went into the cubicle and pulled the curtain closed. Since there was no place to sit, he kneeled and clasped his hands on the wooden banister in front of him. There was a sort of closed window facing him with a screen on his side. Suddenly, the window opened itself, sliding to one side to reveal an opaque window shade.

"Hello," Thomas said.

"Yes, my son," came a deep baritone voice through the shade. "Do you wish to make a confession?"

"Uh, not exactly. Um, well, I'm not sure why I am here."

"We all have those misgivings from time to time," the voice came back. "Perhaps you could start by just telling me what's bothering you."

"I'm not here for a confession. My grandfather was Stewart Braden, and I believe he sent me here looking for Father Dimitri."

There was a long pause on the other side of the screen.

"You said was. Has your grandfather passed away?"

"Yes, a few days ago."

"I am sorry for your loss, my son. So, why do you think he wanted you to find me?"

"Well, to be honest, I don't know for sure. It's been a crazy couple of days, and he left me a rather cryptic note that seems to have led me here. But that's all I know."

"Do you have the key?" the voice asked.

Thomas' heart jumped.

"Yes," he said.

"Come with me," said the voice as the shade slammed shut.

Thomas stepped out of the cubicle and came face to face with a portly man in a long black robe. He was graying just above the temples, but the rest of his curly hair was jet black. He eyed Thomas for a moment and then noticed Dani and Chaney sitting in the nearest pew.

"Who are these two?" he asked.

"That's my wife, Dani, and this is Chaney. He's been helping us."

"Very well, then. Show me the key," the priest demanded.

Thomas produced the key and the note from his pocket and gave them both to the Father. He studied them to decide their and Thomas' legitimacy, then handed them back.

"I need to see all of your IDs, and then we will go to my study."

They complied, and again he studied each one like a checkpoint agent at airport security.

"Very well then," he said for the second time. "Follow me quickly."

He led them out of the sanctuary and then through a maze-like set of hallways and stairs until they reached a small office two levels below ground. They crammed into the tiny space, but there was only one chair, which the priest settled into. A small wooden cross adorned one wall of the sparsely decorated office. The half-sized desk was completely free of clutter, and the desktop was scarred and scratched through years of service. Dimitri withdrew his own set of keys from a pocket hidden deeply within his robe and unlocked the bottom drawer of the desk. From it he lifted a metal container. He set the box down on the desk and turned to face his visitors.

"Your grandfather," he began, "was a great, great man and a genuine believer in the Holy Trinity. I have known him for many, many years. We met on the day that he acknowledged Jesus as his Savior. He had spent the first years of his life as a nonbeliever. For that time, science was his only master, but God possesses miraculous power and authority, and even the most ardent atheist cannot ignore it if God calls. Stewart came to me a few months ago and gave me this box for safekeeping. He said that only one person would ever come for it, and that would be his grandson, Thomas. He told me that if you came, you might be under duress or control of others, but I praise God in this moment that does not seem to be the case. However, I think it is entirely possible that evil and desperate men will follow you in due course, because that is what your grandfather believed. I do not know what is in the box, and it is not my place to know. So, my duty will be done when I hand it over, and you will leave with it and never come to see me again. Is that clear?"

"Okay, sure," Thomas replied. "But if I may ask, Father. What caused my grandfather to change his belief system all those years ago?"

"I think only God knows, but I will say that his transformation was as quick as that of the disciple Paul. Something opened his eyes and, like Paul, he could see for the first time God's own truth."

"I'm learning that there is more and more that I did not know about my grandfather."

The priest gazed at Thomas with genuine sympathy, bowed his head, and whispered a prayer to himself. When he finished, he made the sign of the cross and looked at Thomas again, this time with watery eyes.

"Again, I am very sorry for your loss. He was my friend and fellow servant of Christ. Even though I don't know what is in the box or what your mission might be, I do know that if your grandfather believed it was important, it must be. Now you must go."

He handed them the box and quickly guided them back to the cathedral's main entrance. He shook hands with each of them.

"God's work is sometimes mysterious, and sometimes we must make decisions without knowing if they are the right ones. This is where faith comes in. Go with the grace of God," he said before closing the door on them.

Chapter 11

THEY DECIDED IT was time to try the beignets while they studied the contents of the box and figured their next move. The Cafe du Monde was an open-air affair, rich with the smell of freshly baked pastries. A line of fifteen or twenty people to the left waited to order. Most all the tables in the place were round and made of cast iron. They were smallish, more useful for a quick donut than a full meal. Chaney grabbed one in the back and sat facing the main entrance while Dani went to get in line to order. Thomas set the metal box down on the table with a clang. He inserted the key and opened the box.

"We've got company," Chaney said.

Thomas looked up and watched Agent Harrison enter the cafe and then scan the room. He was once again wearing a dark suit and white shirt. This time he paired it with a blue tie, however. It wasn't a minute before Harrison spotted Thomas and made a beeline for him. Not a chance encounter. Thomas closed the lid and carefully set the box down at his feet. As the agent lumbered over to their table, Thomas spotted two other hulking brutes in suits and ties take a table near the front entrance of the cafe.

"Fancy meeting you here, Mr. Braden," he said politely, as he yanked another chair from a neighboring table and plopped down in it facing the wrong way. "And I don't believe we have met, Mr.," he added, looking at Chaney.

"Bunny," Chaney answered. "Easter Bunny."

"Well, Mr. Bunny, I'm Agent Harrison with Homeland Security." He pulled a card from his pocket and dropped it on the table while eyeing Chaney. "I see you have found another comedian for your act, Mr. Braden."

"Sometimes the comedians find me," Thomas replied.

"Another good one," Harrison said, without a hint of a smile. He then sighed loudly and clasped his large hands on top of the chair. He directed his gaze back and forth between the two men, waiting.

"Are you always dressed for a funeral, because I saw a cemetery on the tourist map. It's just a few blocks away," Thomas said.

"It's the uniform. Department regs, but what are you gonna do?"

"Are you following us?" Thomas asked.

"Let's just say I was in the neighborhood and wanted to stop by and say hello."

"Really? I don't think New Orleans is in my neighborhood," Thomas responded, feeling anger rise in him. "No, I'm thinking that some of our civil rights are being squashed like a bug here, and I'm not a big fan of that. What's next? You gonna get your bouncers to throw us in a black SUV with tinted windows and take us to some undisclosed location for our safety?" Thomas asked, adding air quotes along the way.

"Easy, Mr. Braden. I admit I enjoy a good espionage movie myself from time to time, but the real world doesn't operate that way. Homeland Security agents don't go around kidnapping law-abiding citizens just for fun. You are law-abiding, aren't you?" he asked.

"Then why bring the extra muscle?" Thomas asked, ignoring the question.

"You noticed them, huh?"

"They stand out like turds in a punch bowl and are about half as welcome."

"That's seriously funny," the agent said grim-faced. "But I noticed you didn't answer my question, and I would think that a law-abiding citizen would be more than willing to help the authorities if given a chance. You see, I was wondering, for instance, if you had any knowledge of an incident that occurred at Coney Island a couple of days ago?"

Dani approached wide-eyed, carrying three paper plates of beignets.

"Good morning, Mrs. Braden," Harrison said while standing. "Let me get you another chair."

He took one from a table where an older man sat reading the newspaper without a word, twirled it around like it was made of straw and dropped into a tight spot at the crowded table.

"I only got three orders," Dani said lamely, while giving

Thomas the 'what's he doing here' eye.

"Oh, no worries. I already ate breakfast. Most important meal of the day, you know. No, I just happened onto your husband here and thought I would just say hello."

"Of all the gin joints in all the world, huh," Dani said.

"Yes, well, it's fortunate for me too because I had made a note that the next time I saw you I wanted to ask you what you knew about four men being assaulted at Coney Island."

"Now, why would you think we knew anything about it?" Thomas replied, forcing his voice to stay even.

Harrison made a show of pulling out a pocket-sized notebook and flipped through the first few pages like he wasn't sure what he was looking for.

"Well, I don't know, maybe because you left your car there," Harrison deadpanned.

Thomas swallowed and glanced over at Dani, who looked as guilty as he felt.

"It seems that," Harrison continued, reading his notes as he spoke, "someone assaulted four victims near the beach showers and then dragged them into the men's room and left them to fend for themselves with varying cuts and contusions. Plus, an unknown assailant or assailants had shot one young man in the arm. That's attempted murder. And witnesses described a tall, thin, shirtless black man of about forty years of age leaving the scene."

Harrison turned his head and stared directly into Chaney's eyes with laser intensity.

"Why are you looking at me?" Chaney said. "I've got a shirt on."

"Sure," Harrison said. "I should probably check my

suspicions based on that newly discovered piece of evidence."

The agent consulted his notebook again before continuing.

"Also, someone saw a young couple roughly matching you two in the area."

"You're kidding," Thomas remarked. "Two young white people were spotted at Coney Island? What are the odds?"

"I realize it's not much to go on," the agent said, nonplussed. "But since you were in the area, what with your car being there and all, I was hoping that you knew something. No stone unturned, you understand."

"Why don't you just ask the four men what happened?" Thomas asked.

"I did, but they weren't the talkative type. Apparently, they all slipped in the bathroom at the same time and tripped over each other, with one of them falling onto a bullet. It was a perfect storm, I guess. Look, Mr. and Mrs. Braden, I'm not the enemy here. I think the two of you are involved in something and are in way over your heads. I think that if you trusted me, maybe I could help you. Of course, I had to have your car towed because I believe you are involved, however unwittingly, in a situation that may be a threat to national security. There must be something you have to say."

"Look, Agent Harrison, I appreciate that you have a job to do and are probably great at it, but you're seriously barking up the wrong tree here. We like to travel, and sometimes we do so on the spur of the moment. My grandfather just died, and I'm just visiting places that had special meaning to him. Just part of the healing process, I guess," Thomas said.

"What about you, Mrs. Braden? You backing his story up? Seems a little contrived to me. For instance, why did you leave your car?"

Dani swallowed hard under the gaze of the agent's bad-cop stare. The man obviously didn't mind awkward moments and was prepared to sit and watch her while she searched for an answer.

"We left the car because I forgot to renew our AAA membership," Thomas jumped in. "And it wouldn't start."

"Right," Dani said. "So we had to catch a ride."

"To New Orleans," the agent confirmed.

They both nodded.

"With the Easter Bunny."

Another nod.

"So, Mr. Bunny. Do you have free time in the summer as well to travel or do whatever?"

"Sure," Chaney replied. "My busy time is in the spring. You know, March and April."

"Uh huh," the agent said.

He flipped the notebook closed and carefully put it and his pen back in his pocket. Then he clasped his hands back on the table and waited for another ten count.

"What's in the box?" the agent asked Thomas, changing tactics.

"Memorabilia from my Papa."

"Interesting. Mind if I take a look at it?"

"You got a warrant?"

Harrison just chuckled and took a moment to clean his glasses with a napkin.

"Okay, well, I really appreciate your cooperation here

today. Just let me leave you with this tidbit. One man who was injured in the Coney Island incident that you know nothing about is a known associate of a group called the Freedom Landers. Ever hear of them?"

"No," Thomas answered.

"Well, Homeland has labeled the group as domestic terrorists, and they have been under surveillance for the past few months. They look and sound like everyday Americans. They could walk right up to you and start a conversation. You might even enjoy it. I mean, if you're into that backwoods southern drawl thing. In fact, they talked their way right into the hospital where the one who was shot was being treated. They beat up the guard we had on him, stole some medical supplies and rolled their friend right out of there on a gurney. Make no mistake. They are extremists by any definition, and if you get crossways with them, it will go badly for you. And one more thing, the reason we were watching your grandfather's house was because we had picked up chatter about this same Freedom Landers group being contacted from there. So, you see how a lot of dots are connecting. I do love it when that happens."

He stood up and put his chair back at the old man's table.

"Call me anytime," he said, pointing to his card on the table. "Seriously, don't be strangers."

They watched him walk out the front with the two goons trailing him. As soon as they were clear, Chaney grabbed the others and guided them out a back exit that led to The Moonwalk along the Mississippi. They jogged along the path for maybe a mile before stopping at a riverside park to catch their breath.

"How did he find us?" Dani asked.

"He has to be monitoring our phones," Thomas replied.

"Isn't that illegal?" she asked.

"It's within the purview of Homeland Security, I guess," Thomas answered.

Chaney laughed out loud.

"Missy," he said, "the government can do whatever it wants, anytime it wants and using whatever means it deems necessary, if it thinks there is even a chance of a threat. Believe me."

"It's one reason I think Papa did not trust turning this over to the authorities. There's no reason to believe that they would make decisions based on moral or ethical values," Thomas said.

"Their mandate is to unearth threats to the country, real or imagined, and make them go away. They won't care two bits about the things your grandfather cared about, and they won't give two shits if there is collateral damage along the way," Chaney said.

"What do we even really know about Harrison?" Dani asked. "He showed us a badge and dressed like a G-man, but we did nothing to check his credentials. For all we know, he could be in on it with the four guys at Coney Island. He could even be calling the shots whether or not he really works for Homeland."

"You're right," Thomas said. "The old man said trust no one, and I'm going to stick with that. Unless he sent them like Chaney here or Father Dimitri, we need to be overly cautious."

"Glad I made the cut," Chaney remarked. "So, what's

next?"

"The answer better be in this box," Thomas said.

Thomas retrieved the key and opened the box again. Inside was a two-page letter and nothing else. He couldn't help wondering, even if just for a moment, why his grandfather only gave them bits and pieces of whatever puzzle he was building. Some small part of him still wondered if he wasn't maybe at least a little off the reservation. Perhaps this entire scavenger hunt comprised ten percent reality and ninety percent paranoia.

"I don't know, guys, if we are going down a rabbit hole or climbing our way back out of one," he said. "But I can't stop until I know for sure."

He carefully unfolded the handwritten pages and flattened them on the picnic table.

"It's written in French," he said.

Chapter 12

DEAR THOMAS,

YOUR father was an answer to a prayer, and you and Caleb were blessings I had never even dreamed of. I am certain as I write this letter that you are the only one capable of following the breadcrumbs that I have scattered. I only hope and pray that you are reading it of your own volition and not under the threat of some dark force. However, since that part of the equation is outside my control, I must have faith that God's will be done. It may seem that I am doing a sort of tango with you, but I need you to trust me; it is absolutely necessary.

In 1956, I was a member of a four-man team that went on a dig in the Holy Lands, specifically the Qumran Valley. Nine years prior to that time, the first set of Dead Sea Scrolls had been discovered in the area, and there continued to be additional finds year after year. In total, archaeologists excavated eleven caves that had produced scrolls. The leader and primary funding source of our group had mapped out an area for a dig on a previous trip and then came back and put our team together. Because of concerns for our safety and a hefty dose of paranoia, our leader kept the mission covert. It turned out to be a highly successful excursion for us as we discovered and collected eight jars of scrolls from a place that we called Cave 12. We were able to remove the scrolls to a safe location and keep them away from both the Romeo Catholic Church and the Israel Antiquities Authority, both of which had been accused for years of delaying the release of scrolls discovered before. At the time, many conspiracy theorists believed officials had never made the most controversial documents public.

So, we squirreled our treasure away while we cataloged, documented, and translated every piece of parchment. Eventually, we had the scrolls carbon dated, which turned out to be another problem. They were at least four hundred years newer than most of the other Dead Sea Scrolls, which put them at about 60 C.E. or right after the time that Jesus walked the earth. This further pressured us to get the translations right. Our discovery could be, in fact, rarer than all the other scrolls. Several months into the project, we came face to face with the biggest problem of all. We came to believe that some writings found in the scrolls could be seriously detrimental to the Christian faith, maybe even disastrous.

Well, our leader, who was a devout Catholic first and a scientist second, would have none of the idea of releasing the scrolls and their translations. I was ambivalent on the subject at the time, but the other two archaeologists were both scientists first and argued that it was not our place to determine if the people should or should not be given the revelations of these scrolls. It was our duty to science to release our findings and let the chips fall where they may. These two men remained unified like a shout down a mountain and its echo. We argued for several days until finally we agreed we would wait until all our work was complete and we had all the information before we made the final decision.

In the meantime, the financier I'll call him Mike — arranged for the scrolls to be put into a vault, and he asked each member of the team to come up with a six-number access code that we could always remember. So, when the time came, the four of us went with the scrolls to the vault location, took turns entering our part of the combination lock, and placed the scrolls and translations in the vault. After we closed the heavy door, we were done. None of us ever laid eyes on the scrolls again. Our leader checked every year with the keepers of the vault, and every year he reported that all was well. We just could never agree to reopen it again. We had sworn to keep our codes safe, and when we could all agree that the time was right, we would bring all the codes together and open the vault. At the time, I remember thinking, bravo. This could take up to a year for us to agree.

You see, without the original scrolls, our translations were worthless, and we all knew it. So, every year we would take another vote, and every year the vote was 3 to 1 or 2 to 2. I remember one year when I had to fly back from Lima for what turned out to be a five-minute discussion. Some years I felt holier than others, I guess, but the other three men were steadfast in their beliefs. I admired how all three of them knew what they believed and stood up for those beliefs, while I was so wishy-washy. I was definitely not the alpha male.

As the years went by and we all got older, we each, in our own way, had to plan to pass the codes along. The day you were born was when I decided how I would protect my code. It had been many years by then since we had spent all those weeks digging in the dirt in Cave 12, and it had passed like the blink of an eye. All four of us had unearthed other artifacts, published works and developed some sort *of fame in our own rights, but we never agreed what to do with what was perhaps our biggest discovery. The irony is that we ended up being no different from those organizations that we despised for hiding important discoveries. That damn Yankee just would not listen to reason.*

When your father and mother passed, I fell even further away from the church and from you and your brother; I realize now. I deeply regret both. There were and are fundamental flaws in my character, son. But today, as I write this, I can see with more vision than ever before. I have learned to accept that God is in charge and that our mission is to spread the Gospel. I fear it is too late for me to do what needs to be done, so I am sorry that I am placing this burden on you. You and Caleb are all that I have left in the world, and when I move on to the next life, you and he will have to carry on.

Now, I am the only remaining survivor of the expedition that discovered the scrolls, and even I am not long for this earth. I have recently noticed a few odd things happening around me. I am sure that I am being followed and almost positive that Carson is spying on me. Someone is after the codes. Make no mistake that there may be some danger for you and anyone else with access to one of the four codes. These people must be located and warned. I am counting on you to do the right thing because I know you are an honorable man. There are people out there who would do anything to get the scrolls and sell them to the highest bidder. If a singer's glove can sell for a hundred thousand dollars, what could ancient biblical parchments be worth? Enormous sums of money will drive people to do almost anything, so be aware.

Even as I write this, I do not know what the right thing is to do with the scrolls. However, I firmly believe they should not fall into the hands of men with evil intentions. I trust that when the time is right, the Holy Spirit will guide you to make the right decision.

Bless you, my son.
Ephesians 2:8

Papa

***

Below the sign-off was another coded message, a word problem this time, written in Arabic. Thomas skimmed it but dismissed it for later. There were issues in the main body of the letter that he wanted to decipher first. He read the letter twice more, the second time aloud. After he finished, he thought for a moment. A barge loaded with colorful, stacked containers slid through his line of sight as he tried to decode and understand his grandfather's words.

"What do you think?" he asked the others. "Anything strike you as odd about the letter?"

"He gave up sending the Bible verse in code," Dani said.

"Yes. He must have figured that if we had gotten this far, it was no longer necessary," Thomas said. "What is it?"

"It's a favorite verse for Lutherans," Dani said. "For it is by grace you have been saved, through faith and this is not from yourselves; but is the gift of God."

"Okay, I don't know where it comes into play. Let's table it for now," Thomas said. "What else about the letter strikes you?"

"It says a lot without saying a lot," Dani said. "Even wanders some."

"For one thing, there are no names," Chaney said. "He wants us to find and warn nameless people about the danger they may or may not be in."

"They are in danger, whoever they are," Dani said. "Gunmen at the beach and a Homeland Security goon tracking us down say so."

"Truth is, WE are in danger because of the gunmen, but do we really know that the danger extends beyond us?" Chaney countered.

"Yes," Thomas said. "Everything that my grandfather has said outright or implied so far has turned out to be spot on. If knowing one of those codes poses a danger, we have to do something. If it turns out to be a red herring, then so be it. You're right, though. There are no names in the letter except for Mike, which he clearly made up. What else seems odd or out of place in the letter?"

"Well, unless you were having trouble reading his writing, he misspelled Roman as Romeo. But maybe that was just a typo or a slight brain leak," Dani said.

"No. No way. He didn't have leaks. His brain was sealed tighter than Tupperware with Gorilla Glue. No, he meant to write Romeo, which got me thinking about something else. Whenever he was on the phone and had to spell something, he would always use military words for letters. You know, like on police shows when they put out an APB on a license plate, they'll say things like Victor, Oscar, Zulu, seven, six, four."

"And Romeo is one of those words," Chaney added.

"Right," Thomas said as he re-scanned the letter. "And there are a couple of other sentences in here that seem superfluous. Like saying he was doing a tango with us, and one time he came back from Lima for their five-minute meeting."

Thomas took out his notebook. He reread the letter

from the top and jotted down all the military lingo words he could find.

"Tango, Romeo, Echo, Mike, Bravo, Lima, Alpha and Yankee," he said. "T R E M B L A Y."

Dani pulled her phone out of her jeans back pocket and started googling Tremblay.

"There's about a million Tremblays in Louisiana alone," she said, flipping through dozens of Facebook entries.

"Try archaeologists named Tremblay," Thomas suggested.

She scrolled back to the top and searched again.

"Here it is. Franco Tremblay," she said. "Died two years ago after a life spent traveling the world on archaeological digs. He lived in New Orleans and was survived only by a granddaughter, Jacqueline Kaylee Tremblay, whose parents died in a plane crash when she was young."

"That's got to be it," Thomas said, jumping up. "We need to find her. Do you have an address?"

"Hold on," she said. "Apparently, he owned a mansion in the Garden District. It's on the walking tour."

"Then let's get a map," Thomas said.

"Wait a minute," Chaney said, grabbing his arm. "We don't know what we are racing into here, plus we still got Big Brother in the neighborhood. Remember?"

"He can't arrest us for walking around the Big Easy. We're just tourists right now," Thomas said.

"What about the code at the end?" Dani said. "It's not the same as the others, is it?"

"No. But I think we need to find Tremblay first. After that, we'll figure out the new code," Thomas said. "So, let's take a tour."

Chapter 13

THEY FOUND THE house on Chestnut Street, slipped through the iron gate and walked up the red-bricked walkway to the front of the estate. On both sides, towering oaks spread their canopies above the sidewalk, competing for airspace. Long, elegant strands of Spanish moss danced from the branches in the soft breeze. Beneath them, the grass grew in sparse patches, living in the constant shadows of the giants. Roots wove up and down through the soil searching for water like giant earthworms, causing ripples in the brick path. Three-story white pillars guarded the front porch, which ran the length of the house. Many colorful and well-trimmed hibiscus bloomed brightly along the steps leading to the front door.

As they reached the first step, Chaney halted.

"I'm going to hang here and keep an eye out," he said.

Thomas nodded. They were all feeling an increasing need for vigilance after their encounter with Harrison. He and Dani proceeded up the steps and rang the bell. From deep within the building bounced an echoing sound in search of someone to hear it. He reached for the bell again when the massive door opened without a sound. Standing before them was a stunning young woman with long dark hair and smooth, tanned skin. She was wearing a full-length white gown as if she were going to a prestigious ball, even though it was barely noon.

"Yes?" she said.

Thomas cleared his throat as Dani shot him an 'Are you kidding me right now?' look.

"Did this house belong to the late Franco Tremblay?" he asked.

"Who's asking?" the girl said.

"My name is Thomas Braden. I believe my grandfather knew Mr. Tremblay."

"Franco Tremblay was my grandfather, but he passed away a couple of years ago," she said with a hypnotic southern accent.

"Yes, I'm sorry for your loss. It's just that I think my grandfather wanted me to come here to find you."

"Who are you again?" the girl asked.

"I'm Thomas Braden, and this is my wife, Dani. My father was Stewart Braden. He also passed away recently. Would it be possible for us to come in and speak with you?"

"Stewart Braden? The Stewart Braden of archaeological fame? Our grandfathers went on digs together, did they not?"

"Yes, I believe so."

"Who is he?" the woman asked, spotting Chaney on the walkway.

"He's an associate of ours. Please, we mean no harm. We just need to talk with you for a few minutes," Thomas answered.

The young girl eyed all three of them for a moment before making up her mind.

"Please come in," she said, stepping aside. "My name is Jackie Tremblay."

She guided them as if floating on air through the ornate hallway filled with a mismatched smorgasbord of old lamps, photos, pottery and at least one golden pot that looked as if it could serve as a comfy tiny home for a genie until they reached a dark study.

"This guy must have used Papa's interior decorator," Thomas whispered to Dani, who responded with a punch in the ribs.

"I will ask Marvin to bring you some tea while I change into something a little less ostentatious. I was trying on gowns for the Jazz Festival Gala next month when you rang the bell. It will take only a moment. Please excuse me."

After she left, Dani turned and hit him again.

"What was that for?" he asked, rubbing his shoulder.

"You can put your eyes back into your head now," she snapped.

The study contained several floor to ceiling mahogany bookshelves, none of which had an inch of space to spare. An elderly gentleman with an old-fashioned tea cozy entered the room on suspect legs and set the tray down on a wooden table that was just as rickety. He poured two shaky porcelain cups of tea and retreated without a word.

"I guess ancient butlers come as standard equipment when you purchase an old estate," Thomas said. "At least this guy has more personality than Carson."

"He didn't say a word," Dani said.

"That's what I mean," Thomas replied.

Jackie Tremblay entered the study through a heretofore invisible door next to the bookshelves. She was barefoot and dressed in loose-fitting jeans that had been cut and shredded in several places and a white tank top with spaghetti straps. A heart-shaped locket on a gold chain bounced on her chest. She plopped on the sofa with one leg pinned under her and gestured for them to sit in the two facing chairs by their cups of tea.

"Now, tell me about your grandfather and why you are here," she said.

"Well, it's all a little hard to explain, and I'll grant you it might not make any sense at all once I say it aloud," Thomas began. "But a few days ago my grandfather summoned me to his house, at which time I discovered he was on his deathbed. The thing is, he didn't want to talk about dying. Instead, he secretly passed me a note like a seventh grader and told me that there could be danger ahead. Later that day, he died and left me with a lot of questions. Suffice it to say, I thought he was delusional, but things have happened since then to make me believe maybe he wasn't."

"For one," Dani interrupted, "some thugs threatened us at gunpoint at Coney Island."

"Gunpoint! Are you serious?"

"Afraid so," Dani answered the stunned woman. "But at the time, we didn't know why they were there or what they were after."

"Anyway," Thomas continued, "through a series of stops and more clandestine clues, we were brought to your door, or rather the door of your grandfather, looking for a password or some sort of code."

"A code for what?" Jackie asked.

"A vault," Thomas said. "Let me explain. On a dig many years ago, our grandfathers discovered what they believed to be additional Dead Sea Scrolls of immense historical value. But because some translations were not favorable to the Christian faith, your grandfather did not want to release their findings. So, for all these years this treasure, for lack of a better word, has been stored away, and each original member of the expedition had a six-number code that could open the vault, but only if all four of their codes were entered. Now though, someone is after the codes and presumably the scrolls in the vault."

"Where is this vault? Jackie asked.

"We don't know that," Thomas said.

"So, your grandfather had one set of the codes?" she asked.

"I believe so, but we don't know that either."

"Did your grandfather ever tell you about a code?" Dani asked the young girl.

"I can't remember," she said with a shiver. "All of this is a little overwhelming. How do I know what to think?"

"It's a fair question," Thomas said. "You've only just met us, and we're telling you some far-out tale about secret treasure and codes and henchmen on the prowl. I wouldn't have believed it myself two weeks ago. All I can tell you is that my grandfather asked me to warn those who might have the codes. We're not after the treasure, and we don't even know one code, but I know we were followed and threatened, and I know that a man claiming to be from Homeland Security has braced us twice."

"Wait a minute," Jackie said. "How does Homeland Security figure into all of this?"

"We don't know that either," Thomas answered. "This Agent Harrison showed up at my grandfather's funeral and told me they had been watching the old man's house but didn't elaborate. Then, this morning he appears out of nowhere like it was an accidental meeting."

"But he knew we had been at Coney Island," Dani added. "And he says the guys who threatened us are tied to some domestic terrorist organization."

The girl stared at Thomas, wide-eyed. He felt bad about dropping all of this on her. Until a few minutes ago, she didn't have a care in the world.

"I think you'd better go," Jackie said.

"But Miss Tremblay…" Thomas began.

"No. I don't want to hear anymore," she said. "You come in here with all this crazy talk about codes and running from thugs. Then, you tell me that the government is following you. Get out now!"

The front door crashed open, and Chaney raced into the hall.

"Thomas!" he yelled.

"Here," Thomas shouted, jumping from his chair. "What is it?"

"There's a van coming slowly around the corner, and it ain't the ice cream man."

"Wait here," Thomas said to the women.

"No way, Braden," Dani said as she popped out of the chair.

They ran to the front windows, keeping low, and peeked out. An unmarked white van pulled to the curb where one of the Coney Island assailants slipped out of the passenger seat. He was still sporting the ridiculous "Make America Great Again" ball cap. He subtly held his right hand in his jacket pocket as he looked up and down the street for other traffic.

"I can't believe that this guy wasn't the one on Harrison's watchlist," Thomas said.

"He's very subtle with that right hand in his pocket," Chaney said. "Only in America could a guy like that get another gun that quickly."

They watched him knock on the sliding door and stood aside as two men bailed out of the van. They were not so subtly carrying assault rifles.

"AK-47s," Chaney said.

"Only in America," Thomas said. "We've got to move now!"

Behind them, they heard Jackie gasp. "What is going on? I don't understand."

Thomas grabbed her by both arms. "Look at me," he said. "Is there a back way out?"

She swallowed hard. "This way," she said.

She led them out through the secondary door off the main hallway and down a dimly lit, narrow passage to a connecting door at the other end. Once through that door, they took a quick left and down a set of stairs to an outer door.

"Hold it," Chaney said. "Where does this come out?"

"It leads to a greenhouse that my grandfather kept, which leads to a second garage on the back of the property," Jackie replied.

"Okay, let me take a quick look first," Chaney said as he stepped to the door and opened it a crack. He eased out slowly and slid his back along the wall to the nearest corner. A quick peek told him that no one was on that side of the house, so he waved the others out and then followed them into the greenhouse.

An earthy aroma slapped their nostrils as they quickly jogged to the other end where Chaney performed the same look-see method before they ran to the garage door. Once inside, Jackie fumbled for the light switch and illuminated a Harley Davidson in disrepair and a white 1970s vintage Cadillac with a black vinyl top and tail-fin lights.

"The keys are always in it," Jackie told them. "We crank it up once a week to keep it running. It was my grandfather's pride and joy."

She jumped into the driver's seat while the others piled in the other three doors. The engine rumbled to life on the first try. Jackie hit the garage door opener, and the big sedan slid smoothly out.

"Keep down until we get clear," she commanded.

"I know this routine," Dani said as she and Thomas lay together in the back.

Once they were a couple of miles away on surface streets, they pulled into the parking lot of a closed Piggly Wiggly and sat there idling. No one spoke for a moment as they all caught their breath. Finally, Jackie broke the ice.

"What the hell was that?"

"I am so sorry that we tangled you up in this, Miss

Tremblay," Thomas replied.

"Call me Jackie, and it's a little late for sorry, don't you think? I just got chased out of my own house by men with guns! Until you showed up, I was trying on formals."

"I know. You're right. I didn't expect them to show up," Thomas said.

"How did they find us?" Dani asked, puzzled. "Harrison tracked us too, but that didn't seem as creepy. He has the resources of the government at his disposal."

"Maybe these thugs have more resources than we gave them credit for," Chaney said.

"Or Harrison is in on this and pointed these guys right at us," Dani said.

"There are several possibilities," Thomas said. "We know Homeland was watching my grandfather's house, but we don't know who else might have been. We don't know who is ultimately behind all of this or where they got their intel, but maybe they already knew that there are four codes and that Tremblay had one of them. They could have been monitoring his house from the beginning, and then when we showed up, it triggered them to move in. Or maybe our being here was just a coincidence."

"That's a big coincidence. Not sure I'm buying it," Chaney replied. "And those goons have not been watching this house for long because they were playing pitty-pat with us on the beach."

"One thing is for certain," Thomas said. "There is no longer any question that we are stuck in the middle of something and there is no easy way out."

"So, what do we do now?" Dani asked.

"Is there somewhere you can go for a while?" Thomas

asked Jackie. "I think you just need to lie low for a bit, and we will leave and hopefully take our trouble with us."

"If there's a chance that those guys were going to show up anyway, like you said, then I'm in trouble too, which means I'm staying with you," she said.

"I don't think that's a good idea."

Jackie reached behind her neck and unclasped the chain. She then gently opened the locket and held it over the front seat in front of Thomas.

"My grandfather basically raised me while my parents traveled the world and did nothing of consequence with their lives. After they died, he gave me this locket and told me it was his most prized possession. He made me promise to always keep it with me and that someday it could become the most important thing in my life."

Thomas held her wrist and looked closely at the locket. There were six random numbers engraved on it. He let go of her hand and nodded at Dani.

"I believe it is what you and those other guys are after. So," Jackie continued, snapping the locket closed and re-fastening the chain on her neck, "we are in this together now."

Chapter 14

"FIRST THING WE have to do is dump this car," Thomas said. "It's like riding on a parade float. Do you think you can get to your car without being seen?" he asked Chaney.

"Have you ever seen the Easter Bunny?" Chaney replied.

"No."

"Well, there you go. Let's drive by once to see if it looks clear, and then you can drop me off around the corner," Chaney said.

Jackie drove the Caddy slowly past the Voodoo Museum while the others kept their heads low, eyes just above the door frame. Chaney's sedan sat alone in the lot's corner, cooling its heels right where that had left it earlier that morning. There was a smattering of cars parked closer to the museum entrance, but no people in sight.

"It looks pretty quiet," Thomas said.

"Wait!" Dani said.

Just as Jackie made a turn at the next street, they saw Harrison exit the museum with his goons in tow.

"We're made," Chaney said.

"But how?" asked Thomas.

"You keep forgetting that you are dealing with the United States government, dude. They probably ran my mug through some sort of facial recognition program, or they're watching us on their special Homeland Security satellite channel like the world's creepiest reality show," Chaney said. "It don't matter how they did it. It's done. Question is, what do we do now?"

They circled the block once. Jackie kept the car moving, but slowly as they drove by. There was no one standing in the lot, but upon closer inspection, one of Harrison's men stood posted a few steps into the trees by Chaney's car. When they turned the corner, they spotted the other one directly across the street from the car, standing in the doorway of the Hurricane Bar. They drove on, turned the next corner, and stopped.

"Now what?" Dani asked.

"I've got an idea," Thomas said. "Jackie, we really need to dump this car now, preferably out of sight."

"I know a parking garage on the edge of the French Quarter. A lot of employees park there," Jackie said.

They made their way slowly through a series of one-way streets. Once, they spotted the white van just ahead of them as if it were circling slowly on the prowl. It turned at the next intersection, and Jackie sped through the light just as it turned red. Finally, they pulled into the garage, took a ticket and drove all the way to the highest covered floor and parked as far away from the elevators as possible.

"Thomas, I need to talk to you," Dani said when they got out of the car.

"What?" he said.

"Alone."

Thomas squinted a question mark at her.

"Chaney, you take Jackie and head down to the first floor and keep an eye out for our friends in the van. We'll be right behind you," Thomas said, without taking his eyes from his wife.

"Do you really think we should be picking up strays?" Dani said as soon as Chaney and the girl were out of sight.

"What are you talking about?" Thomas asked.

"I'm talking about you saying that you wouldn't trust anyone except people that your grandfather sent to us. But a five-foot four brunette with big doe eyes crosses your path, and you're Lancelot du Lac suddenly."

"Don't you think you're overreacting here?"

"No. You said don't trust anybody and I don't trust her," she said.

"How can you not trust her? You just met her," Thomas responded, feeling his own anger rising.

"You just met Harrison and you don't trust him," she said.

"That's different," he said. "Harrison sought me out and told me he was monitoring my grandfather's house. We approached Jackie without warning, and we may have invited trouble right to her doorstep."

"We know nothing about this girl. I can spot a

manipulator a mile away, and I'm telling you, she has more red flags than a Chinese military parade. Don't you think it's weird that she wanted to go with us?" Dani asked.

"No, I don't. A vanload of guys carrying guns showed up at her house, and I don't think they were selling Girl Scout cookies!"

"But you said yourself that they may have just been there because they were following us. Don't you think she would be much safer staying with some aunt in Baton Rouge or whatever than she will be tagging along with us? She's got to have some relatives somewhere. There's about a million Tremblays in Louisiana alone," Dani said, with a fierceness in her voice that Thomas had rarely heard.

"I think she could be in real danger, and I don't want to leave her alone," Thomas said. "I think you're just jealous."

"Jealous! Are you serious? I'm not jealous of that tramp stamp. You're thinking with the wrong head again, Braden, and if you ever accuse me of being jealous again, I'll give you the same headache I gave that goon at Coney Island."

Dani turned and stormed off without another word. He followed her to the exit door, and they headed down. The stairwell dropped them off two blocks over from Bourbon Street. The crowds were out now, milling around, which provided decent cover for the foursome. Thomas led them through the tourists and tourist traps, keeping to the edges as much as possible. A young boy of maybe eight was tap-dancing on the next corner. Thomas waded through the gathered onlookers to get a peek at the next street. No sign of black SUVs or vans with AK47s lurking ahead. They moved on through stands of people watching mimes, jugglers and spray artists. Finally, they reached Jackson

Square.

"We're going back to the church," Thomas said. "I'm hoping like hell that Father Dmitri is still around."

They circumnavigated the square without incident and entered the dark confines of the cathedral once again. This time, there were people scattered throughout the church, sitting in pews. Some were praying aloud, others twisting rosaries in their hands, while still others just sat and stared ahead at the altar as if completely lost in their thoughts. They retraced their steps from earlier that morning by memory until they reached the priest's door. Thomas tapped lightly.

"Come," said the priest.

They crammed themselves back into the tiny office as before, except this time there were four of them. Father Dmitri eyed them with a frown and waited a beat before saying anything.

"I told you all that you could never come back here," he said coolly. "We had an agreement."

"I know, Father," Thomas said. "But things have really turned upside down since this morning. You're the only person who can help us right now."

"I warned you that your grandfather believed, as do I, that this mission of yours could be dangerous."

"Yes, you did. But the thing is, we didn't expect the danger to slap us in the face as soon as we left here," Thomas replied.

"Who's this?" the priest asked, looking at Jackie.

"My name is Jackie Tremblay," she said. "I am Franco Tremblay's granddaughter."

The priest studied her closely before breaking into a

smile. He stood and took both of her hands in his.

"Yes, I believe you are. I can see his mischievous eyes right on your face. There was a time when you were much younger when your grandfather and I would sit in his study and you would push this little cart around the room while we talked. You were constantly filling and emptying that cart with things you found. Once, you had a chalice that was several hundred years old in there. He told me it was practically priceless, but he didn't take it from you. He just shrugged his shoulders and said, you had good taste."

"Father, can you help us?" Jackie asked him.

"I feel I must," he said, letting go of her hands. "What is it you need?" he asked, turning his attention back to Thomas.

"There are at least two groups of men looking for us," Thomas said. "We need a vehicle to get out of town so we can figure out what to do next.

There was a knock at the door.

"Father Dmitri?" a woman called. "Are you in there?"

The priest signaled for them to be quiet.

"Yes, Delores. What is it?" he said through the door.

"There is an Agent Harrison asking for you in the sanctuary. He says he is with Homeland Security."

"Fine. Tell him I will be right out," he said.

He waited for a moment and then cracked the door to make sure his young assistant was gone.

"You didn't tell me that the government was involved," he said.

"At this point, we don't know who all is involved," Thomas said. "And until we know more, I don't think we should trust anyone."

The priest studied them a moment longer before nodding.

"Come with me," he said. "It's not much, but I have an old Ford Explorer that you can take that belongs to my brother. He stores it at the church because he travels a lot. It won't be missed."

He guided them even deeper into the maze of the church until they popped out a side door into a covered parking area. It wasn't a garage, but the landscaping concealed it well. The priest handed Thomas the keys.

"I shouldn't keep the agent waiting too long. Is there anything else that you need?" he asked.

"You wouldn't happen to have a couple of nuns who could remove the starter from Harrison's car, would you?" Thomas said with a grin.

"I'm afraid Sister Delores' skill set is more secretarial than mechanical," Father Dmitri replied. "Be careful and go in peace."

With that, he closed the door on them for the second time that day. They piled into the car, this time with Thomas in the driver's seat and Chaney up front with him. The upholstery was duct-taped here and there, and the passenger window sat askew in the frame. Thomas turned the key, and the old SUV contemplated the request, choked and wheezed for a few seconds, and then coughed into a throaty rumble. They backed out into a cloud of exhaust and then drove away.

Forty-five minutes later, they were westbound on I-10, driving at the posted limit out on the open highway before turning north onto a state road.

"Any idea where we're going?" Chaney asked over the

wind whistling by his head.

"We need to stop and work through the word problem," Thomas said. "But I want to get a little further away before we do that. In the meantime, we need to dump our cell phones."

"Agreed," Chaney said. "We're being tracked somehow, and phones are the most logical explanation."

Thomas dug his out of his pocket and handed it over to Chaney, who turned it in his hands twice. He tapped the screen a few times, looking at the installed apps on the phone. He opened one and showed it to Thomas.

"What the hell is that?" Thomas asked.

"It's a listening/tracking app. It not only shows your location but can listen in on your conversation. Someone installed it on your phone when you weren't looking," Chaney said.

"How do you know that?" Thomas asked.

"I got skills," Chaney replied.

"How can that be?" Thomas asked. "I always have it with me unless…"

"What?" Chaney asked.

"Son of a bitch!" Thomas yelled, slapping the steering wheel. "Carson took my phone when I saw Papa. He made a lame excuse about it interfering with the machines."

"If he planted the bug, then someone has been tracking us since that day," Dani said from the back seat. "Did Harrison ask him to do it?"

"I don't think so," said Thomas.

"He's right," Chaney added. "Harrison wouldn't need to install a bug. He would just tap directly into your phone from Big Brother in the sky."

"It makes some sense, though," Thomas said. "Harrison told me they had been monitoring calls from my grandfather's house. I thought he was implying that he was the one they were most interested in. But they were monitoring what Carson was doing. That bastard bugged my phone right under my nose."

"And the letter we found in the box indicated Papa suspected Carson," Dani said.

Chaney forced his window down another inch, then threw phone out on the highway.

"They can listen to the Louisiana swamp now," he said.

"We have to get rid of all our phones," Thomas said.

Dani passed hers forward, and Chaney performed the same search on it, but there were no suspicious apps on it. Chaney threw it out the window just the same. Then he turned and looked at Jackie.

"I don't have one," she said. "In all the rush to leave, I left my phone along with my shoes."

"Okay," Thomas said. "They can't ping our phones, and at least for the time being we should be clear driving this car."

"But driving where?" Chaney asked for the second time.

Thomas slowed the car and pulled onto the shoulder.

"I need you to drive so I can work the word problem," he said.

Once they were going again, Thomas pulled out the letter and his notebook and copied down the word problem.

Back in 1994, a man had a job to do that was projected to take him

12 days. He worked Monday through Friday and every other Saturday. He got a late start on the project because of a previous job, and so he began on the first Saturday of the month. He ended up having to take 3 sick days during the project, and the job turned out to be half again bigger than originally projected. On what day did he finish the job?

When he was done with his copy, he read it aloud to the others and then drew numbers in his notebook.

"It's pretty straightforward, I think," he said.

"You're kidding, right?" Jackie asked.

"He always says stuff like that," Dani said. "I think he does it just to make everyone else feel dumb."

After a few more seconds of scribbling, Thomas looked up. He knew the answer but not the meaning.

"He finished the job on Thursday," he said, looking at the others.

"So, what does that mean?" asked Chaney.

"I wish I knew," Thomas said.

"Think, Thomas," Dani said from the back. "Thursday must mean something to you."

"It's just like any other day of the week," he said. "What can be special about Thursday? On Thursdays, I went to school and hardly saw my grandfather at all, even if he was in town."

"Which Thursday?" Jackie asked.

"What do you mean?" Thomas said.

"I mean, maybe the answer is not just the day of the week but which one of them. Like, was it the second Thursday or the third?"

Thomas looked down at his notes.

"It was the fourth Thursday," he said.

"Okay," Dani said. "So, what does the fourth Thursday mean to you?"

"Nothing," he said. "My grandfather and I had no regular Thursday routine like Sheldon's Thai food Thursdays. There was no monthly meeting held on the fourth Thursday, and even if there was, he was not involved in it."

"Wait a minute," Chaney said. "Isn't Thanksgiving always on the fourth Thursday of November?"

Thomas thought about that. His mind drifted back to his childhood and the few precious days that he spent with his grandfather.

"It was the only football games we ever watched together," he said. "On Thanksgiving. Fortunately, we are already going in the right direction. We need to go to Big D."

Chapter 15

MACKIE WAS GIVING the tour to a prospective young couple and their two kids after the father, Nick, had contacted him through the email address provided on the Freedom Landers website.

"Up the hill," Mackie said, pointing, "is where everyone in the community lives. You will build your own cabin, and we will help, like in the old days when people came together for barn-raisings. We live our lives as God intended, with support for each other. We don't allow outside influences to determine our path. Smartphones and internet access are prohibited. We don't want the filth that the world calls news to poison our children's brains."

The man, Mark, surveyed the hill before asking a question.

"Does anyone work outside of the compound? I have a

good job that I can do remotely, but I need Wi-Fi."

"Yes, of course," Mackie answered. "And if you need a smartphone out in the world, you will simply turn it in when you return each night. Keep in mind, though, that there is an expectation that money made on the outside will be used to make improvements here."

"Do any women leave from time to time?" Mark's wife asked.

Mackie thought for a moment before answering.

"We believe women serve our lifestyle best when they are here, teaching and caring for our children," he answered.

The couple's oldest boy had been eyeing the playground for some time and finally asked Mackie if he could go check it out.

"I think that's a splendid idea," Mackie said. "Take your brother with you and say hello to Casey. She's the little girl on the swing."

When they had gone, Mackie turned to the young couple.

"We believe in the purity of our faith and our race," he began. "And as such, we set rigid standards for who we allow to join us here. We teach our children the King James Bible and all the math and science that they will need. Everyone here, young and old, will learn to speak German fluently. We believe it is important to have a communication option other than English if the need arises. Make no mistake that there are those who wish we would just disappear. They will try every means necessary to run us off our land because they do not believe that we have the right to live the life we have chosen. If you join us, we expect you to embrace this life and all that it offers. It is a commitment, and we don't take it lightly. If you decide it is not for you, then we'll part as friends."

He paused to let what he was saying sink in. The couple were listening intently and trying to let the words wash over them for consideration.

"If you choose to come be with us, we will provide everything you need for your family. The membership fee is fifty thousand dollars. That gets you set up with a cabin and modest furnishings. I will introduce you around the compound, and work roles will be assigned to each of you. We all work together and pray together. So, I guess that's about it. If you need some time to think it over, we have no problem with that."

The man looked at his wife, and she nodded.

"We're in," he said. "It will take us a month or so to sell the house, but I will get you the money to hold our place as soon as possible."

"We look forward to your joining us on this journey," Mackie said. "Let us know if you need any help getting ready for the move."

They shook hands, and the couple called for their boys and left.

"Mackie," the voice came over the loudspeaker. "You have a call."

He went to the phone in the outdoor kitchen.

"You lost them in New Orleans," Patterson said without preamble.

"We never saw them," Mackie replied. "They left before we could get there. Anyway, we will continue to track them. The boys got back late last night, so we will stand down until we pick them up again. It won't be long. In fact, I think it might be wise to alter our plan somewhat."

"And what revision did you have in mind?"

"Braden is working hard to find and get the answers that we will also need. I suggest we let him do that without interference until he has everything, then we force him to work with us. If we can track him, we can wait and show our hand when he has done all the legwork."

"How do you propose to force him to comply?"

"By all accounts, he loves his wife greatly."

"Fine, it would be most regrettable if you cannot acquire the scrolls. I hope you understand the urgency of our situation."

"Are you threatening me, Patterson? That's not the sort of thing that I would recommend."

"Mr. Mackie, I do not make threats. I'm merely pointing out that failure is not an option."

"We won't fail. It's vital to our way of life that we protect our faith at all costs."

"And the money doesn't hurt either, does it, my friend?"

"The money ensures our continued survival in a world that is twirling away from us, Patterson, but make no mistake, our faith is the bedrock of everything we do."

"Very well. Now, on to the next subject. The butler says that he has searched high and low and that our objective is not to be found in the old man's home."

"That's what he says on the phone," Mackie responded. "I'm going to ask him in person. Give him a chance to be more forthcoming."

"Do you think he is hiding it from us?" Patterson said.

"There's enough money at stake here to make almost

anyone think about going off script," Mackie answered. "Let me talk to him to be sure he hasn't sent us on a wild - goose chase."

***

Mackie drove around the block to make sure there was no surveillance in the area. Patterson had told him that the Feds had pulled out shortly after Stewart Braden died, but Mackie only trusted himself on matters of great importance. He parked at the curb a block away, facing the brownstone, and rolled down his windows. It was well after midnight, and only a few of the homes had interior lights burning. An early summer breeze blew through the car with just a hint of spring clinging to it. All was quiet in American suburbia.

He pondered how Americans had gotten so soft. They had long ago quit fighting for their freedom and their birthright. Instead, they craved air conditioning and plush mattresses, and cars that would drive themselves. They had lost sight of the importance of God and family. They weren't stalwart or brave. They chose lives with no commitments and few worries. Yet, they would wake up in the morning and complain of backaches or commuting traffic, or the baseball scores as if such things mattered.

After a few minutes, he got out of the car and casually walked to the house and up the steps. After checking the door and realizing that it wasn't locked, he pushed his way in quietly. Old furniture and cardboard boxes littered the entry hall and front room. Someone had begun packing up the place already. He made his way deeper into the building until he heard heavy footsteps above him. After checking the first floor fully, he softly climbed the stairs. Once at the top landing, he turned right onto the carpeted hallway and moved toward the sounds of ripping packing tape. He stepped through the doorway. The room was small but well-appointed. A hulking man, with his back to Mackie, dominated the space, making it seem much smaller than it was — like a limousine in a parking spot. He had already sealed and stacked several boxes near the door and was using the bed to load books into another.

"Going somewhere?" Mackie asked.

The butler stood to his full height before turning around. He stared down his nose at him.

"I recognize your voice," Carson said, crossing his arms. "But I never expected that we would actually meet. Yes, I am packing to leave since the grandson of my former employer has dismissed me."

"Is that so? I guess the younger Braden did not recognize the value of your service," Mackie said, grinning.

"Why are you here, young man?" the butler asked. "I have much to do before I go, and I don't relish the thought of spending time with the likes of you. I have complied with all of your requests, have I not?"

"And you were paid. Were you not?" Mackie said. "I expect to get my money's worth in all of my business dealings."

"I'm afraid there is nothing more I can do for you, sir. The scrolls are not here. I have searched every room of this house, and I can assure you that your best bet is to follow Thomas. His grandfather was too smart not to have had a plan in place. I am positive that he passed on information to Thomas somehow. It would behoove you to stop wasting your and my time. I care little for Thomas, but he is not an idiot. He will find the scrolls. I am sure of that."

"It seems to me that you're boxing up a good deal more than you have a right to," Mackie said. "How do I know that you have not already found them and boxed them up for yourself, as a — how do you say, severance package?"

"You know nothing about me or what I am entitled to," the butler said. "I served Mr. Braden for decades with dignity and honor. He would want me to have some treasures that he and I discussed over coffee many, many times. He would be the first to say that his grandson has treated me unfairly in all of this. Now, as I have told you, the scrolls are not here, and that is a fact. Whether or not you believe that is none of my concern. Now, I'm afraid I must ask you to leave, or I will be forced to call the police. I have no doubt that you have been in trouble with the authorities before, so I'm sure they would love to come get you. So go!"

Carson turned his back dismissively and began packing up again. Mackie's anger rose like a creature from the hidden regions of a distant planet. His father had taught him well how to tap into the rage, to bring to bear an overwhelming force in the service of his mission, but he had never taught his son how to control the anger once it took over. He pulled the Glock he kept in his waistband, aimed at the man's left leg, and pulled the trigger. The room filled with smoke as the walls vibrated from the shock. The big man collapsed to the floor, writhing in pain and clutching at what used to be his kneecap. Since his tenth birthday, Mackie's aim had always been true. He stepped over to the butler, staying away from the man's remaining good flailing leg, and squatted down next to his head. His eyes boiled with fury as he stared down at this ungodly man.

"No one turns their back on me," he said through gritted teeth. "What's the old saying? God created man, but Samuel Colt made them equal. Thing is, we are not all equal, are we? Now, I need to know exactly everything that you know about the scrolls. You must have some idea of where they are or how to find them."

Carson whimpered incoherently. He was already going into shock.

"I can't hear you, sir."

"If I knew, I would tell you. The scrolls mean nothing to me. I would not try to take them. Please, I'm an old man. I'm no threat to you or anyone else. I just want to gather my things and live out my days in peace."

Mackie laughed at the pathetic giant lying in front of him.

"No, you are not a threat," he said.

He shook his head, stood and looked down at the man's face. He felt no remorse, no pity. Everything this man had done up to this moment led to one inarguable truth. Carson Prewitt was of no use to anyone. Mackie shot him between the eyes, and immediately a blissful peacefulness overcame him, a serenity in knowing what was right. The creature inside him receded back into the depths of his being, and Mackie thanked God aloud for bestowing such gifts of power on him. He was on a spiritual journey now, and it promised to be quite fulfilling.

Chapter 16

"OKAY, I'LL BITE," Chaney said. "Why Dallas?"

"My grandfather was a genius and, like many people that smart, he had a few quirks. One of them revolved around Thanksgiving. Even if the other 364 days of the year were anything but the American Dream, on Thanksgiving, for that one day, we were a Norman Rockwell poster. No matter what trips he had planned, being home for Thanksgiving was a sacred trust for him. He said that it was the only holiday where no one expected you to honor anyone else. So, we watched the Macy's Day parade together and then we watched the two pro football games that were always on that day. While everyone else was cooking feasts for a big gathering, Caleb and I sat on the couch next to him and gobbled down chips and deli sandwiches and ice cream until we were almost sick. It was amazing."

"Right. The Cowboys and the Lions always hosted games on Thanksgiving," said Chaney. "So, why are you thinking Dallas and not Detroit?"

"Because Dallas is closer, I'm hoping it's the right choice. We need to get access to the Internet before I will know for sure. I think that 1994 is the clue. It plays no part in the riddle itself, so it must be there to further clarify the answer. I hope it will tell us which city is the correct one."

"Fine, but right now we have bigger problems," Chaney said. "We're getting low on gas, and I've been thinking. If Harrison was tracking your phones, maybe he is also monitoring your credit cards, and maybe mine too by now. We need gas, a room for the night, some food, and maybe some extra clothes. For sure, the girl needs new shoes. Plus, we have to pick up some burner phones, but if we go off charging all of those things, it might light up his screen like an airport runway."

"I know. I've been thinking the same thing," Thomas said. "But I don't know what other choice we have."

"Maybe I could help," Jackie said from the back seat. "The cops don't know that I am with you yet. They've never seen me. I have a credit card with me. We could use that."

"You have a credit card, but not your phone?" Dani asked.

"Yes, I keep a little money clip with me all the time. All it has is my I.D. and a couple of cards. It's for the bars."

"Since when do they let twelve-year-olds in bars?" Dani asked.

"I'm twenty-four, but I always get carded. You

remember what that's like, right?"

"Okay, it doesn't help for us to go after each other," Thomas said. "Let's get closer to Dallas, then we will use Jackie's card to get a room and some burners. That sound like a plan?"

He glanced over at Chaney, who was nodding his head.

"Sure," Chaney said. "As long as these two don't kill each other before we get there."

Just before midnight, they pulled into a Knight's Inn off I-30 just east of Dallas and parked away from the entrance.

"We'll camp here for the night," Thomas said. "Jackie, go get us one room."

"I think we should go in as a couple," Jackie said.

"Fine. You and Chaney go," Thomas said.

"In East Texas?" she said. "I thought you wanted to stay under the radar."

"Okay," Thomas said, with a glance at Dani. "Let's go get a room."

The two of them got out. As they approached the front door, Jackie looped her arm through his and smiled as he opened the door. A few minutes later, they came back with a key. Thomas and Dani slid into room 114 while Chaney and Jackie went looking for burner phones and shoes. As soon as they drove off the lot, Dani was at him.

"Why are you doing this?" she said.

"What are you talking about?"

"I'm talking about all of it. As soon as Chaney found that bug in your phone, you knew as well as I did Harrison was being straight with us. He's not in league with those other thugs. He told us we were in over our heads, and he was right."

"You're probably right," Thomas agreed. "But I can't give up just yet. Even if Harrison is legit, he wouldn't hesitate to tie us up in red tape given the chance. I can't risk that right now. My grandfather asked me to do this, and he said there could be some danger."

"But did he know that men with guns would be chasing us?" she asked. "Do you think he wanted you to risk your life for this mission? Are you even sure that there is an actual mission?"

"Yes, I'm sure. Jackie has one code. Those guys are not chasing us just for the fun of it. They are after something. Maybe they want the scrolls. Maybe something else, but I have to believe that Papa wouldn't have set all this up if it wasn't really important."

"You're going on blind faith, Thomas," Dani said. "That's not how you operate."

"Not usually, but here it's needed," he answered. "He asked me what I believed in, and I gave him a snarky answer. Truth is, I don't know the answer, but I believe in him, and he believed in a God. So, for right now I guess I'm a believer of sorts."

"Okay, what about the girl?"

"What about her?"

"We have to dump her, Thomas. Putting her arms around you and batting her eyes all the time. She's playing you, and you can't see it. She has a hidden agenda."

"Will you listen to yourself? How could she have an agenda? She didn't know that we were coming to see her, and there is no way that she could have expected that we would all be in a dumpy motel outside of Dallas before the night was over."

"I know all that. But you have to at least accept the possibility that she might be holding something back."

"Like what, Dani?" he said, exasperated.

"I don't know, but I don't believe for a minute that the girl left her cell phone. A girl of that age wouldn't be caught dead without one."

"We were running for our lives, so I think she could have left it. Have you never left your phone somewhere? And under much less urgent circumstances?"

"When they come back, I think we should search her," Dani said, crossing her arms in defiance.

"Are you crazy? I'm not doing that!"

"I don't trust her," Dani said again.

"Fine. You ask her about the phone if you want, but I'm not getting involved with it."

Dani fought back tears as she stared at her husband.

"I'm going for a walk," she said, slamming the door behind her.

Thomas waited a beat before stepping outside himself. He walked back to the office to ask about Wi-Fi access. The night manager directed him to a public computer that he could use. He looked up the Thanksgiving Day games from 1994. Dallas won a shootout with Green Bay, and the Lions and Steelers played to a tie. He pondered the games for a moment. Were the scores of importance? Cowboys 42, Packers 31; Lions and Steelers 16 apiece. He was sure that Dallas or Detroit was significant. The fourth Thursday had to mean Thanksgiving., but what was he missing? He thought back to 1994. It was the year after his parents died. He remembered the emptiness he had felt. He remembered Caleb had barely spoken during those first few months after. It was depressing to think about. He needed sleep. He shut down the computer and went back to the room. The others were all there.

"I got four burner phones," Chaney said. "They are all pre-programmed. You're 1, I'm 2, Dani's 3 and Jackie is 4. Until we know more about what's going on, we stay off the grid. Agreed?"

"Agreed," Thomas said.

Both women nodded without speaking. Thomas had missed something while he was out, and the room was frigid. He took his phone from Chaney, went to the far bed and lay down on top of it with his clothes on. The last thing he remembered was Dani sliding in next to him.

The next morning, he woke with a start. Chaney was just coming out of the shower. He looked over and saw Dani curled up next to him. Jackie was in the other bed and still out.

"Good, you're awake," Chaney said. "You need to go get us some coffee."

"Why can't you do it?" Thomas said.

"Because I ain't s'posed to be here, white man," Chaney said, laughing.

Thomas rolled out of bed. When he got back with coffee and donuts, everyone was stirring.

"I'll be back in a few," he said to them. "I need to look something up."

Thomas made his way back to the lobby computer and drank while it booted up. He could almost feel the synapses in his brain stretching and yawning. He remembered where he had left off the night before and decided to change his tack. This time, he searched for archaeologists in the

Dallas/Fort Worth area. It spat back a list hundreds of pages long. He re-typed the search to find renowned archaeologists in Dallas and only had to sift through the list for a minute before he hit what he was looking for. Robert Packer of Packer Oil Industries. The Packers played the Cowboys on Thanksgiving in 1994. Bingo.

***

Harrison walked up the flagstone path to the Braden house. Yellow crime scene tape was strung across the front door, which stood open. Next to the doorway, a young officer, who looked like he had graduated from the academy about five minutes ago, stood guard. Harrison nodded at him once, ducked under the tape, and stepped inside. The all too familiar odor of decomposition immediately assaulted his nostrils. From the entryway, he could see two rooms, one on either side. There was old furniture crammed into both of them with various boxes strewn about haphazardly, like someone was packing to move but didn't know where to begin. He looked up and saw Agent Conner approaching. He was a strapping go-getter who annoyed Harrison at every turn with his upbeat demeanor.

"What do you have for me?" Harrison asked the junior agent.

"One dead upstairs. It's the butler, Carson Prewitt, who appeared to be packing up when he took two bullets. One to the head and one in the knee. It doesn't appear to be a robbery."

"Show me."

Conner led him up the stairs and down the hallway.

Several members of Boston's finest milled around in the hall and took turns glancing into the far bedroom door. Conner shouldered past the gawkers, with Harrison trailing, until he found the detective in charge.

"This is Detective Brice," he said to Harrison.

Brice was a big man with a fixed jaw. Harrison liked him at once.

"I'm Agent Harrison with Homeland," he said, offering the detective his hand.

"Yeah, Conner told me you were coming, but he didn't tell me you'd look like shit on toast when you got here," Brice said, without cracking a smile.

"Spent all night on a flight from New Orleans," Harrison offered. "Sorry if my wrinkled shirt offends."

"Nah. I just figured it was your way of appealing to the common man. Anyway, what's Homeland's interest here?" he asked.

"Tell me what you've got so far and then I'll fill in the blanks," Harrison said.

Brice eyed him for a moment. Harrison figured he was trying to decide whether he was going to play along or if he'd rather be a dick about the whole thing.

"Okay," Brice said, turning his attention to the corpse in the room. "Carson Prewiit, seventy-eight years old, shot twice. The kill shot was point-blank between the eyes. Coroner says he was already on the floor looking at the killer when the second shot killed him. We've ruled out robbery since there is a ton of expensive crap lying around everywhere. We think the assailant shot him first from the doorway, then took his time to come over and finish the guy off."

"So this is one case where the butler didn't do it." Harrison said. "You got a TOD?"

"Coroner thinks it was between two and three days ago."

Harrison nodded. "I saw him three days ago at the funeral of his employer, Stewart Braden. It had to be sometime after ten that morning. Conner," he said, turning to face his young agent. "Go down and get on the horn with surveillance. I need to know the exact location of Thomas Braden right now."

Conner pushed back through the crowd and out the door.

"Is this Braden a guy I should look at for this?" the Boston detective asked.

"I don't think so. He's more likely to be the next victim than the shooter here," Harrison answered. "We were monitoring calls in and out of this house for about six weeks prior to the elder Braden's death. We were working on a tip that a white supremest group on our watchlist had a member in this household. The old man was on his deathbed and seemed unlikely to be involved, but the butler was a possibility. Now, I'm thinking he was definitely involved in some way. Anyway, before he croaked, the old man summoned one of his grandsons, Thomas, and appeared to send the boy on some sort of errand. Since the funeral, he's visited Coney Island and New Orleans. I don't know what he is up to, but I do know that this group the butler was mixed up with is also interested in tracking him."

Detective Brice nodded. "Anyone come to mind for this?" he asked, tilting his head toward the dead butler.

"No. We haven't gotten a bead on who's running this thing, and since we pulled out after the old man died, we weren't monitoring here when the shots were fired."

Agent Conner pushed his way back into the room.

"Agent Harrison," he said. "Braden's phone stopped moving around the Henderson Swamp in southern Louisiana sometime last night. It's still there."

"Well, unless a gator ate him, he dumped his phone," Harrison said.

"Does that make him a suspect now?" Brice asked him.

"I would be surprised, but I can't rule it out," Harrison answered.

Chapter 17

CHANEY DROVE THEM slowly past the Packer Industries building and then boomeranged around the block for a second look and pulled into a fifteen-minute loading zone. The glass and steel home office stood among the other giants in the Dallas skyline as a show of wealth and American capitalism. An old man pushing a shopping cart full of plastic bags filled with soda cans lumbered and jingled down the sidewalk. Another man wearing a white dress shirt, bright red tie, boots, and a white ten-gallon hat walked past the can collector going the other way. Walking stride for stride with the cowboy was a woman in a knee-length blue dress and matching heels. Behind her, a guy in a bright pink shirt with cranes on it and white-stemmed earbuds was talking loudly and wildly gesturing like an ASL interpreter on methamphetamine. Foot traffic in both directions moved at a frantic pace, but no one took notice of them. They had seen no obvious threats since New Orleans, but they all were scanning the area like lighthouse searchlights. Thomas considered Chaney sitting across from him for a moment.

"I don't know if what my Papa did for you merits your being here right now, but I'm glad you are," he said.

"Without your Papa, I'd be dead. So, yeah. It merits."

Thomas nodded and stepped out of the car into the sauna that was downtown Dallas in the summer. He watched them drive away and turn at the next corner, took one look up but couldn't see the top of the building and headed for one of the three revolving door entrances. Inside, a giant glass-enclosed atrium rose to the sky. Directly in front of him was a long stone counter, like a hotel registration desk, behind which sat several uniformed clerks and security personnel. Behind the counter, a two-story water wall provided white noise. To his right was a set of chrome and glass stairs leading up to a second-floor balcony where people were milling around small tables, drinking coffee and paying homage to their phones. To his left were several turnstiles where people with privileges badged their way to the elevators and the upper reaches of Packer Industries. Farther to the left was a security station and scanner where those who had not yet earned their Packer Merit Badge were forced to line up and partially disrobe. Women's heels clacked on the marble floor as they and men in suits hurried importantly either to or from their meetings. He stepped up to the service desk, where a petite black woman with an electric smile greeted him.

"May I help you, sir?"

"Yes, I need to locate the office of Robert Packer, please," he said, countering her grin with one of his own.

"Do you have an appointment?"

"Well, no, not exactly. I was just hoping I could stop in and speak with him for a couple of minutes."

"I see. Are you a friend of his?" she asked, while turning some internal dimmer switch on her smile.

"No, we have never met."

"I'm sorry, but I'm afraid I can't send you up without an appointment."

The grin went into night-light mode. Thomas held his place at the counter and watched as a sparrow flew across the lobby and landed on a windowsill. He bumped into the window twice before flying off to look for another exit.

"I feel you," Thomas said.

"Pardon me?" the woman asked.

"Nothing. I wonder if I could ask you to at least call his secretary or personal assistant or whatever really busy men have these days and just ask if I can have a few minutes of his time. I really think he would want to see me."

"Even though he has never met you?"

"Yes, please call up and tell whoever answers that Thomas Braden would like a few minutes with Mr. Packer."

Reluctantly, she picked up the phone to relay the message. Waited for a moment. Hung up.

"One of Mr. Packer's aides will take the message to him. If you would care to wait, you may do so over there," she said pleasantly, while pointing to a row of plastic chairs against the window.

Thomas thanked her, went over, and sat down. The lost sparrow flew to a perch on the back of the chair three over from him.

"You come here often?" he said.

A few minutes later, a tall woman wearing a dark gray business suit, librarian glasses, and black heels approached Thomas. Her hair was pulled back severely into a ponytail.

"Mr. Braden, I am Holly O'Malley. I manage all of Mr. Packer's personal affairs.

"I thought all affairs were pretty much personal," he said and instantly realized the joke missed like a Scud missile.

"Matthew O'Reilly is Mr. Packer's assistant in charge of his business interests."

"I see," he said. "O'Malley and O'Reilly. Packer must be a big fan of St. Patrick's Day."

She stared at him. Another miss. He was going to have to get new material.

"If you will just walk this way," she said, turning.

He choked on his Groucho impression and followed her. She handed him a temporary badge, and they passed through the gates in single file. The elevator launched like an Apollo mission before dumping them out on the seventieth floor and directly into a reception area. A curved steel desk sat front and center. Behind it, two women with hands-free phones carried on separate conversations. Above them, a large video display shuffled through various pictures of nature. Behind all of that, floor to ceiling windows ran along both walls from the building's corner.

"Please have a seat, Mr. Braden and I will tell Mr. Packer you are here," she said, without looking at him.

Thomas parked himself on a deep sofa covered with luxurious leather. After only a couple of minutes, a frail-looking man of about sixty hurried through a mahogany door and rushed over to him. He had the arms of an anorexic teenager and the nervous tics of a rabbit. Even his nose wrinkled every few seconds. He offered Thomas a dishrag handshake.

"I'm Robert Packer," he said with a nasal Southern twang. "Unless I am mistaken, you are the grandson of the illustrious Stewart Braden."

"Yes, Thomas. I am very grateful that you took time out of your busy schedule to meet with me."

"Nonsense, I am delighted. Shall we go into the conference room?" he asked, whisking off down the hallway without waiting for an answer.

The conference room featured a lavish mahogany table, polished to a high sheen, and about twenty-five plush office chairs. Packer punched a button, and the shades rolled up one wall, revealing a magnificent view of the skyline. The far wall contained what appeared to be a fully stocked bar. Packer took the chair at the head of the table. His customary spot, Thomas thought as he sat a couple of chairs away.

"I must tell you," Packer began, "my father had a deep and unwavering respect for your grandfather."

"Thank you," Thomas said.

"Now, what brings you here?" he asked, after Thomas declined both water and a stiff drink, as Packer called it.

"Well, Mr. Packer..."

"Please call me Robert," he interrupted. "Whenever I hear Mr. Packer, I look around for my father."

"Okay, Robert I don't really know where to begin without sounding like a conspiracy nut on steroids, but your father and my grandfather along with two other men kept a secret hidden for over fifty years and now it appears that because of it, their heirs could be in some danger. I know that sounds crazy, but there it is."

"Why, Thomas, I don't think it necessarily all sounds crazy. My father was quite the adventurer and, as such, he relayed to me many, many stories that may have been embellished, I suppose, but at their core could still be eye-popping."

"I'm really glad to hear you say that. I was hoping to come up with a way to open this conversation that didn't get me tossed out through the revolving doors."

"No, you're fine. So, tell me more about what our elders were up to and how I can be of help."

Thomas relayed the story from his grandfather's deathbed to Coney Island, to the letter from his grandfather, through New Orleans, including their encounters with Harrison and the gun squad to the oil tycoon. He didn't feel a need to hold anything back, and if Packer were in danger, Thomas felt obligated to tell him everything. To his credit, the man listened to the entire story without interruption and without making faces of disbelief.

"So, that brings us to right now and why I am here," Thomas said. "Does any of this story mean anything to you? Did your father mention the dig in Qumran at all?"

Packer steepled his fingers together in front of his face before answering.

"Let me ask you one question first. How many of the codes do you have right now?"

"One," Thomas said, thinking about Jackie's necklace.

"Okay, now I will answer. I am aware of the dig in Qumran, and I know that one of the four archaeologists was adamant that the scrolls remain unrevealed. I don't know which one, and I don't really care. My father told me that the find was worth a fortune, just as your grandfather believed. However, my father made many fortunes, and if I'm being completely honest, the only discoveries I ever really cared about were the ones that could fuel things. I never shared my father's passion for traveling the world and digging in the dirt. I was sick as a child and didn't really get out much or develop a powerful bond with him."

Thomas was reminded of how strained his relationship had been for so many years with his grandfather and nodded in understanding just as an immaculately dressed young man tapped politely on the glass door with his pinky ring and stuck his head in the room.

"Excuse me, Mr. Packer. Mr. Simmons from Arkansas Central Equipment called and said he wanted to negotiate further on your acquisition offer. What should I tell him?"

Thomas watched as Packer's face turned visibly red and he set his jaw. He stood up and paced the length of the table before speaking.

"You tell Mr. Simmons in no uncertain terms that my offer is final. I will not negotiate further. You tell him that if he doesn't take the offer and do so quickly, I will make it my personal goal to see that no one else shows interest in his failing company. Tell him I will have him on food stamps before the month is out."

The man slipped back out without a word. Packer went back to his chair and sat down. He straightened his tie and ran a hand through his hair.

"I apologize, Thomas," he said. "Some people respond to a simple handshake while others require a punch in the gut to get their attention."

"No worries," Thomas said. "It's your business, not mine."

"Of course," Parker replied. "Now back to the matter at hand. I realize, Thomas, that you have been through quite an ordeal, and I don't for a minute want to minimize that, but frankly if there is any danger in knowing a vault combination I'd just as soon not know it. I don't need more money or more headaches, and whatever is in that vault is no concern of mine. Can you understand that?"

"I guess so," Thomas said. "But I must admit that I am surprised at your somewhat cavalier attitude. No offense."

"None taken. I assure you that every decision I make is based on what is best for this company that my father has left me to run. Potential Dead Sea Scrolls do not improve my company's bottom line. In fact, the entire ordeal will only distract me from more important matters. I'm not Indiana Jones and don't want to be."

Thomas thought his words over for a moment.

"Do you have your father's code or know where it is?" he asked.

"I do. The question is, do you want it or do you want to walk away as if we had never met? Either outcome is okay with me, but I urge you to weigh your answer. "

Thomas saw nothing in the man's words or face remotely disingenuous. If he took the code, would he be putting himself and the others in more danger? What would having two of the four codes be worth to him or anyone else? He still didn't know his own grandfather's code. What was his grandfather's real purpose in sending him on this scavenger hunt? He didn't specifically ask that Thomas acquire the codes. Is his mission just to warn others, or is there some greater good to be done?

"I may be taking a leap of faith here, which are words that I have rarely spoken in my life, but something tells me I'm going to need your father's code before this is all over. If you are willing to give it to me, I promise I will do my best to protect it, and if at the end of all of this there is some fortune to be had, you will get your fair share."

"Fair enough," Packer said. "Please wait here, and I will retrieve it for you."

Before Thomas could respond, the man wriggled his nose and bounced out of the room.

"Man, I hope that was the right call," he said aloud. "Cuz I may have just screwed the pooch."

When Packer returned, he handed Thomas a sealed envelope. Written across the seal were the words: 'Open at Your Own Risk 1 of 4'.

"Did your father think that having these codes could be dangerous?" he asked Packer.

"I honestly don't know what he thought about it," the man answered. "I'm not a brave man, Thomas, and as such, I never dreamed of opening that envelope. Maybe my father was only warning me because he knew I was weak. I will say this: one of the other four archaeologists badgered him for years to give him this."

Thomas considered this. He couldn't imagine his grandfather doing that, and certainly Tremblay would have never wanted Packer's codes. He never wanted the vault to be opened.

"Do you know the name of this man?" he asked.

"Yes," Packer said. "His name was Arnold Smith. He and my father were best friends for decades until Smith drank himself to death. I believe he lived in Memphis, but he has been dead for some time."

"But if he has an heir, he or she might know his code," Thomas said.

"I suppose, but I was never interested, so I didn't pursue the idea."

Chapter 18

TAYLOR MACKIE DISCONNECTED the call with a smile. He set the phone down gently and considered his next move. As he had told Patterson, he believed that an adjustment was in order. Now, an opportunity was opening up for him. He could see it as clearly as he could see his hand in front of his face. It was important, in fact imperative, for a soldier to reassess his strategy. A tactical plan was only that — a plan. When it was time to implement, one had to be aware of the changing dynamics and variables. Mackie considered himself a master strategist. Since he was very young, he had studied battle plans from history. He dug into the strategies and tried to understand the logic, the circumstances, and the influences that drove commanders to make the decisions they made. And he didn't confine his interest to traditional war battles.

He favored elegance and simplicity when possible. Complexity added too many variables, but simplicity is beauty of the rarest kind. No other person had the vision he possessed. He picked the phone back up and called Marcus, who answered on the first ring, as he had demanded.

"Yes," Marcus said.

"I have word," Mackie said. "They are in Dallas, but they are heading for Memphis, driving right through our backyard. Get your gear together; we leave in an hour."

***

They drove east on I-30 into Arkansas. Chaney focused on the road, but his mind was elsewhere.

"So, you're telling me that this Packer dude just gave up his father's code without a care in the world?" he said.

"I'll admit it sounds strange when you say it, but when he told me he didn't care about it or the money it might be worth, I totally believed him," Thomas answered. "I mean, the guy is made of money. He was wearing a two-thousand-dollar suit and stepping on the throat of some mid-sized company owner while I was there. I don't know, but I believed him. Plus, he gave me the line on this Arnold Smith character in Memphis. That seemed plausible as well."

"Why do you think your grandfather didn't give us any clues about Smith?" Dani asked from the back seat.

"Packer said that his father and Smith were best friends for a long time," Thomas answered. "Maybe my grandfather figured we would get to Smith once we found Packer. Plus, the scripture reference at the bottom of the letter was about grace. Maybe that was meant to be a clue to Graceland."

"That's a reach of Inspector Gadget proportions," Dani said. "I feel like every time we go in a direction or take on a person not directly indicated by your grandfather, we are inviting trouble," she said while glaring at Jackie.

"Subtle as a train derailment," Jackie said.

"If you need it more in your face, I can make that happen," Dani snapped.

"Okay," Thomas intervened. "Let's move on. The real reason we are going to Memphis is that we have no other viable clues to work with. Also, something Papa said to me before he died keeps rattling around in my head. He told me about a trip that he and my grandmother took when they found out that she was pregnant with my dad. He mentioned going to Mardi Gras and something about Texas and even going to Graceland. It was like he was giving me a verbal roadmap of places I would visit before I knew it. So, we're going to track down Smith's heir or heirs and see what we can find out about him or her and if they have a code. If it turns out to be a dead end, then I don't know what is next, but for now we have a thread to pull and that's the plan."

"Fine," the women said in unison.

"So, the envelope that Packer gave you. You think it has the right code in it?" Chaney asked.

Thomas pulled out the sealed envelope that Packer had given him with the warning on the outside. He carefully opened it at one end, blew into it, and pulled out a slip of paper inside. There were six digits on it. He looked over at

Chaney.

"It's the right code," he said.

A few hours later they pulled into the "Regal Inn" in West Memphis, Arkansas. Chaney rubbed his eyes and punched Thomas in the shoulder.

"Time to check in," he said.

Thomas stretched and got out, opened the back door for Jackie, and woke her up.

"Let's go," he said to her, pulling her to her feet. They headed for the front door of the motor inn, and she slipped her arm around his back.

"When this is all over," Dani said from the back seat. "I'm going to kick that girl's ass."

"I believe you could do it too, Missy," Chaney replied.

Once they got settled, Thomas called Caleb on his burner.

"We'll be in Memphis tomorrow, brother," he said when Caleb picked up. "It seems there may be another heir of one of the original archaeologists there."

"Where did you get the information?" Caleb asked.

"From Robert Packer of Packer Oil. He said that Arnold Smith was from Memphis and that his family might have his code. He also gave me his father's code without blinking an eye."

"That seems weird. Do you trust this Packer guy?" Caleb asked.

"I think so, but there are a lot of blurred lines here for me. Like, why doesn't Packer care about either the historical or monetary value of the scrolls?" Thomas said.

"I talked to the Monsignor, and I'm taking some time off. I'll meet you in Memphis tomorrow," Caleb responded.

"It could be dangerous," Thomas said. "I don't know if that's a good idea."

"If it's dangerous, then it is the perfect idea. I'll be there."

Caleb hung up before Thomas could say anything else.

***

Harrison answered the phone after double-checking that it was five fifteen in the morning. He shook his head once and rubbed the sleep from his eyes. Some days he really hated this job.

"This better be good," he said as a greeting.

"It is boss," Agent Conner chirped.

That Conner was upbeat even at the butt crack of dawn made Harrison want to shoot somebody, preferably some idiot with a stupid grin on his face.

"What?" asked Harrison.

"Braden and company popped up on a traffic camera in downtown Dallas yesterday afternoon. From there, we have him entering the Packer Oil Industries at three minutes after three. The other three people stayed in the car and drove off. We lost them for about thirty minutes, then they came back, and Braden got back in the car. The last time we saw them was at the eastbound ramp for Interstate 30."

"Who's the fourth person? I thought it was only Braden, his wife and Chaney caught up in this," Harrison said.

"We didn't get a good shot of her. She stayed in the back seat the whole time. Still working to identify her. All we have for now is female, dark hair, mid-twenties."

"Did she seem like she was there of her own accord or

not?"

"She's with them," Conner said.

Harrison considered all the news. If Braden was involved with the death of the butler, he sure was running around the country like a lost Greyhound bus. Most guys running from the law do so in straight lines. And why pick up an extra person along the way? What was her role in all of this?

"Did you run the plates?"

"Yes, it's a 1995 Ford Explorer registered to a John Boudreaux from Metarie, Louisiana. Hasn't been reported missing, though, and no one is at the address that is listed for the registered owner."

"It's not stolen," Harrison said. "Five will get you ten that the good Father Dimitri provided the transportation. Send somebody over to the church to ask him about it."

"Will do," Conner said. "What else?"

"Any idea where they are going next?"

"Not yet, boss, but we're pretty sure they were heading east."

"Okay. Keep me posted," Harrison said. "And find out who the girl is."

Harrison hung up. He crashed back down on the pillow but, after trying to go back to sleep for thirty seconds, he groaned and got up.

***

The next morning, they checked out early and crossed the Mississippi with the morning rush hour traffic.

"Let's find the downtown library," Thomas said.

"Without smart-phones, it might be our best bet. We'll start there trying to dig up info on Arnold Smith."

"I need more clothes," Jackie said.

"You got a date?" Dani asked.

"Unlike you, I care about how I look, and I am the one paying for everything, don't forget."

"Christ Almighty," Thomas said. "Dani and I will do the library research while the two of you go shopping."

"Thanks a lot," Chaney said. "Actually, I'd like to recon the area a little. Get my bearings."

"Good," Thomas said. "It may take us a while to track down Arnold Smith's heirs."

They found the library on Poplar Avenue. Thomas and Dani got out and went it. The library was chilly, as if the air had been running all night to get a jump start on the day's heat and humidity. Thomas spotted the reference section, and they headed that way.

"Where to?" Chaney asked Jackie as he pulled away from the curb.

"Find a mall," she said. "You can let me out. I'll call you when I'm ready."

***

Agent Harrison snapped up the phone on the first ring this time. It was Conner again.

"We got an ID on the girl from Father Dmitri," he said. "Seems she's the granddaughter of some big-time archaeologist in New Orleans. Name's Jacqueline Kaylee Tremblay. The priest told us she was with Braden because some guys with guns showed up at her house while he was

174

there. She escaped with them."

"Did he know who the gunmen were?" Harrison asked.

"No. He said that Braden's grandfather had been his friend, and he helped Thomas because of that. He gave them the keys to his brother's Bronco so they could get away from the gunmen. He said they seemed desperate."

"If they were in danger, why didn't they call the police?"

"Don't know, boss. Father Dmitri felt that their problem might have been bigger than the local police would realize."

"Gee, I wonder what gave him that idea since I visited him the same day that Braden did," Harrison said.

"You want us to pick up the Father?" Conner asked.

"No, he can't give us much more. Find out all you can about the Tremblay girl."

***

Thomas and Dani reviewed the life and times of Arnold Smith through a series of newspaper and magazine articles. He was quite a celebrity in his thirties and forties, but just as Packer had suggested, he fell from grace quickly amid rumors of alcoholism and bankruptcy. He had one son, Aiden. After a few website searches, they found a phone number. He had applied for a restaurant job three years earlier, and there was contact information about him. It still amazed Thomas that for a few dollars, one could get private information on almost anyone.

After several rings, a groggy voice came on the line.

"Who is this?"

"Mr. Smith, my name is Thomas Braden."

"I'm not interested in buying anything," he blurted.

"No, Mr. Smith, I'm not selling anything," Thomas quickly added. "Please don't hang up."

"Well, if you're a bill collector, you're out of luck. I don't have two nickels to rub together."

"Your father and my grandfather were involved together in an enterprise many years ago. It is about this that I would like to meet with you," Thomas said, reeling him in slowly, trying not to lose him.

"What did you say your name was again?" Smith asked.

"Thomas Braden."

"You've got to be kidding me."

"No, I'm here in Memphis, and I would really appreciate an opportunity to speak with you."

"Oh, there are a few things I would like to say to you as well. All the better if we do it in person," Smith said. "I'm at the Rum and Blues bar every night by 5:30. You can find me there, but rethink if you really want to hear what I have to say."

The man hung up. Thomas looked at his phone as if there were answers to be had there. If he had a smartphone, he doubted Siri would know any more than he did about what Smith meant. He looked at Dani.

"He will meet us at his regular bar tonight. Doesn't seem like he is going to be too cooperative though."

"Well, you said you've been going on faith lately. This should test it a little," Dani said.

"Right. I'm going to call Caleb and fill him in. He'll love the going on faith plan."

***

Chaney let Jackie out in front of the Oak Court Mall.

"I'll be close by whenever you're ready," he said.

"Thanks. I'll call," she said.

Chaney drove off as Jackie went in and started walking. It was still early. The air was frosty, and there were mostly just employees moving around. She found a bathroom in a side hall off the main drag and took advantage of it. On the way back out she hesitated, trying to decide whether she should go to Macy's or Dillard's. Macy's probably. They were more likely to have cute shoes, and she really needed some.

She started in that direction when a gloved hand reached from behind her and clasped over her mouth while a second arm closed across her midsection with tremendous strength. She struggled but was pulled roughly back out of sight and into a janitor's room next to the restroom. The pitch-black room smelled of pine cleaner. And old mops. She heard a whisper in her ear.

"Don't scream."

Chapter 19

JACKIE STRUGGLED, BUT the arms holding her were made of steel. She could feel her heart pounding in her chest. She willed it to calm while her feet dug for purchase on the cement floor. The duo's awkward backward dance bumped into a metal shelf, setting off a chorus of sloshing bottled liquids. Rolls of toilet paper fell from somewhere above her and glanced off her shoulder before bouncing on the floor and rolling away. Slowly, the hand slipped from her mouth. She breathed in deeply without a sound. The other arm spun her around to face the man like a disco dance move. He held on to her side tightly as he reached over her shoulder with his free hand and turned on the light. It flickered twice above them before coming to life. She stared wide-eyed at the man's face under its harsh glare. He removed his sunglasses. She stood looking into the intense eyes of Taylor Mackie.

"Hello, Miss Tremblay," he said with a wicked smile.

She put her arms around his neck and kissed him deeply, imploringly. His arms enveloped her. She felt herself melt and release into his control. Taylor did everything with unrelenting, aggressive passion. She was no match for his intensity, but she did not care to be. Being with him was nirvana. He was the only man she had ever believed to be her superior. He finally released his powerful embrace of her and looked into her eyes.

"It seems you have missed me," he said.

"You have no idea," she replied. "Why did you send Marcus and the others to my house?"

"It was a calculated gamble. I figured either Braden would leave you to your own devices or, more likely, feel as if you were his responsibility. Taking you with them was the perfect and predictable response. I am surprised that they didn't make you give up your cell phone, however."

"They asked me to, but I told them I'd left it at home."

"And they believed you?"

"The girl didn't, but if I say it sweet enough, Braden will believe anything, and I had it well hidden, I figured it was worth the gamble. Anyway, it's almost dead at this point. I left the charger at home."

"I figured as much," he said. "But your intel about Braden's movements has proved very valuable. Well done, even if the phone is dead."

She twirled around him, stepped deeper into the room, and spread her arms. "You're welcome to see if you can find it."

He closed the gap between them and pulled her tank

top over her head, then quickly reached behind her and undid her bra. It fell to the floor lightly.

"Well," he said. "No phone in there."

She stared directly into his eyes. "You'd best keep looking."

He squatted, unsnapped her jeans, and slid them down with practiced precision. Next came the panties. She moaned as he pulled them down. A tiny, old-style flip phone fell to the concrete floor.

"You are as cunning as you are beautiful," Mackie said.

"It's my trouble phone. You never know when a girl will need one. Anyway, it seems like a waste for you to have come this far without taking advantage of me," she added, winking at him.

"You are villainous, Miss Tremblay," he said.

She unbuckled his pants, and he lifted her off the floor with ease and pushed her hard up against the shelves. More paper crashed down around them onto the floor. Somewhere, bottles clinked and chattered like a rehearsal dinner champagne toast. After a while, he set her down gently and kissed the top of her head. She was still breathing heavily as she leaned against him.

"Soon this will be all over, and you and I can revel in each other's company night after night," he said.

"Oh, my love, that is what I dream of," she replied, her eyes still closed.

He stepped back, hands still holding her sides, and appraised her many genuine qualities. Her dedication to him was without question, and if he were willing to admit the truth to himself, he felt stronger because of her.

"When Patterson first told me he had a contact as a

starting point for this mission, I did not know how lucky it was going to be for me," he said.

"It was fate that brought us together, my dear," Jackie said. "Once we bring down all the righteous bullshit that floods this world, you and I will be free to go anywhere and do anything."

Mackie watched her eyes as she dreamed her dreams. He put his hands on her face and kissed her again.

"What's Braden's next move?" he asked.

"He's looking up some guy, Arnold Smith, who may have been one of the original people with a code. Sounds like, though, he drank himself into oblivion. Braden is trying to locate the next of kin."

"Okay, you just keep doing what you're doing, except some of it you only do with me," he smiled.

"Yes, Master," she replied.

He handed her another phone.

"My burner number is already in there," he said. "Keep me posted."

Then he winked at her, turned off the light, and pushed his way out the door.

***

Conner was calling back again. Harrison picked up and muttered.

"Yeah," he said.

"Boss, we got a hit on the girl's cell phone. She's in Memphis."

"That means Braden is in Memphis," Harrison said, more to himself than Conner.

He didn't believe that Braden had killed the giant manservant, but the men with guns who were chasing him certainly could have. They were far more interesting. There was no doubt the butler was working for someone other than Stewart Braden. Whoever these guys were, they were not above tying up loose ends.

"Have the guys monitor traffic cams in Memphis and call the local PD and have them put out a BOLO on Braden. Make it understood that under no circumstances should they approach. Got it."

"Got it, Boss."

"This is a Homeland case," Harrison continued. "We want to know who is after Braden and why. Meet me at the terminal. We are wheels up within the hour."

Harrison hung up. He could feel the pace picking up. Every case gained speed as it approached its conclusion, like a sprinter in the hundred meters. This one was racing to a destination that was unknown but inevitable. He loved the chase, and this was getting good.

***

Officer James Cahill, Jimmy to his friends, arrived at the Memphis Police Department for his day tour. He was smaller than many of his fellow officers, only five foot nine and a buck sixty, but he considered himself lean and mean. Most of his brothers in blue would definitely agree with the mean part. Jimmy knew he wasn't especially well-liked in his precinct, but he didn't especially care. Being an asshole had its perks.

He picked up the BOLO and looked closely at the

picture of the perp. Those freaking Feds, he thought. Always trying to tell us what to do, like they've got bigger brains and bigger dicks than anybody else. He would decide the correct course of action if he laid eyes on this guy, Braden, not some self-important jackass from Washington or wherever the hell they came from. It was Jimmy freaking Cahill's call. He had twelve years on the force and a half-dozen years running from the cops before that. He knew which end was up and didn't need some hot to trot G-man calling the shots.

Chapter 20

THE "RUM AND Blues" bar was two blocks off Beale Street. It was the definition of a dive. It had a low-slung roof that sat slightly askew. The door hadn't seen a paint job since the sixties, and decades of dust caked the windows. The street it sat on was narrow and lined with cars. A sign with a curved, lighted arrow pointed to parking in the back. They followed its instructions, pulled into a dusty gravel lot and parked nose into the decrepit wood-planked fence of the neighbor behind.

The door swung open with a loud screech, like an out-of-date alarm system, and the four of them walked into the bar. They waited a moment for their eyes to adjust to the darkness. The place was packed with construction workers from the apartment complex across the street. Along the left wall was a long wooden bar that curved at either end to corral the bartender. Every stool along the length of the bar was taken and formed a chorus line of butt cracks. Behind it, an aging bartender wearing a denim shirt that was possibly older than its owner popped beer tops. His shock of white hair looked like he'd combed it with a leaf blower. At the other end, there was another younger version of the old guy stocking shelves and chatting with the regulars. To the right were booths filled with three or four men each. A neon Budweiser sign buzzed loudly over their heads. Tables were staged haphazardly in the center of the room, as if the person arranging the furniture didn't know what to do with them. Most of them were occupied as well. The place reeked of cigarettes even though there were no-smoking signs plastered on every wall. From the back, pool balls banged into each other, and men were laughing just a little too loudly. Half-mast eyes glanced at them as they entered further. They eyed Chaney with contempt and the two women with lust.

"Wow, you take me to all the best places," Dani said.

"Just keep your head down and don't make eye contact," Thomas said.

"Screw that," said Chaney. "If they're gonna eyeball me, I'm gonna eyeball them right back."

"Let's keep focused on our mission. We don't need to get involved with the locals, okay?" Thomas said.

"Right boss. Don't get involved. I got it."

"Let's just find Smith and get done with this," Jackie said. "This place gives me the heebie-jeebies."

"Stay close," Thomas said, moving toward the back of the room.

At the far booth in the back, facing the door, sat a pale,

pudgy man of indeterminate age with a half-empty bottle of scotch and a shot glass. He downed one as he saw them approach and quickly poured another.

"I thought you were coming alone," he said.

"Things have changed," Thomas said. "May we sit?"

"It's a semi-free country," he said, glancing at the seat across from him.

Thomas and Dani sat with the man while Jackie and Chaney took up positions at the nearest table, Chaney facing the front of the room.

"I'm Thomas Braden, and this is my wife, Dani."

"Aiden Smith," the man responded before gulping another shot.

"I appreciate you agreeing to meet with us," Thomas said. "Could I talk to you about a dig that your father and my grandfather took together?"

"I know all about it," Aiden said. "I know that because of your grandfather, my father died a penniless drunk. Just like I know that because of your grandfather and that holier than thou Cajun, the greatest discovery of my father's life counted for nothing. He was already in his mid-fifties when I was born, and all he could talk about was getting that one big break. Near the end, he told me he actually did get the big break, but two men kept him from claiming it. They ruined his life, and for what — some superstitious belief system? Tell me something. How Christian is it to destroy a man's career and life? My mother bailed on him because he was such a disgusting loser. And now, here I am, a chip off the old block. So, yes, I agreed to meet with you just so you can know how much I hate you and everything you stand for."

He downed another shot and blank-eyed stared at Thomas.

***

From across the street, Taylor Mackie watched the four of them drive around to the back of the bar and park. When they walked around the corner, he laid eyes on his opponents for the first time. Braden had that young, cocky American walk like he knew everything. Meanwhile, the black guy was leery and constantly surveyed the area for threats. He could be formidable, but Mackie was not concerned. He waited for them to enter the bar, then crushed his cigarette and headed for the door.

He stepped into the bar, surveyed the situation and took the lone empty stool, the one nearest the in/out opening for the bartenders. He kept his hat pulled down low and quietly ordered a beer when the white-haired old man approached him. His natural Arkansas accent fit right in with the crowd. No one even noticed him. He sat quietly and listened. Nothing was more important than boots-on-the-ground intel.

***

"Look," Thomas began. "I'll admit that I don't know what all went on…"

"You guys gonna order something or just take up space?" the younger bartender said loudly as he moved from behind the bar over to the center table.

He spoke to all of them but looked only at Chaney. He

was thick through the chest and arms but sported skinny legs under his shorts. Typical weightlifter's build. He had the same wild hair as the old man, but brown.

"Sure," Thomas said. "We'd like four beers."

"What kind?" the young man said, still watching Chaney.

"Surprise us, okay?" Thomas replied. "We're not staying long."

"You okay, Aiden?" he said, shifting his gaze for the first time.

"Yeah, Bud. I'm fine."

The man nodded slowly and then walked back to the bar.

"Is he a friend of yours?" Dani asked.

"I'm probably his best customer, is all. His name's Bud McCready. He and his old man run the place."

"A man named Bud runs a bar? That's pretty hilarious," Dani said, trying to lighten the mood.

Smith gave her nothing but crickets.

"Anyway," Thomas said. "As I was saying, I don't know all the details, and honestly I can't tell you what part my grandfather really played in all of it. But I am truly sorry for everything that happened to your father and to you. I'm only here now because I think it is important that we talk and you could be in some danger."

"What are you talking about, danger?"

"Did your father talk about a code that he had to a vault?"

"He did. But it was about as useless as teats on a boar, wasn't it?" Smith said, shaking his head.

Bud brought back the four beers and put them all on

the table in front of Thomas.

"'That's twenty bucks," he said.

Thomas looked up at the bartender. The man was leering at him as if he had a third eye.

"Really," he said, digging a twenty out of his pocket. "Must be happy hour."

He dropped the bill on the man's tray and played the staring game with him for a moment. Finally, the bartender turned on his heels and walked away. Thomas caught Chaney's eye and tilted his head as if to say, 'Watch him'.

"Mr. Smith," Thomas began again, pushing the beers to the side. "There are men, dangerous men, searching for those codes. They believe that whatever our patriarchs discovered and put in that vault is precious. I really need you to believe me."

"Why now?" Smith said. "Why, after all these years, is somebody interested in that vault?"

"I don't know," Thomas said. "Before my grandfather passed away, he told me he was being watched. Since then, we have found two of the codes, but we have been threatened along the way."

"So, are you seriously asking me to give you my father's code?" Smith said. "No way. Maybe if you had all four codes and knew where the vault was and opened it, there could be a treasure. But I'm not helping you one bit. You think I have any interest in making you rich?"

"So, you know your father's code," Thomas pressed on.

"I know where it is. Right where my father left it, but you ain't getting it."

"Please, Aiden. I'm asking you for your safety and ours. Work with us."

"No," Smith shouted. "Get away from me!"

He gulped a last shot and slammed the glass down on the table. He rose unsteadily and stepped out of the booth. Thomas grabbed his arm.

"Aiden," he said.

The man shook his arm free and fell against Chaney's table. They all stood to help him up, but he continued to shrug them off. He staggered away towards the front of the bar through a throng of locals, who were now all standing. Thomas started to go after him, but they closed ranks and blocked his way. Chaney moved in next to Thomas while the two women stood behind them. Bud slid through the blockade from behind and took charge, arms crossed.

"I don't think Aiden wants to talk to you anymore," he said through gritted teeth.

"We don't mean him any harm or want any trouble," Thomas said, hands outstretched.

"You didn't even touch your beer. That kind of hurts my feelings," Bud said.

"Well, aren't you the emotional one," Chaney said. "Why don't you just take your sensitive old self back over behind the bar."

At least a dozen pairs of eyes glared at Chaney's smiling face, but no one moved.

"Look, fellows," Thomas said. "There's 43 people in here right now, so that's 39 to 4 or 9.75 to 1 if we count the girls or 19.5 to 1 if we don't. That assumes, of course, that everyone will get involved in a brawl, but statistically speaking that seems unlikely, so even if I round down it's probably still 14 to 1."

"Wait a minute," Dani said, stepping between Thomas

and Chaney. "We count, so just figure us in right along with you."

"Alright, well then we'll call it 7 to 1 against us. Still not very good odds if you ask me," Thomas said.

He didn't take his eyes off the bartender as he pulled the wraps from his pocket and started wrapping his hands.

"Stop! Stop with all the numbers. What are you talking about?"

The bartender uncrossed his arms and looked at his allies for support. His face reddened.

"Okay, 7 to 1 it is," Dani said. "Bud, or do your friends call you Buddy? You get to be the first one to punch a girl."

She stepped up in front of him, jaw set.

"You gonna let your arm candy do your fightin' for you, asshole?" Bud said, glaring at Thomas.

Thomas reached over and pulled Dani back just an inch or two. She was hard to move when she was angry, and right now she was as rigid as a wall safe. He slid back in front of her and stood face to face with the bartender.

"There will not be any fighting, Bud," he said, dragging out the man's name. "We're leaving. Step aside, and everybody can go back to their drinking. You don't want a bunch of broken furniture, do you? Your Pop doesn't need that."

"This furniture is older than he is, and I'm the one who's gonna decide if there will be any fighting or not. I'm the one who's gonna decide if you and your friends walk or crawl out of here."

At that moment, the door creaked loudly as it was pushed open, and a big man stepped into the dark room. Chaney was the first one to spot the white collar.

"A priest walks into a bar," he said. "Now, that's funny."

"He's no joke," Thomas replied. "But we could still get a punchline. Our odds just improved."

The priest stepped through the assembly.

"What seems to be going on here?" Caleb asked with a smile. "Is someone having a birthday?"

"This is none of your concern, Father," Bud answered. "We're having a private conversation, and I think it would be better if you found another bar."

"Well," Caleb said, pulling wraps from his pocket. "I'm very good at private conversations. Ever hear of a confessional?" he added while wrapping his hands.

"I don't want to hit no priest," Bud answered.

"But you were all ready to bust up a girl, ain't that right?" Dani said.

The man glared first at Caleb, then Dani, then Chaney.

"I understand your conundrum, my friend," Caleb said. "So, I'm going to help you here."

With that, he removed his collar and stuffed into his pants.

"If you prefer, we can go outside and work this out. You know, have a meeting of the minds, so to speak."

Caleb squared up to Bud. They were roughly the same height and build, like looking in a mirror. Caleb's eyes never left the bartender's. He stood relaxed but ready. His arms hung loosely by his side, more like he was waiting to order a coffee than about to start throwing hands. Tension poured off the bartender, but Caleb remained calm.

"Hold it," came a shaky voice from behind Bud. Then a cane stretched out between the potential gladiators and slowly swept Bud back like he was the last standing bowling pin. The old man stepped up to Caleb and eyed him with a sideways glance, as if he wanted his good eye to take it all in. Then he turned and addressed the crowd.

"The next round's on me, fellas," he said. "Bud, get over there and serve them boys."

A wave of silence permeated the bar. No one moved for a ten-count. Finally, the bartender looked away.

"Shit!" Bud said, then turned and went back to the bar.

The old man turned back to Caleb and gave him another side-eye.

"Father," he said. "Bud ain't much more than a hothead, but he's all I got. You understand?"

Caleb nodded.

"I tried to teach him better, but his mother passed away when he was a young boy, and I guess I just wasn't up to the task. She was the best person I ever knew. Losing her put us both in an awful place."

"Sir, I wonder, could I ask your name?" Caleb said.

"It's Ray, Ray McCready, Father, and I'd be much obliged if you would accept my apology for my son's behavior."

"Mr. McCready," Caleb began. "I'm very sorry for the loss of your wife. I'm in the forgiveness business, so consider your apology accepted, and my friends and I will be on our way now."

"You're welcome to stay for one drink, Father. I'm buying," Ray said.

"Thanks, but we need to go. Rain check?"

"Anytime, Father," Ray said as tapped his cane back to the bar.

Caleb led the others quickly to the exit. They stepped

out into the evening air and took a deep breath before Thomas and Caleb shared a hug.

"I'm sure glad you showed up," Thomas said to his brother.

"Are you kidding? I would have been so sad if I had missed that. Shame we didn't get to brawl though."

"Chaney, Jackie, this is my brother Caleb, or you can call him Father," Thomas said.

They shook hands all around, and Dani hugged Caleb tightly.

"Where to now?" Chaney asked as they re-gathered themselves.

"We follow," Thomas said, pointing to the stumbling Aiden Smith, who was leaning over a trash can throwing up a block away. "You go get the car and come back around. I will follow on foot until you get back to me."

"I'm with Thomas," Caleb said.

The other three took off around the building to the parking lot.

***

Mackie exited the bar, lit a cigarette, and casually started walking in the same direction as Thomas and the priest. He discreetly called Marcus.

"Watch the others when they come around in the car," he said. "I'm going to follow Braden on foot."

Chapter 21

THEY DIDN'T HAVE to follow Smith very far. The man's gait kept pulling him to the left, like his front end was out of align. Every so often, he would have to stop and redirect himself back to the middle of the sidewalk. Once, he stopped completely and did a full three sixty looking around as if he wasn't at all sure where he was or what he was doing there. Finally, after only three blocks, he stumbled up the walk to a broken-down clapboard house just as Chaney and the others drove up. Thomas and Caleb leaned on the passenger-side window and watched as the drunken Smith fumbled with his keys and finally pushed through his front door.

"Well, what now?" Dani asked from the back seat.

"I need to go talk to him again," Thomas said.

"You think that's wise?" Dani asked. "He was adamant

that he didn't want to talk to us. And he certainly wasn't inclined to help."

"I know," Thomas said. "But maybe if I try it alone, privately, he'll change his tune. If he won't help us, we are at a dead end. We have no more messages from my grandfather, and this is the only lead we have to the elder Smith's code."

"Thomas is right," Jackie said. "We need that third code. Then we will have all of them."

"Except we won't," Thomas said. "I don't know my grandfather's code and, more importantly, we do not know where the vault is even if we had all the codes."

"You don't know that you know it," Jackie said. "He has given you enough to go on. You'll figure it out soon. In the meantime, we have no choice. We must get this one."

"If he says he doesn't know it, he doesn't," Dani said. "I think we should drive away right now and forget the whole mess. We have nothing but trouble to show for our efforts so far. Let's cut our losses right here before someone gets hurt."

"She makes sense, Thomas," Caleb said. "You still don't know what's at the end of this treasure hunt. It could be nothing, and it could mean people you care about getting hurt along the way."

Thomas thought about it as he watched long shadows beginning to creep across the street.

"It's not nothing," he said at last. "Since the beginning, people have been tracking us and threatening us and warning us to let it go. There's something here, something that has people either up to their eyeballs in greed or crazy with fear. Let me try Smith one more time. If he won't give me anything, we will bail. Agreed?"

"You'll call Harrison and tell him everything?" Dani asked.

"First thing in the morning," he said. "Caleb, take the women and find a hotel out of the tourist areas and stay with them."

"Are you sure?" his brother asked.

"Yes, I think the only way I can get him to talk is if we're alone."

"After you drop them off, go somewhere and hang out," he said to Chaney. "I'll call you when I'm ready."

"Roger that," Chaney said.

Thomas watched them drive off and then headed for Smith's house. The original white picket fence was now more unpainted wood than white. There were several pickets broken at the top, like a hockey player's teeth. The front yard was almost completely in the shade now, but there wasn't a living tree around. One lone dead ash stood next to the sidewalk, paying homage to a better time. The grass had long ago been choked out by aggressive weeds, which had also consumed the carcass of a lawn mower midway between the fence and the front stoop, as if it had given its life fighting an un-winnable war. The gate to the walkway hung loosely on one hinge. Thomas walked through, up the two cracked steps, and knocked on the door. He could hear sloppy movement inside before the door opened an inch.

"What do you want?" Smith slurred.

"Mr. Smith, if I could just have another five minutes of your time, I'll say what I came here to say, and then you'll never see me again."

The man stared at Thomas with one eye through the crack in the door. Thomas wasn't sure that Smith even recognized him, even though they had spoken just a few minutes ago.

"You have some nerve," Smith said as he walked away from the door.

Thomas took that as an invitation, so he stepped inside the doorway to a living room, which smelled of alcohol and cigarettes. The furniture, what little there was, had been pushed around the room at odd angles as if it were in the way and served no purpose. Thomas continued through the hallway from the front room. There were paper bags, discarded cigarette boxes and fast-food wrappers piled in the corners of the hallway as if blown there by a summer breeze. Thomas heard a chair scratching across the floor further back, so he continued to the rear of the house.

He entered the kitchen, and Smith charged him, screaming some undecipherable string of words. He hit Thomas square in the chest, driving him back against the kitchen wall and knocking his breath out. A wall clock whizzed by Thomas's shoulder and crashed to the floor as if signaling the start of an event, like the flag drop at Indy. Thomas turned his head just as a rain of blows from Smith's right hand assaulted his face. The punches were short, stubby shots with little physical power, but full of rage. Smith had him pinned and was flailing away without regard to where the punches landed. Thomas felt a blow to his kidney and then another caught him in the eye. He grabbed the man around his back and pulled him tightly to his chest, so they stood in a full embrace like two brothers that had not seen each other in years. Smith's blows became even less effective in the tight confines, but his rage did not subside. He screamed in Thomas' ear like a wild predator. Thomas held him tightly and let his body lean to his right. Time for gravity to offer a helping hand. He let himself fall until they fell to the floor like an exhausted marathon dance couple. On the way down, they crashed into an old water cooler, causing an empty five-gallon jug to fall from its perch and clatter across the floor. Thomas rolled over the top of Smith, then let go and rolled away. He scrambled to his feet more quickly than his inebriated attacker. Smith got to his knees, then stood unsteadily. He let out another yell and lunged toward Thomas again. This time, Thomas planted a straight right into the man's nose followed by a quick left to his midsection. No time for hand wraps in this fracas. Smith doubled over and puked. Thomas stepped away and waited. He was lightheaded with adrenaline and tried to slow his breathing.

Smith, hands still on his knees, glanced up at Thomas. His nose was bleeding from both nostrils. He walked hunched over to the kitchen chair and plopped down. He laid his head heavily on his hands and sobbed.

The kitchen table stood open in the middle where a leaf should have been. A stack of dirty dishes sat piled high in the sink with only a dripping faucet attempting to clean them. The stained linoleum floor curled up in the corners of the room. The man shook as he wept. Thomas spotted a paper towel holder hanging beneath a cabinet. He went and grabbed a couple of towels, ran some water on them, and handed one to the bleeding man and kept the other for himself. Then, he sat in the other chair and looked across the gap in the table at Smith. He waited. Dani's words rang in his head: 'Let's cut our losses before someone gets hurt'. He dabbed at his swollen eye.

"Mr. Smith?" he said.

The man raised his head just enough to squint at Thomas. He looked worn and tired, like a horse that had played out. Crusts of blood ran down, across the man's mouth and onto his hands.

"I guess my father would have been a drunk no matter what else happened in his life," he admitted. "Lord knows I am. I just never expected to end up this way. It seems my anger is the only thing that carries me from one day to the next. Anger and self-loathing."

"Mr. Smith," Thomas said again. "I am very sorry for how things turned out for you and for whatever part my grandfather may have played in your father's misery."

"Did you love your grandfather?" Smith asked.

The question, and even more so his answer, surprised Thomas.

"I didn't for a long time," he said. "But recent events have helped me to see some things in a better light. I am coming to love him again, but too late to tell him as much."

"I loved my father, no matter what," Smith said. "Even if he was a total screw-up. Takes one to know one, I guess."

"Mr. Smith, if I were to promise you that if anything of value came out of what we find from your father's discovery I would make sure that you got what you were entitled to, would you give me his code? It might be a chance for you to honor him by allowing his find from so long ago to be brought into the light at last. We could make sure that he got the overdue credit that he deserves. What do you say?"

The man thought for a moment while he wiped blood

from his face. He touched his nose and winced.

"I'm sorry I attacked you," he said at last. "I'm even a failure at kicking somebody's ass."

"You're better at it than you think," Thomas replied. "But listen, in the spirit of full disclosure, even if I have your code, I still don't know my grandfather's. On top of that, I don't know where the vault is. So, I guess I'm saying that nothing may come of this whole thing."

Smith started laughing so hard he choked. He took the paper towel and blew his nose, opening up a fresh stream of blood. He laid his head back and covered his nose, still laughing.

"You know I'm the one who's drunk here, but I have no doubt about where the vault is."

Thomas looked at him in disbelief.

"Where?"

"Let me ask you this," Smith said, while still looking at the ceiling. "How long did your grandfather live in that house in Boston?"

Thomas thought for a moment. He grew up in that house. It has always been a part of him.

"Since before I was born," he answered.

"Right. And he was the swing vote all those years while they debated releasing the scrolls. The other three were solidly in their camps. I always figured that the most logical place to store and keep those scrolls was close to one of the original men. My father never told me where they were, and Packer and he were best friends, so I didn't see him keeping them. Tremblay, for all his bluster, would not cross that line. Even my father admitted he was an honorable man. So, that leaves your grandfather."

"So, you're saying the scrolls are hidden somewhere in my grandfather's house?" Thomas asked.

"Yes," Smith said.

"But that raises so many more questions," Thomas said.

Smith laughed again and got up to get a new paper towel. He blew his nose again and went back to his chair. Thomas was dumbfounded, trying to work out the logic. Smith didn't know all that Thomas had been through to get to this point. Stewart Braden was logical, and it made no sense for him to send Thomas running around the country only to end up back at the Boston house.

"I need to get cleaned up," Smith said, interrupting his thoughts. "I tell you what. Let me think about it overnight. I still hate your grandfather, but I can see that you too are an honorable man. If I think it's the right thing to do tomorrow, I will give you the code."

"Fair enough," Thomas said. "I'll come by in the morning, and you can tell me yes or no, and if it is no, I will walk away and never bother you again. How does that sound?"

The man nodded slightly at him and laid his head down. Within a few seconds, he was snoring.

Thomas got up and put the water cooler back together. He took one last look at the sleeping man and then went back out the front door, called Chaney, and waited out by the curb. He noticed a blue van sitting a couple of blocks away. It was too far to see whether anyone was sitting in it. I'm more paranoid than Chewbacca at a Star Trek convention, he thought. A moment later, Chaney pulled up. He got in, and they drove away.

"I thought we'd avoided the barroom brawl," Chaney

said.

"So did I," Thomas replied.

"He jumped me when I first went in, but then he settled down so we could talk. I think he might help us after all. He wants the night to think about it. So, we wait to call Harrison until after I see Smith in the morning."

"I'm not saying you're crazy, Thomas," Chaney said. "I'll leave those words of wisdom for Missy to tell you, but you are getting deeper and deeper into the shit here. Like I said before, I'm with you to the end, but my Spidey sense is telling me the danger level is approaching the red."

Thomas glanced over at Chaney through his swollen eye.

"You may be right," he said. "I may be crazy. So, if you want to break into a Billy Joel song, now would be the time."

Chaney grinned. "I only sing Motown, brother, but nice try."

***

Mackie stood in the shadow of a large oak and watched as the drunken man stumbled to his front door. He saw Braden go into the man's house and then come back out a few minutes later and climb back into the Bronco with the black guy, and they drove away. He called Marcus again.

"Follow them. Whatever you do. Don't lose them."

The dark blue panel van with "Best Carpet Cleaning" painted on the side took off. Mackie continued down the sidewalk until he reached the old clapboard house with the rusted lawn mower in the front yard. He glanced down the street in both directions, then went through the hanging gate, up onto the porch and in through the front door.

Chapter 22

AS USUAL, CHANEY was first up. There was a coffeemaker in the room, so he started the brew and showered. He came back out of the bathroom and shook Thomas gently.

"Time to get breakfast," he said. Then he called Caleb's burner to make sure that he and Jackie were awake in the other room.

Thomas moaned and threw his pillow at him. Dani stirred next to him.

"Why don't you let the princess go get breakfast?" she said. "Three nights in a row, she checked in arm in arm with my husband. Let her go get the food for once."

"Dani," Thomas said. "Let's not start that again."

"Fine. I'm going for a run."

"I don't think that's a good idea," Thomas said. "We need to stay together."

"Really?" she said. "Because all I ever hear from you is that there is nothing to be afraid of. No worries here, Dani. We're just on a brief trip to Memphis. What could go wrong? You keep telling me I'm overreacting. And you know what? You're right. We haven't caught a glimpse of a bad guy since we left New Orleans. We dumped our phones in some swamp, so even old Stone Face Harrison doesn't know where we are. So, you win. I've been cooped up either in the car or in a cheap motel room for days. I'll be back in an hour."

She jumped out of bed, went into the bathroom and slammed the door. Two minutes later, she was back out dressed in shorts and a tank top. Without a word, she was out the door and gone. The door reopened seconds later, and Jackie stepped in.

"What was all that about?" she asked.

"We're all a little tired of this adventure, I guess," Thomas replied. "Let's go get some breakfast."

The morning air felt good in Dani's lungs. She sucked it in and blew it out greedily. She picked up steam efficiently, like a commuter train leaving the station, and quickly turned on the next block to get out of sight. That woman, Jackie, had pressed her last button. As soon as this was all over, whatever this was, she promised herself that she would kick that Cajun girl's ass all the way back to New Orleans. Something to look forward to. Thomas was always too nice. Always saw the best in people. It drove her crazy sometimes. The juices were flowing now. She could feel her legs churning like pistons, running on their own. The cadence, the rhythm, brought her peace and made her smile. Two blocks over, she turned again and ran next to the Mississippi River.

"We meet again, Old Man River," she said. She pulled up her headphones, turned up her running list, loud and driven.

***

Thomas and Jackie walked to the corner Starbucks. By now they knew everyone's order. He ordered the coffees, and Jackie picked out some muffins. They carried the lot back to the motel.

"I need to spend some time thinking about things," he said to Chaney. "Jackie is right. I can figure out my grandfather's code if I just give myself some quiet time. I need to do that alone. Then, I'll go to see Smith, and hopefully he will help us. If I can tell him that his is the only code we need, I believe that will convince him."

"You told Dani that we should stay together," Chaney said.

"I know, but she made a good point. No one has been on our tail since New Orleans. Right now, I think we are in the clear."

"Okay," Chaney said. "But if you see anything strange, you call me."

"Got it."

Thomas pushed out the door, which closed by itself behind him.

***

'Eye of the Tiger' blared into her ears and down into her soul as Dani ran on. All the negative energy was seeping out through her pores with her sweat, leaving behind her true being. The last few days had been challenging, but she was growing a new sense of hope, even optimism. She had a good lather working now, and the river continued to her right. Boats and barges of all sizes slid along on the current beside her. She came to a bridge, the one they had driven over when they arrived.

She considered running across the bridge, but it was a long way, so she jogged in place and waited for the light. Maybe go down another half mile and then head back. She turned in place while she was waiting and noticed a blue van about a block back, parked along the sidewalk. There had been no parking signs posted all along this route, every few feet. She turned around just as the walk sign lit up. She took off again. After a few seconds, she peeked behind her. The van had moved up and came through the light after it turned red. She pulled her headphones down and turned up the jets. The next intersection was nothing more than an alleyway that dumped out onto the main drag. She chanced another quick glance and then darted across the road into the alley. The van's engine wound up behind her like an angry predator. Bottles and paper littered the alley. On one side was a stack of wooden shipping crates. On the other was a line of dumpsters. She heard the van speed up as it careened into the mouth of the alley. As she reached the crates, she jumped for the top one and, hanging from it, used her weight to make it lean towards the dumpster. After a moment, gravity assumed command, and she let go and took off while the stack crashed into the alley and clanged against the lead dumpster. The van screeched to a halt, and almost immediately she heard doors open and slam shut. At the next building corner, she took a right and barreled into the unknown.

***

Thomas sat down in a booth at 'Angelo's Diner', two blocks from the motel. The place smelled of bacon and coffee. Round stools with bright chrome bases and red upholstery with big brass tacks lined the counter. Behind it stood the back of a large man dressed all in white, presumably Angelo. The big man was slapping the grill with dueling spatulas, throwing pieces of ham, sausage, and bacon onto various spots on the hot surface and cracking eggs in between like he was conducting a symphony. Thomas's booth had the same red and brass look, and the tabletop looked to be original Formica from the sixties.

He ordered coffee and then carefully unfolded and laid out the three messages his grandfather had sent to him. Although he had studied them before, he still felt like he was missing something. He smoothed them over and reread each message in the order that he had received them. First, the hastily written note that his grandfather had shoved into his hand only a few hours before he died. Thomas could vividly recall the man's anxiety and seriousness from that moment. Then the note that he and Dani had tracked down at Coney Island, which turned out to be only a launching point for the trip they were on now. The would-be kidnappers had shown up then, but why? Thomas knew absolutely nothing at that point. He would have been of little help to them. Did they know about the scrolls, and if so, how did they know? Who told them? Who else knew of the scrolls besides the initial four archaeologists? Certainly, there would be a team of support staff for any well-funded dig: hired hands, muscle, guys in charge of food or logistics. But how much did they really know about what they were digging for and, for that matter, how much would they care? He only found out about the scrolls from the third paper — the letter from his grandfather that Father Dmitri had been keeping. He now dismissed the idea that they were after something other than the scrolls. Everything his grandfather had done was about the scrolls. That had to be the connection. This group of terrorists, as Harrison called them, was after the scrolls that had been kept hidden for decades. This was like the search for the Holy Grail to them and, as such, they had to have some inside knowledge about what was in the scrolls. Jacob Tremblay refused to release the scrolls because there were things written in them that were detrimental to Christianity. His grandfather had said as much. Maybe detrimental wasn't a strong enough word. Maybe devastating was more like it.

"Need anything else?" the waitress asked, bringing him back to the diner.

"Sure," he said. "That bacon smells too good. Give me a couple of eggs over easy, with bacon and white toast."

The woman jotted it down on a small green and white pad, then ripped it off the top and walked back around the counter. She stuck the slip up in the slot, next in line for the grill man. Thomas watched her. There was an order and structure to the inner-workings of the diner. It was true of everything. Certainly, in the world of mathematics, laws always applied. It prevented chaos and unexpected outcomes. Without order, there was nothing. Just beneath the surface of daily, mundane life slept a monster of anarchy. Anything that could ripple that surface could also unleash the monster. A hurricane hits, and the looters come out. A riot caused by some injustice opens the door to pandemonium. Their own needs and own weaknesses always influence the way people think. They hear police shot a young inner-city kid, and their next thought could be anything from what an awful tragedy to this is an opportunity to bust the window of a neighborhood store and steal a television. Something devastating could trigger the beast. Not detrimental, but devastating.

***

At the next building corner, Dani took a left into a narrow alley, too small for a vehicle. She ran to the end only to find that it was fenced off. She raced back to the last door she had seen. It was the delivery entrance of a pizza joint. She tried the door, but it was locked, so she ran to the next door. There were no markings on it, but it opened when she pulled, so she went in. Inside was an abandoned retail area. There was no furniture, no walls or corners, nowhere to hide. She started to step back out but heard voices that seemed to come from the mouth of the alley. She moved deeper into the abandoned room. Dust balls skittered across the floor as she walked. The room was littered with flattened cardboard boxes and packing materials the last tenant had left behind. The windows on the far wall were almost opaque with dust. There was little light, but she could just make out a second door to her left and at the end of the room. The voices in the alley were getting louder and closer. She wished she had closed the door, but doing that might have drawn their attention even more than a door left open. She made it to the second door. It opened with a loud squeak. She held her breath for a moment. The voices outside did not change. She slipped through the door and found herself in almost total darkness. She closed the door behind her as quietly as possible and then used her burner phone, number three, Chaney had said, to light up the room. She was at the top of a wooden staircase, and the phone's light could not breach the darkness below. Only three stairs were visible at a time. She started down.

***

Thomas pushed aside the papers when he saw the server coming over with his breakfast. The aroma was hypnotic. She slapped the ticket down on the table and topped off his coffee. Thomas thanked her and gave a thumbs up to Angelo, who was facing the room for the first time. The big man nodded and went back to his grill. Thomas plowed through the eggs and bacon like an Iditarod sled dog. He glanced out the diner window between bites for the first time since he had sat down. Traffic was rushing in both directions, and pedestrians crossed haphazardly when there were gaps, like in a game of Frogger. The chaos was manageable for now. His grandfather had asked him what he believed. He only had a smart-ass answer at the time, like the kid who always sat in the back row and gave the teacher grief. What did he believe, really? Thomas finished breakfast in record time and looked at the papers across from him again. The first sentence of the letter caught his eye, and he remembered something his grandfather had said to him.

Your father was the answer to a prayer.

Chapter 23

THE LIGHT FROM the phone dispersed quickly in the inky darkness. Dani could see only two stairs at a time. They creaked loudly under her feet but felt solid enough for her to continue. Spiderwebs grabbed at her face and arms as she descended. The air was damp and musty and clung to her. She reached the bottom stair and stepped onto the wet concrete floor. The ceiling hung low and closed in over her head, with pipes running away into the dark like railways. She baby-stepped in the dark to her left until she found a wall. There was a rusted metal container there, probably some sort of air conditioning unit, sitting silently and decomposing like a ship's wreckage at the bottom of the ocean. She felt her way past it until she found herself in the corner underneath the stairs. There she found a pile of old rugs rolled up and stacked. They smelled of equal parts urine and mildew. Above, she heard heels clicking on the concrete. She pushed a couple of rugs off the top and lay down in the pile, almost gagging from the stench. Then, she unfurled the rugs she had pulled off and pulled them back on top of her, keeping a small gap for her nose facing the damp wall. She turned off the phone, and total darkness consumed her. She closed her eyes, tried to slow her breathing, and waited.

* * *

Thomas dropped a twenty on the table, grabbed his papers, and stepped outside. His mind raced ahead of him, thinking about what he wanted to say to Aiden Smith. He was closing in on some answers, he thought, so getting all the codes was even more imperative. He had to appeal to Smith's sense of justice. His father had always wanted to release the scrolls. The elder Smith had never wavered on that. Thomas had to convince the son that trusting him with the code would honor his father. It was only a few blocks to the man's house. Thomas called Chaney.

"Grab the others and come get me," he said. "I'm at Angelo's Diner."

"Well, Dani's not here," Chaney replied.

"What do you mean?" Thomas asked.

"I mean, she hasn't come back from her run yet."

"Shit! I told her not to go far. Okay. I'll Uber over to Smith's house. Give me a thirty-minute head start. If Dani is still a no-show, leave Caleb and Jackie there to wait for her and you come pick me up," Thomas said.

"Got it," Chaney said.

* * *

The door to the basement squeaked open. Dani caught her breath. She didn't know that her eyes had opened until she saw a dim light bounce off the wall in front of her limited sight line. She heard the muffled creak of the stairs under the weight of someone's footsteps. The light vanished and reappeared like a searchlight announcing a movie premiere. The smell of her own fear mixed in with the carpet odors as beads of sweat rolled down her face. Then, she heard voices whispering excitedly. The rugs and the humidity dampened the words. She willed her heart to stop beating so loudly. Her breath came in short, controlled releases. One man approached her. She could hear the footfalls echoing ever louder with each step. The light grew brighter on the wall. She felt as if it were shining directly on her, as if the pursuer were teasing her to give up. He knew where she was hiding and would wait for her to reveal herself. Suddenly, the footsteps subsided, and after a moment a heavy foot kicked at the rugs. She froze even tighter and held her breath completely. Every nerve that ran through her body begged to scream out, but she censored them all to silence like a brutal dictator. The foot kicked at her again, towards the front of the carpet pile, near her head. The vile smell of the rugs wafted into her nose even more dramatically, causing her to feel a sneeze coming on. She bit her bottom lip hard and waited. Finally, the light moved away from her, and she heard the sounds of feet retracing their steps back upstairs. She let her breath out slowly. She heard no other sound and saw no other light for what must have been ten minutes. Still, she waited.

* * *

There was no answer at the door. Thomas took a moment to look in the front window but saw no movement. He tried the door. It opened easily when he twisted the knob. He poked his head in and called out. No answer. The house felt empty. There was no movement on the floors, no sound in the walls. He stepped into the entryway just as he had done the night before. The trash in the corners of the hallway remained there, sitting quietly. Thomas made his way to the kitchen, where he and Smith had fought and then talked. There he found him. Aiden Smith was lying spread-eagle on the table. His hands hung off the sides and his legs splayed out on the table facing Thomas, like a man trying to get a suntan in his kitchen. His head was hanging down in the space where the leaf should have been. Blood had pooled and hardened under both of his hands. Thomas walked around to one side and noticed that three of the man's fingers lay on the floor amid the blood crust. He kneeled to look under the table at the man more closely. His eyes were open, with a look of abject terror plastered on his face. Thomas stood and wretched into a trash can. He backed out of the room the way he had come, reached the front door and wretched again into the dead bushes by the porch. He wiped his mouth and sat down on the steps before his quivering legs gave way completely.

***

Dani rolled the nasty rugs off her and coughed as she sat up and strained her eyes toward the stairs, but it was useless. She might as well have been in a cave. She pulled out her burner phone and tried to call Thomas, but there was no signal in the basement. She got to her feet and, again using her phone for light, found the bottom step. She climbed slowly, each step giving her away with its groans. Once she reached the landing, she peered out into the main room. It appeared empty. She stepped into the room and looked at her phone again. There were two bars. She called Thomas. Before he could answer the phone, it was knocked from her hand and clattered on the floor. Then, a bag was pulled over her head, and everything went dark again. She struggled against two sets of hands that held each arm firmly and screamed as loud as she could. A hard slap across the cheek took her breath away.

"Do not scream again or I will hurt you in ways that you cannot imagine," Taylor Mackie whispered in one ear. "I will trade you for your husband's information, but in the end, you are not of great value to me. You are only a means to an end. But if you are too much trouble, I will simply kill you and then kill your husband after I torture him for what he knows. So, what will it be?"

Dani could feel a bruise reddening on her cheek.

"I will do what you say," she said.

"Good," Mackie answered. "Remove the bag."

The man who held her left arm released one hand momentarily and ripped the bag up and off her head. Standing before her was an intense young man with seething, penetrating eyes. They held no life in them, just death. She stared back at him with as much malice as she could muster. He smiled.

"I heard you were quite a handful from one of my men. I believe his balls still ache from the encounter."

"Glad to hear it," she said. "Step a little closer and I could do the same to you."

"Thank you, but I will pass for now. Instead, I believe you were trying to call your husband just now, so why don't we do that? I'm assuming he is number one on your little call list here."

He punched one and waited. He smiled once again, but there was nothing remotely warm about that smile. It was pure evil. The phone rang.

***

Thomas was still in a fog when his phone started ringing. He pulled it out of his pocket. It was Dani. He took a deep breath and answered.

"Dani, we have a big problem," he said without preamble. "Someone killed Smith."

"That is old news, Mr. Braden," a man replied. "There are more pressing matters at hand, and I'm afraid Dani has problems of her own just now."

Thomas' heart raced. The man spoke with a deep Southern accent. Thomas began pacing around the yard frantically. This couldn't be happening. He needed to focus.

"Who is this?" he asked, as calmly as his voice could muster.

"All you need to know is that Dani is with me and that

she is safe for the moment," the stranger said.

"Let me speak to her," Thomas responded.

"I'm afraid that's not possible. She doesn't want to talk right now."

Thomas heard a loud slap, and an injured yelp. It was Dani. No question.

"Stop it!" he yelled into the phone. "What do you want?"

"That's much better, Mr. Braden. You need to understand that you are in no position to make demands. I have explained to Dani that I do not really need her, but that if you do my bidding, that much faster because I have her, then it is worth it to me to go to all this trouble. You have the codes I need to achieve my goal of acquiring the scrolls. I won't wait any longer."

Thomas' anger rose higher than he would have believed possible, like a decibel meter at a ball game.

"If you hurt her, I will absolutely kill you," he said through clenched teeth.

The man on the other end laughed and said something away from the phone to someone else.

"You, my good man, do not have to capacity to kill anyone in cold blood," he said, back into the phone. "It's a belief raised from a myth that all you do-gooders have. You undoubtedly have seen this type of heroics played out in many Hollywood films, but I'm telling you that killing someone intentionally, without fear or remorse, is a learned skill. Trust me when I say that I know this to be true. Now, moving on, you will provide me with all the codes for the vault and give me its location. And Mr. Braden, time is of the essence. Your young wife is a fighter, and I cannot tolerate her for very long."

"Please listen. I do not have all the codes," Thomas pleaded.

"Of course. Well, Mr. Smith was kind enough to give me his father's code last night when I visited him. So, you see, I only need the other three codes, which I know that you have."

"You're wrong," Thomas said.

Another loud slap and another less forceful cry sounded through the phone, then the man's voice was back.

"Where are we going to rendezvous?" he asked. "I will give you your wife and your life back for the scrolls. This is simply business. I harbor no grudge against you personally."

Thomas needed time. He needed to stall this maniac and come up with a plan. This guy killed — no, butchered Smith to get what he wanted. Thomas was under no illusions that he wouldn't do the same to Dani or worse. He thought back to what Smith had told him. Maybe he had been right. Maybe the vault had been in his grandfather's house all this time, but something told Thomas that it made little sense. Why would his grandfather send him all over the country if the scrolls were in the next room? And if they were in the house, wouldn't Carson have found them long ago, way before Thomas would have gone on a scavenger hunt. No, that was too simple. Stewart Braden was not a simple man, and no doubt Tremblay, who financed the dig to begin with, would not agree to leaving the scrolls in someone else's mansion. He had his own perfectly acceptable one in the Garden District with plenty of room to build a hidden room to house a hidden vault. No, the scrolls were somewhere else. Smith and his father were too drunk to see the truth. Thomas' mind hit a hard stop, like a frozen picture in a Zoom call. What was it his grandfather had told him about his motor home trip? Mardi Gras, Six Flags, Graceland, then what? He struggled to retrieve it. Papa had been giving him clues all along, even as he fought a losing battle against cancer. Then it hit him. Papa's words simmered to the top of his brain.

"We're going to Chicago," he said. "It'll take me two days to drive. I can't fly."

"How delightful. You see. I knew you would come up with the answer. You just needed a little motivation," the man said. "Whereabouts exactly? Chicago is a big city, is it not?"

"Call me in two days," Thomas replied. "Then, I'll either talk to Dani and know that she is okay, or I'll assume she is dead and will contact the authorities."

"I give you credit for having some balls, but don't push me, Mr. Braden. You would not like the consequences."

"Do we have an agreement?" Thomas asked.

"We'll be in Chicago in two days, but Mr. Braden, I trust that despite your bravado, you will think twice before calling in a third party. Such action would leave me no choice but to dispose of any loose ends that could come back on me."

"I understand," Thomas said.

The phone went silent, leaving Thomas standing on the steps of a dead man's house.

Chapter 24

OFFICER JAMES CAHILL, Jimmy to his friends, rolled slowly by the old clapboard house with the broken-down picket fence. Standing in the front yard was a nervous-looking man waving his arms and marching in circles during an animated phone call. Cahill continued, turned at the next block, and pulled over.

"Did you see that?" he asked his partner of six months.

"You think it's him?" Officer Morrison replied.

"I do," Cahill said. "Pull up the BOLO."

They reviewed the monitor together and nodded.

"That's definitely Thomas Braden," Cahill said as he executed a three-point turn on the side street. "I think we need to take a closer look, maybe just stop and say hello to him."

"The BOLO says don't approach under any circumstances, James," Morrison replied, grabbing Cahill's arm.

Cahill first looked at his partner's hand on his arm and then at his face. He pulled off his sunglasses and stared into the young man's eyes. Mitt Morrison was basically fresh out of the academy, which means he knew very little about what police work really entailed out on the streets. The kid was bright; Cahill would give him that, but he was greener than a St. Patrick's Day parade, and Cahill didn't know if he had the patience to deal with him. When they first partnered up, Cahill told him to call him James. His friends called him Jimmy.

"Look, Mitt," he began. "The man is standing in someone else's front yard and appears to be in an agitated state. I think we have probable cause to at least question what he is doing there. The BOLO says keep an eye out and don't approach, but if we believe there is something going on that might be dangerous to the citizens of Memphis, we have a duty to check it out."

"But the Feds are going to be all over us if we step into something that messes with a case of theirs," Morrison said.

Cahill inhaled deeply. This was like talking to one of the dumb hookers downtown. They knew only what they knew, which was damn little. Trying to explain the realities of life to them was a waste of breath. This guy, Mitt, was only marginally better. And what kind of name was Mitt anyway?

"Mitt, I hear what you're saying. This is my call. I'll take all the heat on this. You don't have to worry. I'm telling you, I've been on these streets for twelve years and after a while you just develop a sense of when something is out of sync. There is something not right here, and I need to check it out."

Cahill punched the accelerator on the cruiser and came screaming around the corner. Braden was still standing there, but he was off the phone call. He watched them approach wide-eyed. Cahill could see in the man's eyes that he had harbored a brief thought about running but stayed put. The pride of the Memphis Police Department — just ask his friends — slammed on the brakes and slid to the curb while sliding out of the vehicle all in one fluid motion. Morrison clambered out the other side and came around the back of the car. The guy just stood in the yard watching them approach.

***

Thomas heard the police car coming before he saw it. He hoped they would keep going to some other, more urgent matter, but they stopped right in front of him. Of course, what could be more urgent than a dead guy cut into pieces in the kitchen just a few feet from here?

He held his ground as they approached. No matter what, he could not be detained right now. Dani's life was on the line. The first cop, obviously in charge, hurried through the gate and came to rest eight feet from Thomas. The man was lean, almost scrawny, with an overgrown mustache at least thirty years out of date. He stood slightly stooped with his left foot forward as if ready for someone to say, 'On your mark, get set, go'. He weighed maybe one-fifty, with at least forty pounds of it attributed to the chip on his shoulder. An obvious pent-up anger distorted his face like a caricature in a Mad magazine, which he did not try to hide. Thomas could see his own reflection in the guy's mirrored sunglasses. The other officer, who seemed more nervous than anything else, stopped outside the fence and at a forty-five-degree angle from the first guy with a clear line of sight to Thomas.

Once they settled into their spots, the first guy spoke.

"Can I see some identification, sir" he said, barely under control like the first few plumes of gas and fire from a pissed-off volcano.

"Was I doing something wrong, Officer?" Thomas replied.

"I'll ask the questions, douchebag! Now, how about that ID?"

This was no routine roll-up to check on something out-of-place Thomas thought. They were looking for him explicitly. He reached into his back pocket and pulled out his wallet. He slid his driver's license out of the little windowed slot and held it up. The man stepped toward him and yanked it from his hand.

"Mr. Thomas Braden from Boston, Massachusetts. Is that your current address?" he asked, reading the license.

"It is."

"What, may I ask, brings you to Memphis, Mr. Braden?"

"Visiting a friend."

"And who might that be?"

"I'm not sure what business that is of yours, Officer," Thomas replied.

The officer stuck Thomas' license in his shirt pocket,

ripped off his glasses and put his right hand on his weapon. Right out of central casting for a "T J Hooker" episode.

"Cahill and I'm making it my business," he said through gritted teeth.

Check that, Thomas thought. More like 'Starsky and Hutch'.

"His name is Aiden Smith. This is his house, but he is not home at the moment," Thomas said.

"Is that so? Well, Mr. Braden, you seem out of sorts right now, and when we first drove by, you were having a very emotional phone call. Is everything alright?"

"I am fine," Thomas replied. "I really need to get going."

"In a minute. First, I think we'll check on Mr. Smith."

"I told you. He isn't home," Thomas said a little too emphatically.

"Officer Morrison," he said. "Please go check and see if Mr. Smith is home."

The younger man came through the gate, passed Thomas and up the steps in a nanosecond. He began pounding on the old door at the same rate that Thomas' heart was pounding in his chest, but he never took his eyes off the first guy. They were in a championship-level staring contest. The pounding behind him continued.

"Nobody's home," he heard the kid say.

"See if the door is locked."

Thomas heard the squeak of the door as it opened an inch or two.

"Hello," the young cop called into the empty hallway. "Anybody home?"

Beads of sweat popped up on Thomas' forehead.

"Check it out further," Cahill told the young officer.

This was it, Thomas thought. If they find Smith, not only would he be unable to help Dani, but most likely this idiot would arrest him for murder. His fingerprints were all over the place. He brawled with the man just last night, for Christ's sake. He is standing in the dead man's front yard for no apparent reason and, most importantly, he is an outsider. A damn Yankee if there ever was one. They have enough evidence to convict him three times over, and no one is going to spend a minute looking at anybody else. Then he heard it.

Both officers turned their attention to Chaney as he walked up the street towards them, singing 'Midnight Train to Georgia' at the top of his voice.

Chaney stopped in front of the house with his arm still in the air, pulling an invisible train whistle, and stared at the nearest officer.

"Woo, woo," he said.

"You need to move along, sir," the first officer said, now that he was caught in an undesirable strategic situation between two potential suspects.

"Move along," Chaney said with a big grin on his face. "This is my house. I would say that you guys need to move along."

Now the first guy, Cahill, turned completely around to face Chaney. The young officer bounded off the porch and took up a position where he could watch both Thomas and Chaney.

"Let me see some ID," Cahill said.

"Oh, I left my wallet in the house. I just had to run a quick errand."

"You ran an errand without your wallet?" Cahill was incredulous.

"Don't need a wallet to return library books."

"You tellin' me you can actually read?" Cahill said.

"Well, now, officer, I promised my mama, God rest her soul, that I would always try to better myself as long as I lived. So, yes, I've been readin' for some years. In fact, I just finished a biography of Martin Luther King. You know that a man named James Earl Ray assassinated him right here in our city. Say, you ain't related to that white bastard, are ya?"

Cahill's eyes narrowed. He took one quick look at his partner. Mitt was stationed exactly where he should be. He was a bright kid, but that name had to go. With practiced ease, he pulled his Glock nine from his holster and pointed it at Chaney, who raised his hands and leaned back a little. The whites of his eyes were like saucers.

"Watch the other one," Cahill said over his shoulder to Morrison.

The young cop drew his weapon reluctantly and aimed it at Thomas.

"So, you're telling me that your name is Aiden Smith. Do I have that right? Because I ain't never met a brother named Aiden," he said.

"That's my name, Officer. As sure as I'm standin' here. If you just let me go get my ID, you'll see. There's really no need for any hostilities."

"Okay, then, Mr. Smith, if that is really who you are. Let's go inside and retrieve that ID. Once I'm satisfied with that, then we will be on our way."

"Sure. I'm happy to oblige," Chaney said as he came in

through the gate and walked up the path.

Thomas looked on as everything seemed to turn into slow motion. As Chaney passed Cahill, he smiled at him. Then, one step beyond him, he turned violently like a spinning top and punched him hard just below the left ear. The man's head snapped back, and he stumbled/fell over the decomposing lawn mower, out cold. His gun sailed into the knee-high weeds and disappeared like a wayward tee shot. In the same instance, Chaney pulled his gun from his waistband and pointed it at the younger cop. The kid stood frozen in place with his gun pointed at Thomas.

"You don't want no piece of this, son," Chaney said calmly. "Drop your weapon. No one has to get hurt here."

"You knocked out my partner," he said in a high-pitched voice.

"Your partner's a dick," Chaney said. "He'll recover from this, but he will always be a dick. Don't die for this guy. Put down your weapon, and I promise you, you won't get hurt."

The young officer swallowed hard and lowered his gun. Thomas quickly grabbed it while Chaney got the other cop to his feet and marched him up the stairs and into the house. Thomas pushed the young buck in behind him with the man's own gun. The whole incident took less than a dozen seconds, and they were out of sight two seconds after that.

Chaney took their handcuffs and cuffed them together with their backs to each other. Thomas grabbed a couple of hand towels from the hall closet and stuffed them in their mouths. He pulled Agent Harrison's business card from his pocket and wrote a note on the back. Then he bent down to speak to the officers face to face and held the card in front of them.

"We had no choice here, fellows. It is a matter of my wife's life. I have to go. You guys would never have let me leave. Aiden Smith is dead in the kitchen. I didn't do it, and I don't know who did, but whoever it is has kidnapped my wife. When you get out of these cuffs, look up Agent Harrison with Homeland Security, tell him everything that I just told you, and give him this card. You got that?"

The young officer looked as if he would die of embarrassment while the other guy seethed with anger. Thomas tapped him on the side of his face. The man's eyes would pop out if his rage continued to ramp up.

"Nod if you understand what I have told you," Thomas said.

The man slowly nodded at Thomas without taking his eyes off him. If looks could kill, I would be in the late stages of decomposition right about now, Thomas thought.

He stuffed the card into the young cop's shirt pocket. He stood up and nodded to Chaney. They crashed out the front door. Jackie was idling in the Bronco behind the police cruiser.

"I left Caleb back at the hotel," Chaney said. "He's waiting for Dani. Didn't know that some asshole had taken her. We're gonna make him wish he hadn't done that."

Chaney drove the cruiser about six blocks away and parked it inconspicuously behind a donut shop. He piled back into the car with the others, and they took off. They raced back to the hotel, picked up Caleb, and hightailed out of the area. Once they were clear of the city and sure that they weren't being tailed, Thomas opened up.

"I got a call from a kidnapper on Dani's phone. He tortured Smith to get his code and then cut him into pieces. There is no doubt in my mind that Dani is in serious jeopardy. I told him we would meet him in Chicago in two days, but it's only a hunch. I'm not positive the scrolls are there, and I still don't know my grandfather's code, but we have to keep moving. The Memphis cops will certainly think I killed Smith. We must get Dani before they get me."

Chapter 25

THEY DROVE NORTH out of Memphis in silence, Chaney at the wheel.

"Maybe we should call in the cavalry," he said, looking over at Thomas.

"I can't do it," Thomas said. "You didn't see what was left of Aiden Smith. This guy is capable of anything. I have to give him what he wants."

"We've been swimming in deep water for some time now," Caleb said. "Maybe Chaney is right. Maybe we should hand this over to guys who, you know, are in the torture and killing investigation business. Plus, how are you going to give the guy what he wants when you don't have Papa's code, and you don't know where the scrolls are located?"

"And why do you think the scrolls are in Chicago?" Jackie added.

Thomas looked back at her, and the gears in his head wound up like a child's toy car you could roll back before letting it spring forward. How did the madman, as Thomas thought of him, find them in Memphis? They couldn't have traced their phones.

"I don't have all the answers," he said to Jackie after a moment. "Smith told me last night that his father believed my grandfather kept the scrolls in the house I grew up in. He could be right, but it didn't add up to me. On his deathbed, my grandfather mentioned visiting the Bahai House of Worship. Absolutely everything else he told me in that brief conversation had secondary meanings. There were no wasted words, as if he had practiced what he was going to say to me over and over. So, I told the kidnapper that we had to go to Chicago not only to buy us some time, but because something in the back of brain tells me it's where the scrolls are. Papa mentioned four places that he and my grandmother traveled to on their road trip. We've already been to three of them."

"But if the scrolls aren't in Chicago?" Chaney said.

"I know, I know," Thomas answered. "I may have just signed Dani's death warrant."

"What about the code?" Jackie asked again.

"I have an idea about that," Thomas said. "But I'm not positive. Something I was trying to think through, though, is this. The only people who knew we were going to be in Memphis were the people in this car."

"With one exception," Chaney said.

"Right," Thomas answered. "Packer was the one that

put Memphis on my radar. He may be playing both sides of this thing, but I can't figure out a motive. He gave me his code and seemed happy to wash his hands of the whole charade."

"We could ask him," Chaney said. "You've got two days to get to Chicago. We could fly to Dallas and then have Jackie buy us tickets to Chicago. Even if the Feds are back onto us, it seems like it's all coming to a head one way or the other when we get to Chicago."

"I can't take that chance now," Thomas said. "For all we know, they may have identified Jackie by this point. And bracing Packer now doesn't really give us much. He will either admit it or deny involvement. Either way, the clock is still ticking on Dani, and I've still got the figure out my grandfather's code."

***

Harrison and Conner pulled to the curb. There were police vehicles parked at odd angles up and down the street, like a four-year-old's Matchbox collection. A dozen or more cops milled around in the front yard of the little house while more had set up a perimeter on the block.

"Christ almighty," Harrison said. "If this ain't a total clusterfuck."

That got out, badged their way through the crowd and into the house. In the front room, there was a paramedic tending to one officer while another, younger cop sat nervously on the other end of the couch.

"Who's in charge?" Harrison asked an officer standing at the door.

235

"Lieutenant Stanley," she replied, pointing at the man's back standing at the other end of the hall.

Just as the two agents approached the lieutenant, he turned to face them as if he had been expecting them. He was tall and gaunt in the face, like he had seen so many bad things in his life that he could no longer muster a smile. His pants hung on him as if there were two broomsticks underneath. There was an unlit cigarette perched on his lower lip. It moved up and down when he spoke, like a tiny conductor's wand.

"Lieutenant Stanley?" Harrison said. "I'm Agent Harrison with Homeland Security, and this is Agent Conner. I understand that a person of interest to us, Thomas Braden, was involved here."

"He was," the cop said, with a sweeping gesture that invited them to investigate the kitchen.

Harrison saw the corpse lying on the table with its head hanging down in the open middle. Dried pools of blood circled the table, and far-flung splatters painted the room. Flies buzzed in and out, excited by the many options.

"Who's the deceased?" Harrison asked.

"Guy named Aiden Smith. That mean anything to you?" Stanley asked.

"Never heard of him," Harrison responded.

"Well, he owned the place before your guy showed up," Stanley said. He pulled the cigarette out of his mouth, looked at it for a moment as if wondering how it got there, and then stuck it back on his lip.

"So, you think Braden did this?" Harrison asked.

"He did it all right. He couldn't have left more prints in the kitchen if he had been running a cooking show. Plus, our officers spotted him in the front yard acting strangely. They decided that something was up, so they asked for his ID. Turns out he was acting strange because he just carved up this guy like a Thanksgiving turkey."

Harrison sighed and looked at Conner, who shook his head slightly.

"That's what I thought too," he said to Conner.

"What do you mean?" Stanley asked.

"Did the coroner give you a TOD yet?" Harrison asked.

"Sometime last night, between eight and ten."

"So, if Braden cut the guy up sometime last night, why was he standing in the man's yard today?"

"How should I know? In my experience, criminals do stupid crap all the time. It doesn't have to make sense. Maybe he came back looking for something or decided he needed to tidy up a bit before someone else came in here. Then my officers rolled up, and he got all squirrelly."

"I want to speak to the officers involved," Harrison said.

"They're in the front room, but just so you know, I support their decision to approach. It was the right call."

"Is that so? Well, maybe you can tell me then where Braden is now since they were right here and had the man in sight. Why didn't they arrest him?"

"Turns out he had an accomplice they were not aware of," the lieutenant answered. He set his jaw, which caused the cigarette to point straight at Harrison. "He got the jump on them."

"So, let's review. Your overzealous officers approached our guy even though they were expressly ordered not to, and then they bungled the operation. Our guy is now in the wind and aware that we have been tracking him."

"I don't think I like your tone," Stanley barked.

"Well, lucky for me, I don't give a shit. Now, excuse me while I go talk to Dumb and Dumber."

Harrison turned his back on the man and walked away, Conner trailing.

In the living room, the paramedic had just finished with the one officer. Name on his tag said 'Cahill'.

"Officer Cahill. I'm Agent Harrison from Homeland, and this is Conner. You want to tell me what went on here?"

The officer gave Harrison the evil eye but didn't speak at first. He sat on the couch, fuming.

Harrison waited. He was good at waiting. Many times, he had simply used his size to stand over a perp until they finally started talking. This asshole was a cop, though, and Harrison did not appreciate the resistance.

"What about it, Cahill?" he said.

"Did the lieutenant say you could interview me?"

Harrison sighed and squatted down, hands on knees, and got in Cahill's face. "Let's get something straight. Your lieutenant ain't got nothing to say about my talking to you. I asked you for a report, Officer Cahill. Now, considering you have screwed the pooch six ways to Sunday, I think it is in your best interest to fill me in right now or I'll make it my personal mission to retire your sorry ass. I'm in no mood for jerk-offs, so what do you say?"

"The dude was acting crazy, man. He looked dangerous. I have a duty to protect my beat, or didn't they teach you that at Club Fed?"

Harrison glanced up at Conner and smiled, who was

also smiling.

"Club Fed. That's cute," he said. "I'll have to share that one at our next Agent's potluck and spa day."

As he spoke, he reached behind the officer's head and yanked him forward so that their noses practically touched. His eyes pierced Cahill's as if he were performing LASIK surgery. Spittle flew from his mouth and dotted the man's cheek as he spoke.

"When I was a kid, my dad brought home this puppy from the pound. He said he felt sorry for it. Now, I'm telling you it was the ugliest pooch you ever laid eyes on, and it was dumber than a pile of rocks. But you know what? When I called him at dinnertime, he came running. You see, even the dumbest creatures on God's planet know enough to survive. So listen to me, shit for brains. We've got a terrorist cell chasing this guy Braden around the country, and we don't know why. Instead of obeying orders like the dumb mutt you are, you played King Shit Cop. Now, I'm wondering if you have enough brains to survive like that ugly mixed breed that my daddy took pity on. You've got one minute to tell me what the hell happened here, and I don't want to hear anymore material from your stand-up routine. Understand?"

Cahill nodded slightly against the firm grip of Harrison's catcher's mitt hand.

Harrison released his grip, patted the guy on the head, and stood up.

Cahill cleared his throat and continued to eye the Fed with contempt until at last he looked away and began talking.

"This guy, Braden, was standing in the front yard on the

phone. I ascertained from the way he was waving his arms around and yelling that there was some kind of issue with whoever was on the other end of the call. My partner and I went around the corner and checked the BOLO. Even though it said, 'Do not approach', I determined that there was something very wrong going on. So we approached and asked for ID. He continued to act strangely and said that the man who lived here was not home. I asked my partner to check the story. Before he could do that, another man came down the street singing."

"Singing?" Harrison asked.

"That's right, singing. He entered the gate, at which time I told him he needed to move on. He told us he lived here but could not produce ID."

"What did the second guy look like?"

"Black, six feet and thin, maybe early forties."

"The Easter Bunny," Harrison said, looking at his partner. Conner nodded. "Go on," Harrison said to the officer.

"Well, he said he could get his ID from the house, and as he was going to do so, he sucker-punched me, and I fell over the lawn mower. Then, he got the drop on Morris there and disarmed him somehow. Next thing I know, they're hustling us inside the house and cuffing us together. That's it, sir."

He spat the last word out as if it were milk that had expired two weeks earlier. He glared at Harrison for a moment and then dropped his head.

Harrison glanced at Conner with a headshake. This guy, Cahill, was about one road rage away from shooting someone down in the street. Memphis' finest, he thought before turning his attention to the other, younger cop, but before he could say anything, Lieutenant Stanley walked into the front room.

"You through harassing my officers, Harrison?" he asked.

"Not yet, I'm not."

"Is there anything you want to add to that, Officer Morris?" he asked.

The young cop's eyes locked onto his partner's, which were glaring a hole through him.

"There is something else," Morris said. "He said that someone had kidnapped his wife, and he gave me this."

Harrison took the paper from the officer. It was his own business card. There was a spot of blood in one corner. On the back was a hastily scribbled phone number and a note.

'Track Dani's phone!'

Chapter 26

THOMAS TOOK THE call while sitting in the only chair in the low-rent motor lodge. It came at ten o'clock in the morning.

"Mr. Braden," Mackie started. "I believe that we have an upcoming appointment."

"I need to speak to Dani before we do anything else," Thomas countered.

"Of course."

Thomas heard a scraping noise like a chair being dragged across a floor, then a ripping sound and a brief yelp.

"Dani!" he yelled.

"Thomas!" she answered.

"Are you hurt? Did they hurt you?"

"No, no, I'm okay, but."

"See, she is really enjoying herself," Mackie said, coming back on the line. "Now, we are holed up in some nondescript junkie motel in northern Chicago, and I'm sure you are as well. What do you say we get this over with?"

Thomas needed more time to put a plan in place. First and foremost, any such plan had to protect Dani. Maybe the scrolls too, but he was caring less and less about the fate of two-thousand-year-old parchments. If Dani were safe, then he'd think about the other.

"I'll meet you at two o'clock tonight. You bring Dani unharmed, and I will give you the scrolls."

"Very good, Mr. Braden, and where is this exchange to take place?"

"The Bahai House of Worship in Wilmette," Thomas said.

The phone disconnected. Thomas looked at the others.

"Time to make a plan," he said. "First, recon."

They drove the Bronco north to Wilmette and parked a block away from the Bahai House of Worship.

"Papa mentioned this place by name in our last ever conversation," Thomas told them. "I am positive that the scrolls are on the property somewhere, but I don't know where. The website says that it is open to the public from ten to six daily, so let's go check it out."

They stood in line for just a few minutes to get into the building. Once inside the grounds, they split up to cover territory more quickly.

"I'll check the access options and look for a way in after closing," Chaney said.

"Take Jackie with you. I don't want anyone by

themselves. Caleb and I will go inside the temple. Meet back here in one hour, and we will go from there."

Thomas and Caleb followed the general direction of the tourists' migratory path. There were nine reflection pools with fountains and nine separate entrances to the sanctuary. The gardens around the pools were planted with beautiful blooming white roses, hydrangeas, and yellow zinnias. Tall maples and magnolias lined the outer walkway. The giant domed cathedral towered before them. Once inside, they took in the sanctuary's vastness. The pamphlet said the cathedral could seat forty-four hundred people, and it welcomed people of all religions.

"Look at this," Thomas said, pointing to an inscription on one pillar. "The building was completed in 1953. That means it was still very new when our grandfather brought the scrolls back. I'm more certain by the minute that they are here. I can feel it."

They got back to the motel room at three o'clock after stopping by the local library and getting copies of the design plans for the House of Worship. Thomas spread them out on the bed.

"I think I found a way in," Chaney said. "On the west side of the building there is a locked door, probably used for deliveries and worker access. It looks to be two levels below the sanctuary entrance."

"Okay," Thomas said. "That's where we enter. If I'm right and the scrolls are stored there, they will most likely be on one of these underground floors."

"Agreed," Chaney replied. "One thing though — we need to get some more firepower. I've got my Glock, but they're goin' to be loaded for bear."

"Won't that put us and Dani at more risk if we show up armed?" Jackie asked.

"It's a good question," Thomas answered. "But to go in completely unarmed seems like suicide for all of us. Do you think you can scrounge up some additional weapons?" he asked Chaney.

Chaney nodded. "I know a couple of guys who live around here. I'll see what I can do. The priest goes with me. We might need a prayer or two."

* * *

Dani sat on the only chair in the dingy motel room. The one lamp threw out limited light from the desk next to her. She was bound to the chair, arms to arms and legs to wooden legs, just like she had been for the last several hours. Earlier she had spotted an old Chicago Area Yellow Pages directory. She didn't know how she had gotten to Illinois. The last thing she remembered before waking up in this chair was being roughly tossed into a van and having a needle jammed into her arm. The stench of her running clothes and the mildewed rugs still assaulted her nose. She could feel the gummy residue of the duct tape on her lips. Her captors had released her only to eat and use the bathroom, after which they promptly re-taped her to the chair. She saw the leader, Mackie, pull out her phone and make a call. He spoke quietly and then stepped over to her, dragged her chair and all away from the wall so he could stand behind her and ripped the tape off her mouth. She could not help crying out.

"Dani!" she heard Thomas say.

"Thomas!"

"Are you hurt? Did they hurt you?"

"No, but…"

Mackie covered her mouth and walked away. Tears filled her eyes. In a moment he came back to her.

"It will all be over soon, my dear," he said. Then he bent slowly and kissed her on the forehead like a grandparent kissing a child. "Tonight, you will be free to go back to your life, and all of this will become nothing more than a bad dream, an unbelievable tale you can share with your grandchildren."

She watched as the four men checked and double-checked their weapons. Mackie was the leader but barely kept the others in check. Two of them were angry white-power guys with swastikas on their arms and hatred in their hearts. She knew they would relish the chance to slaughter Chaney. The thought gave her chills. The fourth guy was as big as a locomotive. He was quieter than the others and more reserved. Mackie called him Junkyard. There was enough firepower in the room to produce two Rambo movies, and Dani was afraid that Thomas and his tiny band would not be able to compete. She felt completely helpless and totally isolated.

Then, there was a knock at the door. All of them froze in place. Mackie grabbed a blanket and tossed it to the man nearest her, who covered her up with it and sat in her lap. He pushed himself hard against her, forcing her to turn her head to get any air at all. All she could smell was the musty odor of the blanket and the man's smoky sweat. She heard the door open. There were two men talking in low tones. Then, the door closed again.

"Lucky!" the man sitting on her shouted. "You made it!"

The man stood up and pulled the blanket from her. She blinked her eyes open. Now, there were five of them.

***

Chaney returned a few hours later. It was dusk outside, the last tendrils of the summer daylight pulling back out of sight.

"Good thing I have friends in low places," Chaney said after pulling the curtains closed. "I was able to pick up one old 12-gauge shotgun and two beat-up Smith and Wesson handguns, but beggars can't be choosy, right? I also picked up a couple of flashlights. Probably going to be dark where we're going."

"Good. Beat up guns are better than nothing," Thomas said. "Any chance that these could come back on you or your friends?"

"Nope. I served with one of them, and he vouched for the other. No worries there."

Thomas handed the shotgun and a box of shells to Caleb.

"Push comes to shove, brother, you may have to make a hard choice," he said.

"I know," Caleb answered. "I'll do what I have to do."

Thomas looked at Jackie. "Can you handle a firearm?" he asked.

"I was born in the South. Of course I can."

"Good." Thomas pulled the magazine and checked that it was full before handing it to her. "The safety is on. Let's keep it that way until we get there. We've got a few hours before showtime. Let's get some rest."

***

Dani found herself at the bottom of a well. Someone was pouring water from above, bucket by bucket. Each load of water cascaded down the hole and splashed icy cold in her face. She tried to scream, but she could not. She tried to raise her arms to block the onslaught, but failed. She tried to roll over but found herself pinned in place like a picture on a bulletin board. All she could do was close her eyes and hold her breath. She shivered in the standing water as it rose around her. Each new blast of water provided a shock to her system.

Mackie jolted her awake, punching her in the shoulder with the barrel of his gun.

"It's time to go," he said. "And I will ask you once again not to do anything that will force me to kill you right here, right now."

Her eyes came into focus on his smiling, hateful face. She nodded.

"Lucky, get the girl," Mackie ordered.

Dani saw the newest member of her kidnapping team come towards her. He was the one Thomas laid out cold at Coney Island. Then Chaney shot him, yet he was here again like a migraine headache. He pulled a knife out and snapped it open. She instinctively pushed herself back into the chair as if the millimeter of distance could aid her in some way. She heard Mackie directing the others to load the weapons into the van, but her full attention was on

Lucky. He gently pulled the tape from her mouth.

"You must be silent," he said. "If you do, I will take excellent care of you."

She just stared into his eyes. He reeked of stale cigarettes and old clothes. He carefully cut the tape holding her legs to the chair, then he put the knife to her throat.

"I'm going to free your wrists now. Be still."

He cut the tape on her arms and pulled her up out of the chair and guided her towards the door. Mackie stepped back into the room.

Dani saw his eyes grow completely dark, like a solar eclipse. He took two paces toward them and with a practiced snatch from his back pocket and a wicked thrust; he planted a switchblade deep into Lucky's gut. The other man's face froze in surprise as he fell to the floor. Dani screamed, but in the next instant Mackie had his hand over her mouth.

"I will do the same for you if you do not remain silent, and then I will hunt down your husband and do the same for him. Do not doubt me."

Dani's fear numbed her, and she sat rigidly in the chair as if she were still taped to it.

Mackie kneeled down next to the dying man.

"You should not have come back, Lucky. By doing so, you compromised our mission. You should have disappeared. I would never have come looking for you because you are not valuable to me anymore. But today, your luck has run out."

The man called Lucky said nothing. He simply slipped into nothingness.

***

The street was as quiet as a morgue when they pulled up two blocks from the temple. The air was still, as if holding its breath in anticipation of what was about to happen. Thomas looked at the other two.

"Last chance to back out, guys," he said. "It's my wife in there and my problem. I can get out, and the three of you can drive away, no questions asked."

Chaney nodded once, then popped open his door. Caleb and Jackie got out of the back seat at the same time.

"I think the girl should drive away," Caleb said. "You don't want her blood on your hands, and neither do I. Someone is going to die tonight. I feel it to my core, and I have prayed long and hard about this. So, I will do what I can to save Dani, but this girl does not need to be here."

"Forget it, buster, uh, Father," Jackie said. "I don't know what this night will bring, but I do know that I'm seeing this through. My grandfather was part of this too, right from the beginning, and he meant the world to me. I'm going in."

"Okay, I guess we're all going in," Thomas said.

Crickets made a ruckus as they walked along. One lone dog, maybe two streets over, barked twice as if out of obligation but with no genuine interest. Chaney led them to the access door and pulled out his tools to pick the lock, but the door was already open.

"Looks like we're late to the party," he said

"Fashionably late," Thomas replied.

They pushed their way into the darkness and stood for a minute to let their eyes adjust. Just to their right on the wall, a security keypad hung, blinking. All the lights on it were green.

"They've bypassed the security system too," Thomas said. "Which works for me. We don't need any more invitees to this party."

Thomas clicked on his flashlight. The area near the access door was mostly clear, but there were several columns of chairs stacked five or six high along the wall to the right. On the wall to their left was an array of electrical panels. Ahead of them, a corridor led off into the dark. They followed it. The hallway teed into another one. To the left, the new corridor extended beyond the reach of their lights. To the right, it ended abruptly at an elevator door with buttons on the wall that pointed both up and down.

"The deeper we go away from the masses, the more likely we are to find a vault," Thomas said.

He pushed the down button. The car arrived and announced itself with a loud ding. The door opened, casting a flood of light onto them. Inside the car, there were four buttons. The one lit was a G. There were two below it, B1 and B2. Thomas punched B2 and the doors closed.

Chapter 27

THE BELL DINGED, and they stepped out guns first, where they were greeted by absolute darkness. Even in the absence of light, they could sense that the room was large. Thomas' flashlight only penetrated a few feet. Chaney turned his on, and together they could cover one hundred eighty degrees in a search pattern. Each step set off a round of echoes around the chamber. They crept a few steps further into the gloom, their beacons reaching out in search of walls or furniture. Somewhere up ahead, they heard several light switches flip, and a moment later the room was painted brightly from above. There were rows of fluorescent lights running the length of the ceiling, illuminating every inch of the concrete floor and leaving no shadow unconquered. The room was perfectly rounded, like the domed cathedral that stood three elevator stops above them. There was not a stick of furniture, and only one other door besides the elevator. It stood at the far end of the room and directly across from them. It stood open, and from it a wheelchair was being rolled slowly toward them. Dani sat stiffly in the chair. Her wrists and legs were bound with black duct tape. Her eyes were wide and pleading over her taped mouth. She was being pushed by a man dressed all in black. He came to a halt a few feet inside the room.

Thomas immediately moved toward his wife.

"That's far enough," the man called out.

The man took a Glock out of his waistband with his right hand and laid the barrel against Dani's temple. She flinched away from the unforgiving steel, but he took his left hand and crushed her face back hard against the gun barrel. She winced and cried out under the tape. Behind the gunman, three other men filed out through the doorway and fanned out around the circular room brandishing AK47s.

"You will lay your weapons on the floor, please, and kick them across the cement. Do not try to be heroes," the man standing over Dani said.

To his right, just past Jackie, at forty-five degrees, Thomas recognized the MAGA hat guy. He was holding the assault rifle aimed steadily at Thomas' chest. To his left and beyond Chaney, the other two gunmen stood. He had seen one of them before as well. He was at the lockers on Coney Island, and he seemed just as resolute as the MAGA man about his purpose. Thomas was certain that he had not seen the fourth man before. You don't forget a man his size.

A quick scan of the room gave a depressing report. There was no cover and no place to make a stand. Thomas looked at the others. They waited to follow his lead. He nodded slightly and laid his revolver on the tile with a clack and kicked it toward the man in black. Chaney followed suit, then Caleb. Then Jackie mimed doing the same but instead took her weapon and pointed it directly at Thomas.

Jackie laughed as she swept around Thomas' right at a safe distance.

"That's all they're packing, Taylor," she said, winking at the gunman holding Dani hostage. "They shared all of their limited options at our little strategy session earlier. Chaney had the Glock and Thomas had an old Smith and Wesson, and Father Caleb brought the shotgun."

"You did well, sweetheart," Mackie replied.

He turned his attention to Caleb.

"You're a little out of your element, aren't you, Father?" he asked.

"You get your boys to sit this one out and I'll show you my element, up close and personal," Caleb replied.

Mackie laughed out loud.

"Now, you see. I love that kind of attitude. Really, I do, but I never give up my superiority advantage. Nice try, Father."

He raised his left hand and signaled for Jackie to come over. She ran to him and kissed him hungrily. He kissed her back but never took his eyes off Thomas. Finally, Jackie pulled away and focused on Dani.

"I bet this one was a handful, wasn't she?" she asked Mackie.

"She's a fighter," he replied. "But nothing I couldn't handle. Once she knew who was in command, she accommodated my every wish."

"You son of a bitch!" Thomas yelled as he strode toward them.

Mackie raised his Glock. "I can put a round in either eye from here, or you, your bride and the good Father can all walk away from all this. Your choice. The black dude, on the other hand, is not leaving here."

Mackie's men laughed out loud.

"No, I'm afraid that he represents one thing that is truly wrong with this country and, as such, he needs to be erased."

Thomas stopped moving and took a deep breath. He glanced to his left and saw that Chaney had mirrored his movements and was still standing by his side. Meanwhile, Caleb had slid almost imperceptibly a foot or two to the left.

"Let her go now," Thomas said. "I'll do whatever you want after she clears the area."

Mackie sighed, patted Dani on the head affectionately, and then ripped the tape off her mouth, causing her to scream.

"She leaves when I say," he yelled. "I decide when and if anyone here lives or dies. Tonight, in this room, I am your God. No one else. Do you understand me?"

"He's crazy," Dani yelled. "He's never going to let us leave here alive. Don't help him!"

Jackie swung around to the front of the wheelchair and placed her hands on top of Dani's and leaned in close. "You know I have been having loads of fun with your man since you've been out of the picture." She smiled and licked her lips.

"I doubt it. He doesn't go for two-faced skanks."

Jackie eyed Dani for a moment and then stood up and viciously slapped her across the face, drawing blood from her lips.

"I've been wanting to do that for a very long time," Jackie smirked.

"Enough," Mackie said. "I know you say they are not carrying any other weapons, but please search them, my dear. We don't want any mishaps this close to the completion of our mission."

Jackie walked back toward Thomas, her gun out front, pointing at his chest.

Thomas surveyed the situation. To his right, now at three o'clock because he had moved up, was the MAGA man with the AK trained on him. To his left stood Chaney, who had a man at his nine o'clock and another at ten. Caleb had worked his way over to be facing the giant, who was the farthest man to the left. The leader, Mackie, was at high noon, and Jackie was walking directly in his line of fire. He glanced to his left just for an instant and saw that Chaney was on board. He waited just two seconds longer, long enough for Jackie to get within arm's reach.

Thomas nodded almost imperceptibly, and the two of them drew guns from under their shirts at the same moment, like synchronized swimmers. He spun to his right and dropped MAGA man with one shot to the abdomen. The man fell to the floor while his trigger finger sent a spray of bullets into the ceiling. Pieces of plastic light covers and glass from the bulbs crashed down around Thomas. Meanwhile, Chaney, who had two men to deal with, fired at nine o'clock chest high while diving to the floor and rolling once before popping back up on one knee. He fired at the ten o'clock man but was a moment too late. The man ripped off a line of shots in Chaney's direction. One caught him in the shoulder and spun him around and down. He hit the ground at the same moment that Caleb launched himself at the shooter. The man's gun clattered to the floor as Caleb did some heavy bag work on the man's rib cage. He went down, screaming in agony.

Jackie opened fire on Thomas as she continued rushing straight at him, screaming wildly. But her Glock only clicked through one trigger pull after another: empty and utterly useless. Thomas grabbed her forward arm and twisted her around in one motion, holding her around the neck with one arm and jamming his gun into her ribs with the other. The whole thing took less than two seconds. All three of Mackie's men were down, and Chaney was moaning on the floor, his back to Thomas. During the commotion, Mackie kneeled behind Dani and waited.

"You ever see 'The Good, The Bad and The Ugly?'" Thomas asked Jackie, his mouth only an inch from her ear.

"What is that?" she asked, squirming in his embrace.

He pressed the gun barrel harder into her ribs until she stopped. "Too bad," he said. "The twist at the end is the best. My grandfather loved that movie. You should check it out sometime. Spoiler alert: Clint Eastwood unloads the other bandit's gun while the guy was sleeping. Sorry to say that makes you The Ugly."

"You're never leaving this room now," she snarled.

"Ever since we left Packer in Dallas," Thomas said, holding her in a death grip, "I had been wondering how we were being tracked so well. It always seemed like the bad guys were two steps ahead."

"Well, now you know," Jackie replied.

"I know how, but I don't know why."

"The reason is that I thought it was time to turn the tables," Jackie said. "My grandfather's family made their fortune on the backs of slaves at first and then later, itinerant farmers, which was the same thing. Those poor people were given no options to better their lives or change their status. No, they worked for crumbs and lived and died without so much as a nod of thanks from the Tremblays or any of the other southern elites. And all the while, the rich men, including my grandfather, claimed their love of the Lord and their willingness to serve God to the best of their abilities. It was all propaganda. They would abuse people all week long and then smile and cross themselves as they took their accustomed seats in the pews every Sunday. It was disgusting."

"So your answer to that now is to do what, kidnap and kill people you don't even know?" Thomas asked.

"My answer is to expose Christianity and Christians for what they are — frauds. I know that whatever was discovered in that cave all those years ago scared my grandfather more than anything else in the world. He believed it would wreck his beloved religion. So, I waited for just the right time and just the right allies. When the situation presented itself, I jumped. I wanted to destroy my grandfather's fictional legacy and reduce all those bead-wringing hypocrites to the quivering cowards that they really are."

"So, you jumped into bed with white supremacists?"

Jackie smiled. "More than you can even imagine. It was like a cause with benefits. My true love and I will revel in the fall of Christianity. Then we will go off victorious and revel in each other's arms."

"So now, Mr. Braden, the choice is all yours to make," Mackie said. "You will give me your code and Packer's. As you know, I already have Mr. Smith's, which I will admit he gave up reluctantly, and my dear beauty, Jackie, has the fourth. So, you will give them to me, and we will open the vault, which is in this room behind me. You do this, and you will live. If you don't, I will kill Mrs. Braden immediately, then I will torture and kill the priest, and finally I will torture you until you give me what I want. Your black friend is dead or will be. Is there any part of you that doubts what I will do?"

Thomas held Jackie tightly around the neck and pressed his revolver into her rib cage.

"Looks like we are at an impasse," he yelled across the room to Mackie. "You and I can come to an agreement right now. We both walk away with the women we love, and no one else has to get hurt. What do you say?"

"Forget it, Taylor," Jackie yelled. "Look at my neck. I'm not wearing the locket. I destroyed it. Only I know my grandfather's code. He will never kill me. The girl is of no use to us at all. She's a loose end that can be tied up at any time."

"Jackie," Thomas said. "Do you remember when we were escaping from your house? We all jumped in the old Caddy and drove away. Then, when we finally stopped, do you remember what you did?"

Jackie looked puzzled. "I don't know what you're talking about."

"Yes, you do. You pulled your locket off your neck and

opened it to show me. Remember?"

"Okay, so," she said. "It was only for a second."

"I'm great with numbers," he said. "One look and I can easily remember a six-digit code."

A quizzical look crossed her face. She looked across at Mackie and stared directly into his eyes with a silent plea.

"You are a beautiful person, my love," Mackie said to her. "And your heart has always been in the right place."

Mackie stood up, raised his hand and shot her directly in the right place.

Chapter 28

THOMAS JERKED HIS head to the side as the girl's blood splattered on him. He felt the life run out of her as she slid down his body and crumpled on the floor like a rag doll. It left him too stunned to move. He looked up at Mackie across the room and saw only madness in his eyes.

"What you need to understand, Mr. Braden," Mackie said as he watched the life drain from the girl on the floor. "I don't give a shit about all that left-wing nonsense that Miss Tremblay explained so eloquently. She was a means to an end, that's all, and unlike her, I don't think Christianity is a problem. Quite the contrary, I think the only thing wrong with Christianity is what all the socialist do-gooders have done to it. They tear at the fabric of our beliefs by watering down the most basic tenets of the word of God."

"So, you're a man of God," Thomas said. "Could have

fooled me."

"It looks like we are no longer at an impasse," Mackie said while placing the hot barrel back against Dani's face. She winced in pain as it burned her skin. "Either you drop your weapon now or she dies."

A loud moan emanated from the big man to Mackie's right. He pushed himself off the floor, picked up his weapon, and rose to his full height. Blood covered his shirt.

"Nice to see you back from the dead, Junkyard," Mackie said. "Now, if Mr. Braden does not put his weapon down on the count of five, I want you to kill the priest."

The man called Junkyard trained his gun on Caleb, who stood with his hands up.

"One," Mackie said. "Put it down, Braden, or the girl and the priest die right here."

Thomas' mind raced through options, but he couldn't see any other choice. He felt like they were going to die no matter what he did.

"Two," Mackie said.

Then, for the first time since this standoff began, Junkyard spoke.

"Boss," he said. "This don't seem right. We can't shoot a priest, man. It goes against our beliefs. He's a man of God."

"Three," Mackie said. "It's going to be alright, Junk. Just do as I say."

The big man nodded and focused his attention on the priest. Mackie had never steered him wrong before. His leader had a way of seeing the bigger picture, even if he himself didn't quite follow the logic.

"Four," Mackie said.

Caleb looked into Junkyard's eyes. He mumbled a prayer and made the sign of the cross.

"Junkyard," he said. "You are a child of God, and your sins are forgiven."

The man-mountain lowered his gun and looked over at Mackie.

"This is not what we're about," he said. "This man represents the very religion that we're trying to preserve."

"I understand your hesitation," Mackie said. "You're unsure of the righteousness of this play. But I say, five."

Then, with smooth, quick precision, he aimed and shot Caleb, who spun to the floor in a heap and ceased moving

"Caleb!" Thomas shouted.

"She's next," Mackie said to Thomas. "Drop it."

Thomas complied. He stepped over Jackie's corpse and laid the gun on the floor. He heard a low moan from Chaney, but no sign of movement.

"Go ahead," Mackie said. "Take his gun away too, just in case he decides to be a hero later."

Thomas rolled Chaney over. The man's eyes fluttered open. There was bleeding from just below the shoulder.

"He needs medical attention," Thomas called out while taking off his outer shirt and pressing it into the wound.

"He's going to need the morgue if I have to wait any longer," Mackie responded.

Thomas took the man's weapon and tossed it hard across the floor. It clanked and scratched its way along until it hit the far wall with a thud. Chaney's breathing was shallow and irregular.

"Was it still worth it?" Thomas asked him.

"You know it, man."

"I'll come back for you," Thomas promised.

"Sounds good. I'll just stay here and chillax."

Thomas stood and turned to Mackie. The man's eyes had no soul behind them. Thomas was ready to quit.

"Whatever you want," he said. "I don't care anymore. I never asked to be part of this. My grandfather left me a mess to untangle, but it was never my mess, and I'm done with it."

"Excellent. You push your bride, and I will follow. We're going to the archive room. Junk, check the others and make sure that they are all dead. Then follow us."

"Copy that," Junkyard replied.

***

They entered a long, narrow hallway, Thomas pushing Dani and Mackie close behind with his gun trained on Thomas' skull. At the end, they made a left and then a right until they reached a heavy wooden door. There were no markings or indications on it as to what was on the other side. It was locked. Thomas looked back and saw that Mackie had fallen back a couple of steps. He reached into his pocket with his left hand, keeping the gun steady with his right, pulled out a giant set of keys and tossed them to Thomas. The contraption was the sort of thing that a janitor would wear on his belt with a retractable metal line and a large loop to secure multiple keys.

"One of these will open it," he said. "I don't know which one. The man who gave them to me died before I could ask."

Thomas caught the keys, stepped around Dani and

started trying them one by one. On the ninth key, the tumblers turned with a loud click, and Thomas pushed down on the latch and opened the door. He slid the keychain onto his belt, stepped back behind the wheelchair and entered. Inside was an enormous underground warehouse-like area filled with floor to ceiling cages as far as he could see. Each fenced-in area was padlocked, no doubt waiting for one of the keys on the keychain. The space seemed as massive as the nine gardens above ground.

"We are looking for cubicle H3," Mackie said from behind him.

"How do you know that?"

"I have a benefactor with a lot of money and considerable reach in all religious communities. Once I knew that this was our destination, he could get information about the organizations that owned space here. Tremblay's name came up after some digging by the men in our cyber department. You see, we are not just a bunch of rednecks running around in the woods pretending to be an army and shooting cans off fences. We are much more organized and technically savvy than that."

"You weren't technically savvy enough to get here without me though, were you?"

"No, inside information is always valuable, and you had it," Mackie replied.

They moved up and down the aisles until they found H3. Thomas, again, went through the process of trying each key until the padlock clicked open. He swung the gate open, but the entrance was too narrow for the wheelchair. He looked at Mackie.

"Leave her out here. She's not going anywhere," he

said.

So, the two men stepped into the cubicle. It was large and open. The ceiling, which was also enclosed in wire fencing, was maybe fourteen feet high. The cube itself was probably thirty by thirty, and sitting in the very center of it was a large safe. It stood six feet tall and was close to four feet wide and ten feet deep. On the front were four separate steel handles, and next to each one was an inlaid silver plate with numbered thumb wheels in it. There were twelve separate wheels inside each plate, which meant that twelve numbers or six two-digit numbers would have to be entered to open each handle.

"Time to earn your right to live," Mackie said.

Thomas nodded. It was now or never. He had an idea about what his grandfather's code was, but he was nowhere near certain. Any miscue might either lock down the vault with some unseen safety feature or, worse, set off this trigger-happy lunatic into a tirade that Dani might not survive.

"There's another question that we either need the answer to or we have to make an educated guess. Which of the four men's combinations goes with which handle?" he said.

"I trust that, with what is at stake for you that you will come up with a very well thought-out solution. The simplest answer is that they are probably in alphabetical order, top to bottom. Don't you think?"

"It's possible, but if we guess wrong, we don't know how many chances we will get."

"You're thinking too new school, Mr. Braden. This custom-built safe was made decades ago. I doubt that any lockdown features were built in, and I'm even more sure that no one has updated it. Go with your first instinct."

Thomas thought about it. While alphabetical seemed logical, alpha male was much more likely. Tremblay instigated and funded the archaeological dig. No way his code would not be first. He scrolled through the six pairs of numbers that he remembered from Jackie's locket. His hands were sweating, and the dials did not move easily, but he finally got the correct digits facing front. He grabbed the cold steel handle and caught himself saying a prayer. He pulled down, and the handle moved into a vertical position accompanied by a loud metallic pop inside the door. He glanced back at Mackie. For the first time, he saw a slight smile on the killer's face. It gave Thomas a chill.

"One down," he said.

He studied the second set of numbers next to the second handle from the top. This could be Packer or Smith, he surmised. A case could be made for either, but he decided on Packer. He thumbed in the numbers that he had gotten from the man's son in Dallas and reached for the handle. It didn't budge. He turned to Mackie.

"I think we need Smith's numbers here," he said.

"Step aside," Mackie said. "Where I can still see you."

Thomas moved away from the safe to the side wall of the cage and waited. Mackie pulled a bloody piece of paper out of his back pocket and entered the numbers. He pulled on the handle, and it swung down easily. He nodded his head at the progress and then waved Thomas back with the gun. Thomas entered Packer's numbers again at the third handle. It swung down like the others. Now is where the rubber meets the road, he thought. He dialed in the numbers that he was hoping were right. The handle stubbornly refused to turn. Thomas broke out in a sweat. He tried to calm his mind and let it replay the last few days. His grandfather's code had to be in there somewhere, yet they had gotten no clues that specifically dealt with it. All their clues had led to the next place where they could acquire a code, but none had offered to solve the mystery of his own grandfather's.

"Stop stalling." Mackie said.

"I'm not," Thomas replied. "As I'm sure Jackie told you, I do not know my grandfather's code. I'm still trying to figure it out."

"You've got about two minutes, then I'm going to treat your girl worse than I did mine."

Time was running out. There was something his grandfather had said, something out of context from everything else. It was like a blurry picture of someone he knew. The outline, the shape, the pose — all were telling, but the face was blocked out like a bystander on a 'Cops' video. He glanced out at the entrance of the cage and saw Dani sitting there, restrained. Her lips were moving, but there was no sound, as if she were singing silently. No, not singing; praying. Whatever you ask for in prayer, believe that you have received it, and it shall be yours. The key word was prayer. He thought back to the first coded message his grandfather had given him, which referenced that verse from Mark. He remembered him saying that Thomas' father was an answer to a prayer. And then again in the letter that Father Dmitri had been saving for him, the first sentence repeated the mantra. Your father was the answer to my prayers. Maybe prayer was the answer to the safe.

Using the base of eleven, he calculated the values for the safe using the word prayer. P was the sixteenth letter. By adding eleven to it, he arrived at the number twenty-seven. In the same way, he determined the other values. R netted twenty-nine, A equaled twelve, Y gave thirty-six, E was sixteen and the last R was another twenty-nine. Thomas ran through the numbers in his head and, one by one, thumbed them into place on the combination lock. After the last one was entered, he pulled down on the handle, and nothing happened. The handle remained rigidly locked in place. Thomas heard the click of a gun being cocked. He looked back and saw Dani crying silently while a madman pressed the pistol against her temple.

"You're stalling again, Braden. Now say goodbye," Mackie said.

"No! Wait a minute! I'm not stalling. Just give me one minute, please."

"Okay, you've got one minute to save her life, but no pressure," Mackie said, laughing.

Sweat poured from Thomas' brow. He thought for sure that prayer was the key to the combination. Everything that he knew pointed to that one word, but he missed something. He scrolled back through his memory of everything that had happened, starting with his grandfather's last words, through the coded messages, the letter, Packer, Smith, until this very moment. What was he missing?

"I'm losing my patience here," Mackie said.

It seemed inevitable now to Thomas. He had failed Papa and Caleb and, worst of all, Dani. He didn't know the code, and he was going to be forced to watch Dani die right here in this damn basement, and then he was going to be killed next.

"Time's up," Mackie said. "Turn around and get on your knees."

Thomas turned slowly and did as he was told. He couldn't bear the look into Dani's eyes. He mouthed the words 'I'm sorry'. After everything they had been through, it was going to end right here. Once again, God was nowhere to be found, an absent landlord, letting the lunatics win the day. Thomas sighed.

"C'est la vie," he said aloud.

"That is indeed life," Mackie replied. "I speak a little French myself, but in your case, life is over."

Mackie pointed the gun at the kneeling Thomas.

"Too bad for you and the missus that it didn't work out," he said.

A revelation hit Thomas right between the eyes like a window shade snapping open. When his grandfather first said to him that his father was an answer to a prayer, he was speaking French. Then again, in the letter, he had written it in French. Thomas was so quick to translate words that sometimes he lost sight of the source language. The word for prayer in French is priere. That had to be the answer.

"Wait," Thomas shouted. "I know the code. Give me just one more try, and I believe I can open the vault."

Mackie stared at him and shook his head.

"You're playing me, Braden," he said.

"I'm not. I swear to you."

Mackie lifted the gun he had trained on him.

"Last chance," he said.

Thomas go to his feet and turned back to the vault. He prayed silently as he calculated the new code using the French word as the base. He dialed in the numbers slowly, careful to align them perfectly. When he had finished with the last code, he closed his eyes and pulled down on the handle. It swung down easily.

"Thank God," he said under his breath as he leaned on the heavy vault for support before pulling the steel door open.

He stepped back from the vault and shone his light into the gaping opening. On the floor of the safe were four ceramic-looking jars, each of which was maybe three feet tall and had been encased in a glass shell obviously custom-made for the occasion. Above the jars, a shelf ran along each wall, including the back of the safe. Stacked on the shelf were dozens of binders. Thomas stepped into the safe and grabbed the top binder on the left. He thumbed through the pages.

"At a glance," he said, "these would seem to be the translations of whatever is in the jars."

He turned to look at Mackie.

"You can do whatever you wish with this stuff. Let me take Dani, and we will just walk away right now."

"Not yet, Mr. Braden. Because of you, my helpers are no longer available. I will need you for just a bit longer, I'm afraid. In the cage directly across from this one, there is a wheeled cart. Would you be so kind as to retrieve it, please?"

Mackie pulled Dani's wheelchair away from the entrance and off to one side, all the while keeping the gun pointed at her. Thomas stepped across the alley and fumbled with the keys for a third time before he finally got the cage open. He pulled the cart out and into the cage with the safe.

"I don't think we can get it all in one load," Thomas said.

"Get the jars first, then we will stack up as many of the manuscripts as possible."

Thomas did as he was told. Fortunately, the cart had three shelves, and two of them were tall enough to stack the jars, which, while inside their glass cases, were surprisingly heavy but also stable. When he pulled out the last jar, which was deep inside the vault, his knee struck a wooden box that had been painted black and was placed flush with the black wall. It couldn't be seen from outside the safe, and since he was positive that Mackie would never enter the safe for fear of being locked inside, he didn't mention it. After stacking and rearranging a few times, he finally managed to get everything on the cart but for a dozen or so binders. As it was, the cart looked like the Grinch's sleigh. There was no way to add another item to it.

"That's all we can get," he said to Mackie.

"Take the remaining items and put them in Mrs. Braden's lap. She can carry them out for us."

Thomas put a stack on Dani's lap that came up to her chin.

"They won't sit there unless she can use her hands to hold it," Thomas said.

"Very well. Unstrap her wrists, but her legs stay tied to the chair. Then we will all process out together."

Chapter 29

THE HUMAN TRAIN crawled through the maze of cages. They found Junkyard lying in a pool a blood at the outer door.

Mackie halted them for a moment.

"I hate losing the Junkyard. That dude could hack into NORAD if he wanted. Sorry, Junk, but you served your people well," he said. "Okay, let's move."

Thomas led the way, pushing the cart loaded with jars and manuscripts. Dani came next, being pushed by Mackie while holding the teetering tower of binders on her lap. They reached the open room where the bodies still lay, and Mackie called for them to stop again.

There was no movement in the room. He couldn't tell whether his brother or Chaney was still breathing. The giant room smelled of gunpowder and death. He said a silent prayer for both of them. Behind him, he heard Mackie's phone dialing. He turned to see. Mackie lifted the gun as if to tell Thomas to stay where he was. Someone answered his call, and he began speaking in German. He looked into Thomas's eyes as he spoke.

"Yes, we are ready," he said. "We will come up in the elevator. Bring the truck around to the loading dock. Yes, that is correct. No. Once we have the truck loaded, I will kill them."

Thomas stared intently back, hoping that he was not giving away that he knew what the man had said. What he heard wasn't terribly surprising. Thomas figured they didn't have long to make a getaway, but hearing it spoken out loud made it even more real.

"Time to go," Mackie said. "Move to the elevator."

Thomas did as he was told, and the train started up again. When they reached the elevator, Thomas pushed the up button, and they waited. The bell sounded, and the door opened.

"Get on the other side of it and pull the cart into the car," Mackie ordered.

Thomas backed himself into the far corner of the elevator and watched as Mackie pushed Dani in facing him, and then he stepped in, just clearing the door as it closed. He pushed for the ground floor, which was two floors up, and the car began its slow ascent. Thomas first looked at the man with the gun, then at Dani. He could just see her eyes over the stack in her lap, and they were brimming with anger.

"It's going to be okay," he said.

"Sure, it is," Mackie added. "As soon as we get these things loaded, you and I will go our separate ways."

The bell dinged, and the doors opened. Mackie began backing out while pulling the wheelchair. It took both hands to pull it out, so his gun hung pointed at the ground. Still, there was no way that Thomas could climb over the loaded cart and Dani to get to him before he could raise the gun and fire. Just as the man cleared the door, the barrel of a gun appeared in the dim elevator light and pushed into his left ear.

"Drop the weapon," a familiar voice said.

Thomas recognized it at once. Agent Harrison, right on cue.

Mackie seemed perplexed but not stunned. He let the gun fall. It clattered loudly to the ground. He seemed to smile oddly at Thomas for a moment, then he shoved Dani hard back into the elevator while in the same instant his left hand swiped up and back, knocking the gun barrel from his ear. Then with incredible speed, his right hand grabbed the wrist holding the gun and twisted it down. Then the elevator door closed.

The car just sat in place waiting for directions from its travelers, like a taxi driver sitting at the curb of an airport. Gunshots rang out from just beyond the door.

"Can you reach behind you and push a button?" Thomas asked.

Her left hand had been holding the top of the stack of binders. She reached back with it and tried to punch a button with the back of her knuckles. Neither she nor Thomas could see what she was doing. She could barely feel the wall. She strained to reach just an inch further. Her hand flailed backwards, tapping the panel once, twice. Finally, on the third strike, the car moved. It was ascending. They waited as it rose excruciatingly slowly. It stopped with a ding on the sanctuary level of the House of Worship. Dani rolled herself out backwards, sending the binders crashing to the floor. Thomas pushed the cart into the doorway and slid out around it. He spotted the exit sign leading to a stairwell and raced toward it.

"Check on the others," he yelled over his shoulder.

He crashed into the stairwell and took the stairs three at a time. When he hit the ground level, he burst through the door back into total darkness. He switched on his light and rounded the corner from the elevator. In the open space, he could just make out Mackie sitting on top of the agent, his back to Thomas. They were still struggling. Thomas ran to them. He didn't see either of the men's guns. He bull-rushed into Mackie's back like a linebacker blindsiding a quarterback. It knocked the wind out of the madman. They went sprawling across the cement, both of them trying to gain a hold on the other. Thomas ended up on top and punched Mackie hard in the nose. Blood spewed from it before he raised his right leg up and over Thomas's head and scissored him off. Thomas slipped out before Mackie could lock him in a death grip. Both men popped to their feet. Thomas stepped in with a left jab and a right cross, but Mackie ducked the second punch and launched one of his own to Thomas' solar plexus. Thomas bent over but blocked the roundhouse coming in on his left. He stepped back just as a karate kick found the side of his head. He stumbled further back and into a stack of chairs. They crashed into the stack next to them and started a chain reaction. Thomas fell to the floor, chairs crashing down on top of him. He scrambled in the darkness to push them off and regain his feet, but before he could, a charging Mackie knocked his breath out. They tumbled into the mass of chairs, arms and legs swirling and twirling in the wreckage.

The crazy man ended up on top of him, his killer's eyes red with rage. Blood continued to pour from his nose and land on Thomas's face. Thomas grabbed him by the throat and tried to push him off, but the man was built like a battleship with incredible strength and hatred poured from every inch of his body.

"I will kill you and everything you love!" he shouted. "Before you can kill my country."

A new energy and strength rose inside Thomas. He took his hands from the man's throat and plunged his thumbs into his eyes. Mackie screamed and grabbed Thomas' wrist. They fell over and rolled. Thomas ended up on the man's back. He grabbed the keychain and ripped it off his belt loop. Then he pulled the keys out and looped the metal wire over Mackie's head and around his throat. He pulled with all his might. Mackie clawed at the wire trying to get his fingers under it, but Thomas pulled even harder. Thomas pulled for his grandfather. He pulled for Dani, for Caleb, for Chaney, and for Harrison.

"That's enough, Braden!" Agent Conner shouted, holding his weapon out. "Let him go, or you'll be the one going to jail instead of him."

Thomas nodded and rolled off Mackie, who lay there coughing and gagging. Thomas stood up shakily, adrenaline still rushing around his system like a wild bull. He looked over and saw Harrison pushing up on one elbow. He went to him and helped him up while Conner cuffed Mackie. Harrison's neck still flared red in the shape of Mackie's fingers.

"Looks like I owe you one," the agent said.

"There are others coming to the loading dock with a truck," Thomas replied.

"We've already picked them up."

"Then we need an ambulance for my brother and Chaney. Plus, some dead bad guys. They are all in the basement," Thomas said, running for the stairs.

He reached the cavernous room and saw Dani hovering over Chaney against the wall. He ran to Caleb and slid down next to him. There was blood oozing from him, and his eyes flickered open and closed in the harsh lighting. He grabbed Caleb's hand and squeezed.

"Shit, Caleb!" Thomas exclaimed as tears rushed to his eyes. "I'm so sorry! You shouldn't be here. I shouldn't have let you come. You're the good one. This is all my fault. Please, God, I'm so sorry!"

Caleb rasped almost imperceptibly. "We're brothers," he said, squeezing Thomas' hand ever so slightly.

Tears drained uncontrollably from Thomas' eyes as he held his brother.

"Shush. Don't try to talk," he said to his brother. "Jesus, this is my fault," he repeated.

"It's okay. I'm in the forgiveness business," Caleb replied.

Then, his head rolled to one side, and he lost consciousness.

Chapter 30

THOMAS AND DANI sat in the corner of the waiting room. There were at least two children crying from across the room and one elderly gentleman sitting near them who was praying out loud. A nurse had already been by to patch up the cuts on Dani's face and apply salve to the gun barrel burn. They sat holding hands until a physician walked through the swinging doors and called out their name.

"Braden," he shouted over the din. Thomas raised his left hand but clutched Dani's firmly with his right. The doctor walked over while looking at a clipboard and sat down in a chair directly across from them.

"He lost a lot of blood," he said. "We removed the bullet, but it ruptured his spleen and nicked an artery. And, to add insult to injury, he has two broken ribs. It's going to be touch and go for a few days. I wish I could be more optimistic, but he's been through a lot. I've seen bodies perform miraculous healing before, so let's keep a good thought."

"Can we see him?" he asked.

"Yes, but make it brief. He needs a lot of TLC. He also might still be groggy from the anesthesia, but he can talk if he's awake."

"Thank you so much," Thomas said. "There was also another man that came in with us, a black guy named Chaney. Do you have any information about him?"

"They took him second in for surgery. He was luckier than your brother. I'll let the surgeon know that there is someone out here for him. The nurse will show you back to your brother's room."

They followed the nurse through the doors and down the hallway. It was quiet and smelled like every other hospital. While the waiting room was chaos-filled and untethered, the nurses' station hub of the intensive care unit was calm and controlled. She pointed to a door. In a box on the outside, the chart read 'Braden'.

Stepping inside, Thomas recalled the moment he had stepped into his grandfather's bedroom the last time he saw him. Machines were humming and beeping, demanding attention. Thomas went to one side of his brother's bed, and Dani went to the other. They each held Caleb's hand and wept.

"I'm so sorry, brother," Thomas said through the tears. "I should never have risked you or Dani like I did. It was just so damn arrogant. So, we found old jars with parchments written in a language that died long ago. Was it worth all of this? I don't think so. Not with you lying here like this.”

Caleb squeezed his hand and blinked his eyes open. He coughed for a moment before speaking.

“My choice. Not yours. We’re brothers.”

Thomas bent down and hugged his brother as hard as he dared.

“Group hug,” Dani said and joined in with them.

“Excuse me,” a woman called from the doorway.

“Yes,” Thomas said, standing back up.

“Hello, I love family reunions, so I am sorry to interrupt, but I was told that Cleveland Chaney came in with you all, and since you’re the closest thing to family that I know about, I wanted to give you an update. I’m Dr. Stoerner, and I operated on Mr. Chaney. He had some internal bleeding. I think we have plugged all the holes, but he will be in intensive care for a day or so.”

“What do you think though, Doc?” Thomas asked. “Can he make it?”

“He’s strong, but we’ll know more in twenty-four hours. I’m optimistic,” she said.

“Thanks, Doc,” Thomas replied.

“No problem. I’ll make sure that you get an update tomorrow.”

She turned and started to leave, but then changed her mind.

“There was another man who came in at the same time. He’s almost too big for a hospital bed, but he just came out of surgery as well. I didn’t perform the operation, but his doctor told me it didn’t look promising. Do you know his name?”

“All we know is his nickname. They called him

Junkyard," Thomas answered.

Caleb stirred in his bed and tried to sit up, but his ribs screamed at him.

"Where is he?" Caleb asked just above a whisper.

"Three doors down," the doctor answered.

"I need to see him," Caleb said. "Help me up, Thomas."

"Whoa," the doctor said. "You need to stay in bed. You're in no condition even to be moving. Besides, he can't have any visitors right now."

"Help me, Thomas!" Caleb said louder, calling on all of his strength.

"Maybe you should wait until you're a little stronger," Thomas said.

Caleb fortified himself.

"I'm his priest. If he is dying, I'm going to give him his last rites. Now, you either help me or I will do it myself, but I'm going."

Thomas glanced at the doctor.

"Nurse, will you get us a wheelchair?" she called from the doorway.

With Thomas on one side and the nurse on the other, they transferred Caleb to the wheelchair.

"Get my Bible and my rosary beads out of my pants pocket," he said to Dani.

They paraded him to the big man's room with his two IV poles and locked the wheelchair next to the bed.

"I need to do this in private," Caleb said.

When they had gone, he made the sign of the cross. Then he took Junkyard's enormous hand into his own. It felt like a child's hand holding his father's. He placed the rosary in both of their hands and closed them together.

"Junkyard," he said. "This is Father Caleb. I'm sorry that I do not know your given name, but the Lord does, and that is all that matters. You are a precious child of God, and our Lord and Savior, the Christ Jesus, has already died for all of your sins and transgressions. Without his saving grace, we are nothing, but with it we have eternal life. I therefore declare to you that your sins are forgiven and your place in the Father's house is assured."

Caleb struggled to stand from the chair, biting his lip through the pain, and made the sign of the cross on Junkyard's forehead. He then sat back down and began to read.

"The 23rd Psalm," he said to the sleeping giant. "The Lord is my shepherd; I shall not want. He makes me lie down in green pastures; he leads me beside still waters."

He felt Junkyard's hand squeezing his.

"He refreshes my soul. He guides me along the right paths for his name's sake."

Caleb stopped reading and sobbed. Junkyard squeezed his hand even more strongly as Caleb's mind drifted back to the room where he had been shot. He could still feel the cold cement floor under him and his life oozing out of his wound. He could sense the big man standing over him and then kneeling by his head. He remembered the touch of the man's fingers on his neck and the warmth of his breath as he whispered into Caleb's ear. 'Play dead. You're going to make it,' he said.

Caleb reset himself and continued reading.

"Even though I walk through the valley of death, I will fear no evil, for you are with me; your rod and your staff, they comfort me. You prepare a table before me in the presence of my enemies. You anoint my head with oil; my cup overflows. Surely goodness and mercy will follow me all the days of my life, and I will dwell in the house of the Lord forever."

When he had finished, Junkyard's hand relaxed, and Father Caleb crashed to the floor.

Chapter 31

THREE WEEKS LATER, Thomas and Dani sat in the antique chairs in his grandfather's house. Stacked around them were the binders that they had found in the safe. Standing in front of the old fireplace were the four ancient jars. They had decided not to open them for fear of disturbing the scrolls inside. They had started reviewing the translations, but Thomas' heart wasn't in it. He had lost so much, so quickly, and for what?

The doorbell interrupted his thoughts. He went to the door and opened it to find a young man in a tight-fitting suit and an older gentleman standing just behind him and to his left. His suit was dark gray and well-tailored. His shoes gleamed in the midday sun.

"Can I help you?" Thomas asked.

"Are you Thomas Braden?" the younger man asked.

"Yes, and who are you?" Thomas answered.

The older man stepped forward while extending his hand.

"Mr. Braden, my name is Walter Patterson, and if you will permit me, I have a business proposal for you."

Thomas shook the man's hand.

"What sort of business proposal?" he asked.

"A very lucrative one, but one that I'd rather not discuss on your front porch if you don't mind."

Thomas allowed them to come in. He pointed to a chair by the front window, and the older man took a seat while the other stood by the front door like a sentry.

"This is my wife, Dani," he said. "Now please state your business, Mr. Patterson."

"Very well," the man began. "I represent a large and prestigious organization, and it has come to our attention that you are now in possession of very rare and extremely valuable artifacts that your grandfather and his colleagues unearthed many years ago."

"I'm not sure I know what you mean."

"My dear boy, my information is unassailable, and this conversation would move along more quickly if you would simply acknowledge what I already know to be true."

"Okay. Let's say I do know what you're talking about. What then?"

The man glanced at the jars by the fireplace.

"I presume that those are the scrolls," he said.

Thomas did not respond.

"Well, cutting right to it. I am prepared to offer you ten million dollars for the scrolls and all the translations that you have. It's a handsome reward, if I do say so, considering that you didn't actually discover them yourself."

"Well, considering that my brother died helping me to locate them, I don't think it's reward enough," Thomas answered. "And that amount sounds suspiciously like what the redneck goon was hoping to get paid. Did you send the guy who killed Caleb?"

"That was an unfortunate choice on my part. I contracted him to find the scrolls, and yes, I offered him a substantial finder's fee. However, I did not expect that he would resort to such extreme measures. I am quite aware of your loss, and I am truly sorry. Your point is well-taken. Let's start over, shall we? I will offer you fifteen million for the artifacts, and you have my word they will be preserved in a safe place for future generations. That is my company's primary goal. And to be clear, I'm afraid that fifteen is my final offer," Patterson said.

"What prestigious organization did you say you worked for?" Thomas asked.

"I did not say, and my employer is adamant that their name be kept out of these negotiations," Patterson replied.

"Mr. Patterson, did you ever see the movie Shenandoah?" Thomas asked.

"I'm not much of a movie watcher, Mr. Braden."

"Well, it takes place during the Civil War, and the main character, played by Jimmy Stewart, works a farm in Virginia. He has several sons, and since they do all the work themselves and don't own slaves, they see no reason to fight in the war. But then, this Union cavalry outfit shows up one day and says that they want to buy his horses. Now, one son tells them that the horses are not for sale, and then Jimmy Stewart steps forward and says, 'Now, what my son says is God's honest truth, and you can carve it in stone if you have a mind to. The horses aren't for sale.'"

Patterson rolled his eyes for a moment and then responded.

"You're telling me that the scrolls aren't for sale," he said.

"That's what I'm telling you," Thoma replied.

"Well, I'm afraid that is unacceptable. You leave me no choice, Mr. Braden. Joel, if you please," he said, waving at his man.

Joel pulled a gun out and aimed it at Thomas. It was the first time that the man had moved since he had taken up a position by the door.

"I tried to make you a fair offer, Mr. Braden, and I am a reasonable man, but under no circumstances will I leave here without those scrolls," he said, pulling a small-caliber weapon of his own from his coat pocket.

Thomas and Dani both stood.

"Don't you think that there has been enough bloodshed…?" Patterson asked but was interrupted by a noise coming up the steps. Someone was singing loudly about mountains not being high enough.

Thomas exchanged glances with Dani.

"Who is that, Mr. Braden?" Patterson asked.

"I have no idea," Thomas said.

"Joel, get rid of him. And you two, not a peep or I will be forced to kill you both and the front porch crooner. Do you understand?"

They both nodded as the doorbell rang again. Joel hid

his gun behind his back and opened the door a crack. Thomas could hear Chaney's voice through the crack.

"Hey, I was wonderin' if y'all needed any yardwork done," Chaney said.

"No, we're good," Joel answered.

"Cuz I know that some of these big houses can look really grand in the front, but then you go take a peek at the backyard, and Lord-a-mighty that can be a mess," Chaney continued.

"No. Like I said, we're good, and I am very busy right now, so you have a good day," Joel said as he pushed the door closed.

Chaney grabbed the door with one hand.

"Are y'all sure now? I just got into town from Georgia, and I could really use some work. I can clean up the yard, and y'all can pay me whatever you think is fair," Chaney said.

"Sir, if you don't leave, I am going to have to call the police, so I suggest you go."

"Well, you ain't got to be all dramatic about it. I'm just looking for work."

"I'm closing the door now," Joel said.

Chaney let go, but just before the latch hit the strike plate, he threw his shoulder into the door, sending Joel sprawling. In the same instant, Thomas leaped at Patterson and grabbed his gun hand. One shot rang out, leaving the bullet lodged in the ceiling. Thomas dislodged the gun and sent a crushing right hand into Patterson's solar plexus. Meanwhile, Chaney dove on top of Joel, pinning his right arm and the gun underneath the bodyguard and in one fluid motion smashed his elbow into the man's nose. He rolled him over and bent his arm up his back until he dropped the weapon. Then, he placed his knee on the man's back and pushed hard until he stopped squirming.

Both assailants were down, and Dani was already dialing 911.

"You sure know how to make an entrance," Thomas said.

"I told ya. I got skills," Chaney answered.

After the police hauled off Patterson and his goon, they asked the trio a few questions and said they would be in touch. Thomas and Dani got serious about reading through the translations while Chaney kept watch just in case there were more surprises heading their way.

"There has to be something important in these writings," Thomas said. "I don't know why my grandfather and the others would have kept it a secret for all those years if there wasn't."

"True," Dani replied. "They were willing to hide it, and Patterson was willing to pay Mackie a lot of money to get it and then make the same offer to us. As he said, he had no intention of leaving here without them."

"Here's something," Thomas said, holding up a folder and reading aloud.

'The woman was a follower of Jesus of Nazareth. Her name was Mary Magdalene, and Jesus called her the apostle to the apostles. She traveled with him, and he shared much wisdom with her. The other apostles were jealous of her relationship with Jesus.'

"The ancient church would not have been happy with Mary Magdalene possessing any power with Jesus," Thomas said.

"And the Christian movement would not have recognized any woman as a leader," Dani said.

"No, they wouldn't," Thomas replied. "In the 4th century after Jesus' death, the elite movers and shakers of the time pushed to canonize certain writings into what is our Bible today. It was a highly charged moment where the people with wealth or political power decided which writings would become part of the sacred text and which ones wouldn't in order to craft the narrative they wanted to sell to the people."

"So, they just left a bunch of shit out?" Chaney asked.

"That's right," Thomas continued. "Many writings, such as the Gospels of Thomas and Peter, were excluded because they were too controversial. Certainly, a text like we have here that indicated that Mary Magdalene was an apostle would be scratched from the jump."

"Some things never change," Chaney said. "Old, rich, white guys making all the decisions."

"Nope," Thomas answered. "Same as always, although this doesn't seem like enough to make Patterson pay to get the scrolls."

"Maybe not. But this is," Dani exclaimed. She took out her highlighter, marked a page and looked up at Thomas with enormous eyes.

"Read this."

Thomas took the binder and read the highlighted part.

The man was a prophet and was called Jesus of Nazareth. He traveled the countryside, healing those who believed and preaching of God's love. People flocked to him to hear his teachings. Many of them witnessed his performing miracles. He possessed

dark, wavy hair and dark eyes that could look into your soul. His skin was dark as a moonless night. He was called Rabbi.'

"This is about race? Can that be right?" Dani asked.

"Of course it can be," Thomas said. "When these scrolls were discovered, racial segregation ruled the day, and there is no description of Jesus in the New Testament, so Europeans just assumed he was white. All the artwork throughout the centuries depicts a white Jesus, both as a baby and as an adult. Patterson was protecting a large Christian organization that didn't want these scrolls to see the light of day, and Mackie was a straight-up white supremest."

"I guess," Dani said. "There was the forced integration at Central High School in the late fifties, then enormous civil unrest in the sixties."

"Racial profiling still goes on today, Missy," Chaney said. "You don't have to wonder if someone is questioning whether you belong when you walk through a pleasant neighborhood, but I do. It has always been like that and it always will be, but this here says that Jesus was a black man and that ain't gonna sit too well with some folks. Them right-wing evangelicals are positively going to lose their shit."

"No doubt," Thomas said. "You add that to the text that a person who most people portray as a prostitute could be a close confidant to Jesus, and people's brains will explode. But I think over time my grandfather believed that Christianity itself would and could survive this sort of scandal. I think he thought that faith and love could overcome anything."

"First Corinthians 13:13," Dani quoted. "And now these three remain: faith, hope and love. But the greatest of these is love."

"Amen, Missy," Chaney said.

Dani looked at him. "So, what do you think, Thomas?"

"I think he was right. We will release the documents ourselves and let the chips fall where they may."

"You know that anything could happen," Chaney said. "There are plenty of people who will use this to serve their own agendas, while others will deny it completely, calling it fake news. Hatred will never go away as long as humans are running things."

"I know," Thomas said. "But it doesn't matter. Love has to win. My grandfather used the word prayer as the key to the vault. I think he thought prayer was the key to life, so I will pray that making these scrolls public is the right thing to do."

"God ain't afraid of no scrolls written by some dude from two thousand years ago," Chaney said.

"Right," Thomas answered.

"Now, on to the other question I've had in my mind since I got here. What's in the box over there by the jars of scrolls?" Chaney asked.

"It was in the safe as well. I had it removed and shipped after we got back. I haven't opened it."

"Well, no time like the present. Right, Missy?"

"I'm with Chaney," Dani chimed in. "Let's see what's inside."

Thomas and Chaney pulled it away from the wall. The box was made of solid wood and was only about a foot wide and two feet long. They were screws holding the top in place. They took them out and carefully lifted out the contents that were wrapped in linen and laid them on the dining table. Removing the linen carefully revealed a wooden plaque. On it, there were three separate inscriptions carved into the wood.

"What is it? Dani asked.

Thomas scanned the plaque. Some letters had faded as if the wood was reclaiming them.

"It's the same message written in Greek, Hebrew and Latin," he said.

"Can you translate it?" Chaney asked.

"Yes. It reads, 'King of the Jews.'"

EPILOGUE

THOMAS AND Dani entered the ballroom and worked their way through the crowd, shaking hands and exchanging pleasantries. There were celebrities, real estate tycoons, and many well-to-do philanthropists in attendance. There were dozens of round tables for eight placed around the room, with place settings of gold-inlaid plates and gleaming silverware. Servers revolved through the crowd with trays of champagne.

Thomas sported a dark blue suit and a red tie. Dani wore a cocktail-length black dress and a pearl necklace. They found the table with their name cards on it and sat down. Thomas leaned over to whisper to Dani.

"That dress is killing me," he said with a smile.

"You're thinking with the wrong head again, Braden," she replied with a wink.

"Can't be helped," he said as he stood to greet two more donors.

The room buzzed for another ten minutes, and then the guests were asked to find their seats, and Thomas was called forward to the stage. He stood, as did Dani, and they hugged for a long moment.

"You got this, Braden," she said. "And I'll bet that even in the pockets of that brand new suit, you've got those sweaty old boxing wraps."

"You know me too well," he replied. "Here I go."

He reached the podium and looked out over the room. His heart felt proud as he thought of his grandfather and his brother.

"In the late 1950s," he began. "A group of young archaeologists went on a dig in the Qumran Valley and discovered a cache of Dead Sea Scrolls in what they called Cave 12. Those scrolls contained writings they believed would damage Christianity, so they did not release them to the public. My grandfather, Stewart Braden, was one of those archaeologists and, as the years went by, he came to believe that faith could overcome anything. So, tonight with the help of your generous donations, we are dedicating the Stewart Braden Museum of History. Many of the artifacts that he collected over the sixty years of exploration will be on display, and the centerpiece of these exhibits will be the Dead Sea Scrolls along with their English translations. Some writings found in the scrolls will be controversial, but he believed, as do I, that transparency is most important in the time we live. We must pass on to the next generation all that we know, not just what we want them to hear."

Thomas paused for a moment and sought out Dani in the crowd. Her eyes were glistening, and he felt a slight catch in his throat.

"Also, within the museum we will build a chapel dedicated to my brother, Father Caleb Braden, who gave his life in order to bring the scrolls into the light. It will be a place for quiet meditation, prayers, and, if needed, pleas for forgiveness. Lucky for us all, God is in the forgiveness business. Thank you for your support of this project and for honoring my family in this way."

He climbed down from the podium amidst a standing ovation and hugged Dani while tears poured from his eyes.

"You did good, Braden," she said.

"We did good," he replied. "Time to go home."